HONOUR THY BROTHER

Warren Abbey

Copyright © 2019 Warren Abbey

All rights reserved.

ISBN: 9781087286983

This is a work of **fiction**. Names, characters, businesses, places, events and incidents are either the products of the author's imagination or used in a fictitious manner. Any resemblance to actual persons, living or dead, or actual events is purely coincidental.

DEDICATION

For my brothers…

PART ONE
It's a Family-Thing

PROLOGUE

"It's a family ting now"

The black on black Lexus was parked at a dismally unkempt building complex in the heart of Downtown Toronto. This wasn't the part of the city with it flashy lights and crowded streets where one would feel at ease walking from one block to the next. At its finest, this was the part of the city best left forgotten. The kind of place where one could spot drug addicts walking up and down the street looking for that next fix or a means to it; the sort of place where shoot-outs went unreported. But not because there was a lack of witnesses, but because the witnesses knew better.

On this particular street, because of this particular complex, the police patrols were more frequent. Moreover, it was because of this particular fact that the driver of the black on black Lexus was on high alert, constantly scanning the streets in the cool night air of a decaying summer. He lit another cigarette and readjusted his rear-view mirror for the umpteenth time.

"Yo Boom, that's like the third bogie you crushed up in this bitch in like two minutes... What the fuck, fam? Rude boy'll be out in a second," said his passenger in the front seat. The driver remained silent as something had caught his attention in the alleyway across the street.

"Yo Zulu, at least crack a window or somethin' man. You're gonna kill a nigga off wit that second-hand shit, man, like fuck!"

Zulu ignored his companion, still trying to discern through the darkness just what had caught his attention. It had been ten full minutes and Blacks still hadn't returned from the deal. He told that nigga that all three of them should've went up. The blood gang that run these beat up streets were as grimy as they come. Besides, the kind of cash that they were dealing with would seduce even the most honest nigga into doing something stupid. Zulu felt apprehensive in the driver seat, reflecting on the conversation he had with Blacks before the meet.

"Shit Zulu, you worry too much man. These niggas is cool," is what Blacks had said. "I did like two years wit these niggas in the South, man, what you forgot? We was poking niggas up and holdin' shit down dawg, it's a family-ting now," he had said with a smile.

"Brother there ain't no family-ting but the family you got right here, Cuz," Zulu had replied. "My bro showed me that the Bing is one thing but when a nigga touches road it's a different story, you feel me?"

But Blacks wasn't even trying to hear all that shit. He always said Zulu was the most 'paranoid motherfucka' he had ever met. He wasn't the one on 2A North putting in work. He never saw what those niggas did for him when niggas were trying to get at the kid.

"Listen fam, these niggas would never violate like that man. And besides, you already know my nigga; I'm strapped all day in this bitch. They buss, I buss," said Blacks.

Still, Zulu felt uneasy. They were like sitting ducks trying to get fed in the middle of shark city.

What would really happen if these niggas started snaking? He knew Blacks was surgical with his nine-millimeter, but when a killer has the drop on you, there's no way you're pulling that shit out in time. Regardless on how sick you think you may be.

"Ah wha you a pree out there sa, Boom?" The passenger inquired in his attempt to sound Jamaican.

Beads was always an annoying lil fuck, Zulu thought to himself about five years their junior, Beads was the little man of the crew, even though he had the biggest fuckin ' mouth. They called him Beads because either high or sober he always looked out at the world with those little beady red eyes. Not to mention he always wore Islamic prayer beads around his neck for some odd reason; niggas never once seen Lil Beads make Salaah. Little nigga probably thought it was a fashion statement or something Zulu thought to himself as he turned from the window.

"Man, Blacks has been up there too long. If he's not back in the next two minutes, we're goin' up them and wettin' everything! Fuck these niggas, man," Zulu decided tensely. Beads didn't say anything but replied with a smile. Maybe now he would be able to finally catch his first body. It had been three whole weeks with his new 'ting' and he still hadn't even let it off on a nigga yet. Tonight, just might be the night, he nodded to himself as he reached under the passenger for the .38.

Zulu turned his attention back to the alleyway just in time to see a man running full speed with a gun in his hand aimed right at him.

BAP! BAP! BAP!

Zulu barely had time to react as the driver's window exploded and three slugs entered his body; one to the face, two in his shoulder.

Beads, being inexperienced in gunplay, dropped and fumbled the .38 special as warm blood splattered across his face and du-rag. Almost instantaneously, another man in all black- except for the red balaclava across half his face was at the passenger side door. Sawed off in hand, he gave the little nigga absolutely no chance to draw for whatever that may have been under his seat.

CHIK CHIK- BOOM!!
CHIK CHIK- BOOM!!

With the job done the two men ran back down the alleyway as fast as they came. About thirty odd people heard the gunshots early that morning when Zulu and Beads got hit. The number of people who called in to report it:

Zero.

CHAPTER 1

"...isn't this wonderful."

Rakim hated venturing inside hospitals ever since his mother passed. It always reminded him of the last time he had seen her alive. Hooked up to all those fucking machines and shit. All the technology in the world and those pussies still couldn't even save her from cancer. Needless to say, he still held onto a little bit of resentment towards the 'overpaid quacks' in their silly white coats. Shit, he even hated the smell of the joint it smelt like death mixed in with sanitizer. No matter how much you try to dress it up, you always knew what really went down here.

"May I help you?" the nurse at the receptionist desk asked unkindly as he walked up to her station. She was chubby in the face and even chubbier everywhere else. A redhead who wore her freckles with pride. The expression on her face suggested to Rakim that she had smiled her last smile years ago.

"Yeah, I'm looking for my bro. He was shot early this morning and I was told he was brought here."

"Uh huh," the nurse replied while typing something up into the computer on her desk. "Does your bro have a name?"

"Anthony Zulu Anderson."

Rakim had always questioned why his father would add such an African-ass name to one of his children. Shit, he came from Trinidad not Zimbabwe! His dad was always doing shit like that though. His philosophy was the more unique the name, the more unique the person. Rakim's full name was Ronald Prince-Rakim Anderson and as a child he hated it. Growing up, if anyone were to call him that besides his family and teachers, they would be met with the hardest punch to the gut in his side of Scarborough.

"Uhmmm, that patient is currently under police guard due to an ongoing investigation. I'm required to take your name and record your relationship with the patient before I let you up there."

"Sure, whatever," Rakim said while taking the clipboard from the nurse. "I fuckin hate hospitals," he mumbled under his breath, filling out his information.

"What's that now?' the nurse replied.

"I said, isn't this wonderful." Getting the room number, he headed toward the nearest elevator. There was only one other thing he hated more than being in hospitals, and that was being around his half-brother's half-insane mother.

Aight, let's get this shit over with he sighs, bracing himself as the elevator doors close.

"Hold on little brother. Soon come."

*****

It was 4:30 something in the A.M. when Alicia got the call from her hysterical sister.

"They shot Zu! They fucking shot Zu! Oh my God! Oh my God! 'Why?! WHY!?!"

Alicia could barely make sense of what she was hearing, and at this early hour, she thought that she was still half-dreaming.

"Hold on, hold on...What?" Alicia asked groggily. I can hardly make out what you're crying about Keish. Slow down and-"

"They fucking shot Zulu!! Wake up! I need a ride to the hospital! Oh, my fucking God! Why couldn't he just stay his dumb ass at home like I told him to! That fuckin' asshole!"

"Okay, okay. Calm down... Calm down!!" Alicia said, mind racing, trying in vain to pacify her younger sister. She always knew something like this would happen. Messing with those hoodlums from the ghetto always ended up in some sort of drama. She had tried to warn Keisha of that on the same exact day her little sister had introduced her to Zulu. Upon first sight, Alicia had absolutely no idea what Keisha saw in him. He was a tall, lanky, ugly-ass kid with cornrows. He wore too much gold in his mouth and he apparently had a problem with keeping his pants above his ass. And who the fuck names their kid Zulu anyways? But Keisha had always been attracted to the bad boys; The rough necks. Alicia could never understand it. They were brought up in Pickering, far from any hood, ghetto or slum. Though they weren't rich, Alicia and Keisha's parents were well off and spoiled their daughters through the teeth. Their afro-Canadian father was a lawyer and their Sicilian mother ran a successful daycare center in the Township of Ajax. Being half-breed, the sisters encountered their fair share of racial tension in grade school growing up. They were either too black for the white kids or too white for the black kids. Aside from that though, they had a stable childhood. The issues that existed for the kids in the city were only imagined or seen on TV. Why Keisha insisted on entrenching herself with that mess was way beyond Alicia. But regardless, Alicia was always looking out for her baby sister and that would never change, even if she didn't agree with Keisha's infatuations.

"Which hospital is he at?"

"St. Mikes! Alicia, we need to hurry! Please God we need to hurry!"

"Okay, okay I'll be at your house in five minutes. Be outside."

"Hurry!" Keisha yelled into the phone as Alicia hung up.

That was five hours ago. Five long ass hours ago. They've been sitting in the waiting room of St. Michael's ever since. What made matters even worse was the fact that they had to wait with Zulu's crazy ass' mother. Patty was a character. At 40-something she still dressed as if she was much younger. Even now, awaiting the news of the fate of her only son, she wore a short black skirt that revealed too much and a bright pink halter-top that revealed even more. Coincidentally she was at a bar, "livin' it up" just down the street from where Zulu got shot. Accompanying her was her flavour of the month, Steve. Steve and Patty made an unlikely couple. Steve looked like a white crack head from Parkdale who had just gotten out of jail. Patty resembled a broke down Jamaican dancehall queen. Where the two met and how they ended up together was anybody's guess.

"I'm gonna go down to da Timmies and get some more coffee. Do any of you sexy young girls wanna lend your Uncle Stevey two bucks? I'll pay you back some as soon as I get."

Steve's breathe could be smelt from across the ICU's waiting room. Alicia was desperately trying not to make eye contact.

"Leave those girls alone Steve. What, you tryin to hit on' em right in front of me?" Patty dug into her obviously fake Prada handbag and produced a toonie.

"Take it and hurry back. The doctor should be by anytime now." With Steve gone, Patty took a seat beside Keisha.

"Girl, where did you get those shoes at? They're so sexy." Patty exclaimed. Keisha looked up in shock as Alicia shook her head in disbelief.

"You're asking me about my shoes when my boyfriend, who just happens to be your son, is fighting for his life on what could be his deathbed? What's wrong with you?" Keisha snapped.

"Hold up, don't you yell at me you pale ho! I'm just tryin' to deal with this as best as I can. I don't see you trying to make the situation any better!"

"Who you calling a ho?!?" Keisha roared, jumping out of her seat Alicia jumped up with her sister, tying in vain to hold her back.

Patty got up in Keisha's face, shouting even louder.

"What the fuck...You think Zulu loves you more than me! You'll never be good enough for my baby. Never!"

"You're crazy. You're f'in crazy!" Keisha yelled back, just as a uniformed police officer ran into the mix, hand on his holster. The constable couldn't have been more than twenty-five years old; a cadet fresh out of the academy and itching to make his first arrest.

"Do we gotta problem here ladies?"

"No, no officer. Everything's fine. They were just blowing off some steam, that's all," Alicia explained as she guided her sister to the other side of the waiting room.

Standing by the doorway, Rakim observed the whole drama unfold. Although he was slightly annoyed with the situation, he couldn't take his eyes off who he assumed was Keisha's friend. Looking like a King Magazine centerfold, Rakim watched as her curly midnight black hair danced along the slim width of her shoulders. He estimated that she was about 5'3 maybe 5'4. Coca Cola bottle figure, Beyoncé in her bootylicous days had nothing on this girl. She had a smooth butterscotch complexion that was damn near flawless, not to mention her almond shaped eyes and those Megan Good lips. If Rakim was the sort to believe in love-at-first sight, he would've considered himself sprung at that very moment. Luckily, Rakim thought to himself, he wasn't the type to wear his heart on his sleeve. Plus, if she was one of Keisha's friends than she probably wasn't his type.

"Just make sure you guys keep it down in here, any more outbursts and ill arrest the lot of you for public disturbance. Got it?" The rookie warned as his eyes went back and forth between the troublemakers.

"Yes officer, everything's calmed down now," Alicia replied patting her sister's knee.

As the cop exited the waiting room, Rakim made his entry.

"I hate cops," he stated as he walked up to the sisters. "How's he doing?"

"Not good!" Patty interjected before Keisha could reply. Walking up to Rakim's side, she attempted to give him kiss on the cheek. Rakim stopped her by putting his hand on her shoulders.

No way in hell was he letting that cheap lipstick anywhere near his face. He compromised with an awkward hug. "How you doing Patty, long time no see."

"Oh, well you know baby. Just tryin to get through this mess the Good Lord has me in. And I'll tell you it ain't getting any easier with all these damn hoodrats your brother keeps messin' with."

"What! Who the fuck is you callin a hoodrat?!?" Keisha yelled, temper rising once more.

Alicia held on tight to her sister, too stunned to say anything. Were there really, people in the world like this? She thought that these kinds of people only existed in those bad movies she used to watch as a kid or those bad actors she had seen on the Jerry Springer show. She heard Zu's mom was a bit out there, but this was too much.

"Okay listen... Listen.... LISTEN!!" Rakim yelled.

He played the peacekeeper, getting in between the two, not because he didn't want to see anyone get hurt but more so because he didn't want that cop coming back.

"Patty, go sit over there and I'll be by in a second. I'm just gonna holla at Keisha real quick, aight? Go sit down and pray."

"Help me Jesus, help me Jesus! If it wasn't for my Lord and Saviour, I would've done knock this pickney out" Patty prayed aloud as she made her way to the other side of the waiting room.

Alicia held on tighter as she felt her sister tensing up. Rakim took in the appearance of his little brother's girlfriend. She had always reminded him of a lighter skinned version of that movie star Zoe Saldana. She may have been sexy to a lot of other niggas, but she was way too skinny for Rakim's taste.

"Keisha, be easy. I see that look in your eyes. How would Zu feel if he found out you scrapped his Moms," he cautioned as Patty walked away.

"Prince you have no idea how crazy that woman is."

"Trust me Keisha, I have an idea. Who's this?" Rakim inquired, indicating Alicia.

"Oh, this is my sister Alicia. Alicia this is Rakim, Zulu's brother, but everyone calls him Prince."

"Nice to meet you," Alicia said, not really paying attention. She was still trying to get over what just happened. Never ever would she ever allow her sister to have a baby in the same family as that woman. Ever.

"Do you know wa gwan? Did he tell you what he was doing down in that area?"

"No Prince. You know your brother doesn't tell me anything. All I know is that Beads is dead, and Blacks is nowhere to be found."

"Did the bwoy'dem question you yet?"

"Yeah, but I told them that I didn't know anything. I think they think I'm lying though."

"Aight, don't worry about it. Just stick to that and things'll work out. What did the doctor say?"

"Apparently he was shot three times; twice in his upper left arm and once in the face." Rakim grimaced at the news.

"Will he..."

"I don't know," Keisha replied. "I just don't know. This is all so fucking messed up!"

"I think that's the doctor now," Alicia said as an older East Indian man in a white coat made his way towards Patty.

"Are you here for Mr. Anderson?" the doctor asked.

"Yes, we're all here for him." Keisha replied, nearly running to the M.D.

"Okay, well the good news is he's going to make it." A collective sigh could be heard amongst the group.

"The bad news; he's currently in a coma and will have to undergo reconstructive surgery on his face. One of the bullets tore through his jawbone...To say he's lucky to be alive would be an understatement. But uh, I got to get back in there. I'll keep you updated as things develop."

"When can we see him?" Patty implored as she clutched onto Rakim's arm.

"Not for a bit, I'm sorry. However, once the surgery is completed, you'll be able to visit him briefly. I really got to go. Take care and stay positive."

As the doctor walked away, Rakim dislodged himself from Patty's grasp. He wanted to get out of there before the cops started their questioning again.

"I'm going to hit the road, but I'll be back, aight. You have my number if anything."

"What, you're leaving, what about Zu?"

"I said I'll be back, Patty." Rakim already had his fill of the eccentric woman. He needed to holla at Big Will. If anyone knew what his brother was involved in it would be him. Making his way to the elevators Rakim's cell phone started to ring.

"Hello...yeah, I know, I'm leaving the hospital now...Man, you already know what it is. I'll meet you at the spot in twenty... Aight, yeah, one."

News in the hood always traveled fast Rakim thought to himself. Getting out of the elevator and exiting the building, Rakim walked the two blocks to the parking lot quickly. War was on his mind and it was about to spill out into the streets. As he got closer to his car, he caught a bad vibe. Something's not right he thought to himself. It felt as if someone was watching him. Just as he got to his 740 BMW, a maroon-coloured 2009 Intrepid pulled up, blocking his way out. Two plain clothes officers jumped out, guns and badges waving.

"Freeze, put your hands behind your head and get on your knees motherfucker!" Rakim rolled his eyes and assumed the position.

"I fuckin' hate cops..." He mumbled under his breath.

*****

One hundred different excuses reeled through Alicia's mind in a bid to escape the dreadful situation. But the notion of leaving her younger sister to deal with this mess alone was unfathomable. Even though things calmed down considerably between Keisha and Patty, there was still mad tension in the air. Plus, with the return of Steve from Tim Hortons, things just got even more uncomfortable. Why does he smell so bad? Alicia thought to herself for the umpteenth time. And why is he staring at the television when it's clearly not even on. Alicia was starting to get creeped out. To keep her mind off things, she picked up the nearest magazine on the waiting room table and started flipping through its pages. It was an old issue of MacLean's. Most of the articles dealt with the most recent political strife plaguing Ottawa. Blah Blah Blah.

This was not helping. Putting down the magazine, she stood up and stretched. She was so damn tired; all she wanted to do was find her bed. Like a blessing sent from heaven, the doctor reappeared. Everyone but Steve rushed toward the MD with renewed energy, anxious to hear the latest.

"Well ladies, nothing much to report," the Middle Eastern doctor said with a warm smile full of sympathy. "We managed to remove all the bullet fragments successfully and scheduled Mr. Anderson for his first bout of surgery later this evening."

"So, can we see him now, is he awake?" Keisha quizzed, tears welling in her eyes.

Alicia feared the worst for her baby sister. If things went south, Alicia wasn't sure if Keisha would be able to handle it. Poor girl.

"I'm willing to relax the rules for you folks for just a bit and authorize a quick visit with him. However," the doctor's warm smile turned stern. "It can't be for too long, he's still in Intensive Care which means he isn't out of the woods yet. What you ladies need to do is, go home, get some rest and return with some items to help you with your vigil. Books, an iPad, things like that. St. Michael's isn't exactly known for its excitement. Unless a crazed psychopath charges in here and shoots up the place, these old corridors could be quite boring sometimes. "

The three dumbfounded women stood and stared at the M.D. as his joke fell flat.

"Sorry," he mumbled before speed walking away. "Bad joke."

*****

On the way to Zulus room, Alicia could feel her sister trembling as she held her hand. She gave it a little squeeze for reassurance. Keisha replied with a weaker attempt.

This was going to be hard.

Inside the room where Zulu was kept, one could hear the melancholic whispers of lifeless life-supporting machines hard at work. The room, which was more of a ward, was surprisingly dark, Alicia noted absently. There were about ten beds lining its walls. Only three were currently occupied. Zulu was in the middle, bandaged like a mummy from the waist up with all sorts of machines and gizmos attached to him.

Patty let out a dramatic "My Baby!" and hurried to her wounded son. Keisha stood frozen by the door with Alicia by her side.

"I can't do it Alicia. I can't see him like this.. I can't. I just can' t...I ca-"

"Shhh ...its okay, its okay...shhh." Alicia hugged her sister, turning her away from the sight of her shot up boyfriend.

"Do you wanna leave and come back? I think you just need some time to process everything. Do you wanna go?"

"Yeah, please. I just can't do this right now..." Keisha replied, voice trembling. It wasn't until they were outside of the hospital, walking towards the car that Keisha regained her composure.

"Thank you, sis... All that back there...I'm just glad you were there with me. That scene was way too heavy."

"Don't mention it Keish, you know I'll always have your back."

The drive back home was shared in a reflective silence. Both sisters were re-living the events of the past morning.

"Are you really gonna go back to that hospital Keisha?" Alicia questioned as she pulled in front of their parents' house in Pickering where Keisha still lived. "I mean, to go back and wait with that demented woman...You sure you can handle that?"

"I have to Alicia, don't even start. And don't worry, I'm going to call Kim and have her wait with me. I know you're working tonight."

Alicia tried not to let the relief show too much on her face. She loved her sister and wanted to be there for her, but tonight was the Big Night. She worked her ass off for months putting together this event for her up and coming promotion company, Imperial Promotions and if successful, it was slated to open up many doors for her.

"Okay, call me if you need me or if anything changes. Love you."

On her way home, Alicia tried her best to ignore the foreboding feeling that something bad was about to happen.

CHAPTER 2

"Aight rude-bwoy, you can go..."

Sitting inside of a holding cell located in the TPS's 51 Division, Rakim sat calmly, thinking through all the possible reasons why he could've been arrested. The pigs never offered up any reason for his detainment. They didn't even read him his rights. He knew that they were watching him through the closed-circuit camera situated directly in front of his cell. He knew the game. They wanted to see his reaction; body language was everything. Most dudes would pace back and forth in the tiny cell, revealing their anxiety. Others would show some sort of dread and signal weakness to their captors. Not Rakim though; Leeco had taught him well...

*****

Memories of the first day Rakim had met Leeco invaded his mind in the cold concrete cell. He was only fifteen or so around those times and had just been suspended from school. For that particular suspension, Rakim was a bit foggy on the details but he suspected it had something to do with the bootlegging and selling of TTC bus tickets on school property.

On his way home, walking through one of the many side streets of Malvern, Rakim schemed and rehearsed the excuses he would give his grandmother for his most recent suspension. As he perfected his lines and delivery, the quiet noontime ambience was suddenly alight with the sounds of gunshots. Then there was a pause, followed by even more gunshots. Growing up in the Vern, Rakim wasn't unaccustomed to hearing the sounds of shots fired. Shit, even though he was only a teen he had fired a couple of them himself. What really piqued his interest was the fact that he could have sworn he heard at least three different types of hammers being let off. Shortly after hearing what a lot of people that day thought were fireworks, three men materialized from a pathway between two houses that was just four houses

ahead from where Rakim froze in shock. In the few seconds it took the assailants to run in front of Rakim, cross the street and run into another pathway where, presumably, they hopped the fence into the backyard, Rakim
could make out that two of the three men were wearing ski masks. The third was not. In a flash Rakim had realized that had he recognized the third man as one of the older heads that hung around the block.

His name was Leeco, a member of a notorious street gang called the M.O.B. that ran his neighbourhood. Rakim had seen him a few times around the hood in various places like the Malvern mall or the Recreational Centre, but never spoke to him. Every time he had seen him, dude was always surrounded by a gang of thugs or a flock of dimes. The word on the block was that he was a freshie from Yaw'd, meaning he was an immigrant from Jamaica. Rakim had heard stories about him being a shotta and that he was only in Canada to avoid persecution for mad bodies abroad. Basically, he was someone you didn't want to fuck with. As Leeco sprinted across the street, he tripped over the curb and hit the ground hard, sending an object that fell out of his pocket flying and landing underneath a nearby parked car. Immediately rolling back onto his feet like a cat, he continued his mad getaway, oblivious to the fact that his pocket was that much lighter.

It took Rakim all of thirty seconds to regain his composure and assess the situation. Going against his better judgement, Rakim ran over to the spot where he had seen Leeco fall.

Already hearing sirens in the distance, Rakim got on all fours and looked beneath the car. Staring right back at him was a gold-plated Desert Eagle .50.

Feeling the rush of excitement and fear, Rakim reached under the car and grabbed the still warm to the touch firearm. He stood up quickly, heart racing faster than an Olympic relay.

"Hey, you!" a woman yelled from a second story window across the street catching him off guard. "Did you hear that? Are you okay?"

"Yeah," Rakim shouted back shakily. "I ran and hid behind this car when I heard it!"

"Did you see anybody? Is the shooter still out there?" the woman asked, scanning the street and hiding behind her window curtain as if it were bullet proof.

Thinking fast, Rakim concocted a story.

"Yeah, I saw him! It was some Filipino dude in all red! He jumped into a car and sped away!"

"Okay! I'm calling 9-1-1. Don't move!" As soon as the woman departed from the window to retrieve her phone, Rakim power-walked out of the scene, alternating into a full-on sprint as soon as he hit the corner.

*****

Later on, that evening, Rakim found himself at the community recreational centre, hoping on the slim chance that Leeco might be there.

No such luck.

The gym inside the rec was packed, however, as it always was after a shooting. Everyone came through to hear the latest gossip, making assumptions on who did what and who was involved based sorely off attendance. All of his niggas were there as usual, holding down the corner of the gym where the high school boys gathered. Living in Malvern back then one could only be one of three things; a baller, a dancer or a gangster. Anything else and you were irrelevant.

At the time, all of Rakim's friends were ballers. There was Tyson, the light-skinned pretty-boy with the green eyes. Girls gravitated towards him like the planets gravitated towards the Sun. Tyson loved pussy and in the back of his grade school yearbook, he was voted as most likely to be caught in an affair with a celebrity. He aspired to make that true. Standing next to Tyson was his complete opposite, Abdul. Abdul had migrated to Canada from Nigeria when he was ten years old. He was dark, really dark and on top of that, it wasn't uncommon for girls to describe him as the boy who had been beaten with the ugly-stick a one too many times. Nevertheless, what Abdul lacked in beauty he made up for in his ability to conquer any sport he dared to played, especially basketball.

Last but not least, there was Akiel, the bad boy of the crew. Everyone said that he resembled the famous rapper Memphis Bleek. He even wore his hat in the same manner as the iconic hip-hop star; cocked to the side, with a gangsta lean.

Akiel and Rakim had the least amount of skills and enthusiasm for sports and since they both lived in Emprigham, a low budget-housing complex located in the heart of the Vern, they became the duo in the foursome.

"Oh, there you are brother! Everyone was beginning to say you was the shooter and shit," Akiel half-joked, with his trade-mark bad-boy smile.

"Nah man, you know I was over at your girl's crib, beatin' up da pussy as if it stole sumthin'," Rakim razzed, giving Akiel props and returning his smile. "So, what's the word? Who got it?"

"You're never gonna believe this man...Navy's dead."

Rakim shook his head. He damn well could believe it. He wasn't at all shocked over the news, seeing that Navy moved from the opposing neighbourhood to Malvern. Everyone who was plugged into the game had known it was just a matter of time.

Joining the conversation, Tyson and Abdul gave Rakim the accustomed welcoming props.

"So, you heard?" Tyson asked Rakim.

Rakim nodded affirmatively, scanning the crowded gym.

"Notice anyone missing?" Abdul quizzed with a big white smile on his coal black face. Before Rakim could even answer, Akiel jumped in. "The Mob," he whispered almost reverently, pointing to the section of the gymnasium where they usually congregated.

Rakim had already observed this. He had also taken into account that one of Leeco's main girls was actually there. Her name was Jasmine, and Jasmine was fine as hell. One of the best-looking girls in the Vern, her family hailed all the way from the politically war-torn Egypt. She had a Kim Kardashian complexion with the booty to match. Jasmine was never caught in anything but the latest. It was always Baby Phat this or Applebottom's that, with her hair and nails done just right. That day was no different.

"What's in the backpack?" Akiel inquired, snapping Rakim back into attention. Rakim had elected not to tell his boys about the events of the past afternoon and his unwitting involvement in the shooting. For the time being, he chose to play his cards close to his chest.

"Nothing, just some books I gotta bring back to the library," he lied. "Listen, I'ma holla at you niggas later though. I gotta take care of something, aight." Rakim gave each member of his entourage daps as he turned to leave.

"Need any company?" Akiel asked, sensing something was afoot.

"Nah, I'm criss," Rakim answered back as he peeped Jasmine walking towards the exit. Rakim in the past had never had a reason to speak to Jasmine, even though they were about the same age living in the same hood.

She was the older man's catty and never really paid any mind to the boys her own age or younger. He caught up with her just outside the entrance, near the privately-owned snack bar that sold heavily salted and sugared goodies to the fast food prone youth.

"Yo Jasmine, lemme holla at you for a sec..." Rakim beckoned, grabbing her attention. Flicking her hair with attitude, she turned towards Rakim and gave him the wickedest I'm-way-out-of-your-league look and responded with an even ruder "Why?"

"It's about your man. Trust me, it's important." Signaling her to follow him, he led her to the empty skating rink at the other side of the II building. As he made his way up the deserted bleachers, he started to have second thoughts on his current plan of action. He was taking a major risk.

Can I really trust this chick? He silently asked himself as he reached the top of the stands. He turned to her and the look of indignation was clearly written all over her face.

I can't back down now, here goes nothing, he thought as he wordlessly opened his schoolbag and revealed its contents.

Instantly Jasmines eyes widened in recognition, followed by astonishment and then finally disbelief.

"Where did you find this?" she demanded, hand reaching inside the bag. Rakim quickly closed it and stood back, regarding her with a now-who's-in-control expression.

"You need to take me to him, now," he commanded, sounding more confident than he had actually felt.

Jasmine grew silent and glared at him for a few moments.

Rakim could almost see the gears in her mind churning at a hundred miles per second.

Finally, she reached a decision and nodded.

"Okay," she conceded simply. "But it's your funeral."

She led him to Brenyon Way which was located directly across the street from the recreational center. B-Way, as it was known to the natives, was comprised of low-budget town houses and apartment buildings. There were two sides of B-Way: The multi-coloured townhouses behind the white eight storey low-budget building. And on the other side, the brown townhouses situated in front of the fifteen storey, equally low-budget building. Both sides had seen their fair share of violence and murder. She brought him to the multi-coloured houses behind the white building where the Jamaicans stayed.

After knocking on the door of one of the Toronto housing units, Jasmine stood back and stared at Rakim with an unreadable gaze as they waited for an answer. He stared back.

Damn this girl's fine, he thought to himself as he peered back into her hazel brown eyes.

Rakim wasn't at all the timid type. Even though Tyson was the undisputed lady's man of the crew, Rakim more than held his own in the female department. Despite his teenage hormonal urges towards the opposite sex, he kept his poker face intact and hoped that his gaze was as unreadable as Jasmine's.

After a few moments, the door slowly opened.

Standing in the threshold was a skinny, black woman in her mid-thirties with blood-shot eyes and her hair in an Erykah-Badhu-bun. Completely ignoring Rakim, she asked Jasmine if she was there to see "my yute?"

Jasmine replied with a "yeah" and then pointed to Rakim. "He's with me, everything's cool."

The Rasta-lady looked at Rakim for the first time. Her black, weed-stained lips broke out into a yellow-toothed smile,

"Aight den, cool," she said as she opened the door wider, allowing them to enter.

Following Jasmine into the living room, Rakim noticed at once that the house was full of ganja smoke and the soft sounds of the popular reggae artist Sizzla Kalongi. Sitting on a one-seater couch, Leeco was in the process of twisting up a Century Sam. Rakim had also spotted other members of the M.O.B. in the crammed living room, smoking and drinking. Some of the faces he recognized, while some others he didn't. All seemed to be on edge and Rakim sensed that his intrusion wasn't helping their mood.

Jasmine signaled for Leeco to join her in the kitchen. She indicated to Rakim to stay put. Rakim stood awkwardly in the cramped living room with a gang of presumed killers as Jasmine held court with Leeco in the kitchen adjacent.

This wasn't his idea of fun.

He again began to have second thoughts.

Moments later, Jasmine emerged from the kitchen and summoned Rakim to join them. Leaning against the sink, Leeco glowered at Rakim for what Rakim felt like was an eternity. Leeco was short in size but the confidence in his eyes and the way his presence commanded respect made him seem as if he were seven feet tall. Typically, freshies wore their clothes tight with a pair of square front shoes, but Leeco was dressed like any other Toronto local. He wore the latest Enyce shirt with a pair of Levi light blue jeans to match. His grey and white Jordan "Six Rings" complimented the design on the long sleeve shirt. Rakim couldn't tell what kind of watch the gangster was rocking but it was definitely blinged out and it, along with his diamond studded earring, only enhanced the prestige of his platinum "M.O.B." pendant chain.

After a few moments of an uneasy silence, Leeco finally spoke.

"So wa gwan my yute. Wha'chu really deh pun?"

Rakim knew this was a make it or break it moment. By making it, Rakim could become one of the newest shottas in the Vern, which brought with it money, power and respect. Breaking it and well, he could just end up shot.

Looking the killer directly in his eyes, Rakim said: "Big mon, I didn't see nothing. I don't know nothing and I'm not on nothing. I just had a feeling you might want back whatever's in this bag here."

And with that, he slowly took off the backpack and placed it tentatively on the kitchen table in front of him. Leeco made no movement towards the bag but continued to fix Rakim with his penetrating glare.

"Aight rude-bwoy, you can go," Leeco said after more than a few heartbeats.

Rakim nodded, and leaving the bag where it was, exited the house without another word. Outside, Rakim didn't know whether to feel heartbroken or relieved as the last threads of daylight gave way to the darkness of night. Walking home, he was filled with uncertainty.

Did he do the right thing by giving a murderer back his weapon? Or did he just make himself a target? Rakim had no way of knowing. He tried to swallow the seedlings of fear that had begun to cultivate in the pit of his stomach by reassuring himself that he had adhered to the code of the streets and in turn, would be protected by it. Still, later that night, and a few more afterwards, Rakim cautiously slept with his grandmother's steak knife underneath his pillow. Just in case.

*****

Hearing keys rattle, Rakim opened his eyes and took in the pig standing in front of his cell. Dressed in a cheap grey suit with a cheap blue tie and even cheaper cologne, the detective was your run-of-the-mill-cop; a pompous, drunk-off-power, red-necked conservative. Rakim's eyes squinted in resentment at the sight of his abductor. He never met a good cop. That kind didn't exist, and anyone who said they had seen one was suspect in Rakim's eyes. He hated these goofs with a passion.

"Mr. Anderson... Huh! I always wanted to say that," the goof remarked with his goofy smile.

"Do you have any idea why you're here?"

Rakim didn't reply.

The detective's smile quickly vanished.

"Answer me when I'm speaking to you boy!"

Rakim smirked. Emotions run high in hog town, he mused to himself.

"Listen, we both know the rules," he replied casually. "Without my attorney present, you might as well be speaking to me in different language. You know the deal: No lawyer. No talky." And with that Rakim rested back down on the slim, concrete cot as if it were a California King sized mattress, hands folded behind his head, eyes closed. After a moment, he heard the pig's hooves clatter away.

Rakim had called his lawyer over an hour ago and he was beginning to wonder to himself where the slime-bag was now.

CHAPTER 3

"Nigga I was born ready..."

The hypnotic vocals of Lauren Hill's Killing Me Softly floated through the air of Alicia's one-bedroom apartment. With a four-hour nap and a much-needed hot shower, Alicia felt refreshed and ready to tackle the night; her "Big Night". After months of meticulous planning, the event that Alicia secretly called her baby was finally at hand. The party was to be held at the Rebel entertainment complex in downtown Toronto. If all went as planned and the party was a success, Alicia anticipated big time clients for her up and coming promotion company. So far, things were looking good. There was a lot of hype surrounding the function and Alicia, along with her team, was expecting a massive turnout. Bobbing her head to the music, she logged into her laptop, eager to check her Facebook, Twitter and I.G. accounts. Keisha always teased her sister about being a social media junkie, telling her that there was way more to life then the internet and her "silly lil computer."
Alicia didn't pay her any mind.
If trippin' over a bullet-ridden boyfriend at all hours of the night is your version of 'living life' then I'll stick to my dot-coms, thank you very much, Alicia thought to herself as she scanned the contents of her inbox. There were at least fifty or so people hollering at her for last minute ticket purchasing and details. As Alicia sifted through her messages, her cell phone began singing Beyoncé's Crazy in Love, indicating that Jerome her boyfriend, was calling. Alicia and Jerome had been an item since high school and although Alicia's feelings for him were waning, she just couldn't tear herself out of the comfort zone she had created from their mundane relationship.
"Hello?"
"Hey, I've been trying to reach you all morning. Where've you been?"

Jerome demanded, sounding a bit annoyed.

"Oh sorry, but you wouldn't believe the drama that happened last night...Zulu got shot!"

"What? Whoa., but wait, what does that have to do with you not answering my calls?"

"Jerome, like seriously, you can be such a dick sometimes!" Alicia fumed starting to get annoyed herself.

"Obviously I was with Keisha in the hospital. Thanks for caring, asshole."

Alicia could hear Jerome sucking his teeth on the other end of the phone. He used to be so attentive to my feelings, when did he change?

"We both know that's what happens to guys like him. Don't tell me you're surprised?"

"That's not the point Jerome-"

"Whatever," Jerome said cutting Alicia off in mid-sentence. "I'm downstairs; I'll be up in a few seconds."

Click

With that, the phone went dead in Alicia's hand. A minute later Jerome let himself in with the key she had given him. Standing in the threshold of her bedroom, Jerome stood with his head slightly tilted, appreciating the sight of his girlfriend in her bright red booty-shorts and an all white wife beater.

Staring back, Alicia couldn't help but admit to herself that Jerome was sexy in a nerdish preppy kind of way: He was 5'10 with an athletic build. His facial features were feminine, giving him that pretty boy charm. Like Alicia, Jerome's parents were successful enough to spoil their only son with whatever he desired. So as a result, Jerome was always in the latest when it came to fashion, adding to his appeal but unfortunately also to his haughtiness.

"Damn girl, I love it when you wear those shorts," Jerome drawled as he made his way over to where Alicia was seated. Alicia knew what be wanted by the look in his eyes. Giving him the stiff arm as he tried to embrace her, Alicia could smell the Givenchy cologne Jerome always wore when he wanted some pussy. Despite herself, she was beginning to feel aroused by the all too familiar scent of her man in heat.

"Come on baby why are you acting like that?" Jerome whined as he easily pushed aside her hand and began kissing her neck and the spot just below her ear.

Alicia could feel herself getting wet but continued her front, acting as if she were uninterested in Jerome's advances.

"Jerome...you can be such an asshole sometimes...," Alicia gasped between moans failing in her charade.

Jerome replied by lightly biting her earlobe. Reaching under the fabric of her white 'wife beater' he began caressing Alicia's bare, 36 double-D breasts, moving his thumb in a circular motion above her sensitive nipple. Giving in completely, Alicia put aside her laptop and began kissing her boyfriend, sensually raising her arms as Jerome slid her crop top up and over her head. Breaking from their kiss, Jerome descended towards Alicia's breast and began alternating between licking and sucking her erect nipples. Alicia placed both of her hands behind Jerome's head urging him on, grinding her pelvis into his. After a few seconds, Jerome began to feel constricted and started loosening the buckle of his Gucci belt. Freeing himself, he once again began kissing Alicia with a fervid passion as she arched her back and began sliding her skin-tight booty shorts off her curvaceous bottom. Reaching down, Alicia could feel just how excited Jerome was and started rubbing the tip of his desire teasingly around her wet pulsating entrance. Jerome, unable to control himself, reached down and grabbed his member from her, thrusting it into Alicia. Pumping erratically, Jerome struggled to find a rhythm as he rode his girlfriend to oblivion. Alicia, unfortunately, was accustomed to Jerome's lack of skill when it came to sex. She naively figured that all men were like that, seeing as Jerome was her first and only lover. After about a minute or two of his initial entry, Jerome let out a stuttered moan and collapsed on top of his girlfriend, satisfied in their minute-long love making session. After a minute of laying there and waiting for Jerome to cuddle her or at least say something, Alicia got up and without a word, headed to the shower once again.

As the hot water massaged her naked body, Alicia, with her two fingers finished the task that Jerome was never able to satisfy. For reasons unknown to her, thoughts of Zulu's brother entered her mind as she neared her peak. She couldn't recall his name, but she could definitely remember his full, thick lips and sexy seductive eyes. With so much going on in the waiting room between Keisha and Zulu's crazy mom Patty, Alicia was surprised that she could vividly picture the dark and handsome man that was currently invading her fantasies. Her subconscious must have picked up on him through all the commotion...

Whatever.

The thoughts served their purpose as she shivered and spasmed her way to ecstasy.

Finally satisfied, Alicia's mind once again returned to the anticipation of the coming night's event. If all went well, this was going to be one hell of a party.

*****

"It took you long enough you fat, big-nosed Jew. You should've been here over an hour ago." Rakim half-jokingly said to his tardy attorney, sharing a smile and a handshake.

"Listen here you nappy-headed negro. If you had your face nose deep in the primo pussy I just had the luxury of sampling, you wouldn't even had made it!" The lawyer replied with a mutual smile as he took a seat adjacent to one of his most profitable clients inside the interrogation room of 51 Division. At the moment, Michael Steinbach looked nothing like the most requested and notoriously gifted Toronto lawyer as per his reputation. Decked out in khaki pants and a simple all white Polo golf shirt, the only thing that indicated Steinbach's success was his diamond-encrusted limited-edition Rolex. Rakim wasn't far off the mark by calling his lawyer fat. Steinbach's weight was the kind of weight that the affluent earned after years of overindulgence and contempt for manual labour. He ran a law firm with his older brother, Morgan. Their firm, Steinbach & Steinbach, was one of the top law firms in the country. To have either of the two representing your case was the equivalent to driving a Mercedes Benz in a highway full of Toyotas in the legal world. Steinbach had always been Rakim's lawyer. Leeco fronted the exorbitant lawyer fees in the early days stressing to the young Prince that there was nothing more important than having the best fighter in your corner. So now, looking back at all the bullshit that this man who now sat in front of him had gotten him through, Rakim felt no ways in paying an arm and a leg for the security of his freedom.

"So, what's the deal, why am I here?" Rakim asked, getting straight to business.

"Well, let's see, aside from you being a suspect in three murders across the GTA and the fact that you've been the prime subject of two failed gang-related investigations, I would have to say, in my most humble legal opinion, you're here for approximately fuck-all. They were just fishing for a weapons charge or anything really that would put you away for a few months." The lawyer chuckled, shaking his head.

"Rakim, you gotta realize that these fuckers have it out for you. Why don't you take my advice and lay low for a year; or two. Go O.T. as you boys say and get the fuck outta Dodge before these pigs just say fuck it and kill you? With what you're paying me, I know you're not strapped for cash." Rakim sucked his teeth and looked away from the pleading eyes of his lawyer.

"Man, you know I can't do that. No matter where I go, it'll always be the same. You try to run from life you'll only end up facing death."

"Wow..." Steinbach said after a moment's reflection. "That's deep. Did you come up with that yourself? Well, fuck it, it's your life and more money in my pocket, huh!" And with that the well-paid advocate wobbled out of his seat and reached across the table, patting, Rakim on his shoulder.

"Let's get out of here eh. I got lil missy waiting in my condo, aching for me to finish my final summations on why lawyers are so damn good with their tongues. Everything here's taken care of."

"So, they don't even wanna question-"

"I said everything's taken care of. Let's go!" Steinbach reiterated, anxious to get back to his barely legal cuisine.

Rakim couldn't help smiling to himself as he walked past the infuriated constables. He could almost see the steam blowing out of the ears of the one detective who paid him a visit in the holding cells. Now with his freedom regained, Rakim realized he had wasted more than half of the day playing cops and robbers with the fucking pigs.

It was time to get back to business.

After exchanging a quick handshake with his lawyer, Rakim power-walked the seven blocks to where his car was parked, jumped in his whip and skated out of the scene. Once on the DVP, Rakim reached over and hit the button that heated the seats of his car twice, followed by the air conditioning button three times and finished off with the heated seats button another two times.

Like something out of a Star Trek episode, the MP3 Sony stereo system lifted with a mechanical buzz, revealing two chromed 45. calibre handguns. On further inspection of his stash box, Rakim concluded that the two extra clips along with the emergency $2500 were still intact. These cops are waste, Rakim thought to himself as he smirked and shook his head, closing the hidden compartment. Reaching over to the passenger seat, Rakim picked up the clear plastic bag that held all the items the bwoy'dem had seized. Keeping one hand on the steering wheel, Rakim ripped open the bag with his teeth and reached in for his cell phone. After hitting redial, Rakim didn't have to wait long for someone to answer.

"Yo, where the fuck you been man?" The voice on the other end demanded. "You already know what it is; I've been linkin' your phone for the past three hours! What's poppin' man?"

Rakim couldn't help but smile to himself.

He loved his nigga.

Kilo, aka, Akiel, had been Rakim's right-hand man since grade school. Coming up in the game together their bond only grew stronger with all the death and betrayal all real niggas face when playing the 'Game of Thrones' as they liked to call it. Kilo loved Rakim and his family as if they were his own flesh and blood and took the events of the past night personally.

"Shit bro, I just had a little run in wit da beast, ya know. Had me tangled up for the morning but the Jew worked his magic and freed a nigga up."

"Yeah?" Kilo replied; his tone noticeably more cautious. "Is every-ting bless?"

Rakim understood the multiple connotations hidden in his comrade's question, so he answered with a simple "yeah, every-ting bless," to ease his niggas fears.

"Listen though," Rakim said getting back to the matters at hand. "I'm on my way over. You ready to roll out?"

"Nigga I was born ready. Just honk when you're outside, fam."

Ten minutes and two honks of the horn later, Kilo-eased his husky frame into Rakim's passenger seat. Throughout the years, Kilo had gained a lot of weight. Though most of it was muscle, his potbelly bared testimony for his love of beer and his complete disregard for cardio.

After showing respect for one another with the customary hood handshake, Kilo made a show of looking around the car and mouthed the words "Did they take the whip?"

"Nah, they didn't get a chance to," Rakim responded out loud as he began driving in the direction of the local mall.

Kilo adjusted the trademark tilt of his hat as he sat back in his seat and tried to relax.

"Nigga I don't know how you takin' this shit so calm and collect right now, man."

He fumed moments later. "I'm here flippin' out... Baby brother? Baby bro? Nigga, we hot right now, man! Fuckin' feds lurkin' in da bushes and shit... Now we gotta lay a nigga out?... This shit is crazy!"

"I know, I know," Rakim agreed "but hear wha; If we go into this all emotional and shit, we're bound to fuck up...Either with da bwoy'dem or dem niggas, whoever they are; they gonna catch us slippin'. So, we gonna play this cool. You feel me?"

"Aight, aight I hear that. So, what now? What's our next move?"

"Well, first we're gonna pay Big Will a visit and see if we could track down that nigga Blacks. The way I see it, if we can find that nigga, most of the pieces of the puzzle will fall into place, ya zee it"

"Aight, I hear that," Kilo nodded as he scanned the deceptively peaceful streets of Malvern.

"So, you're sayin', Cut Creator then?"

"Yeah," Rakim replied narrowing his eyes; "Cut Creator".

CHAPTER 4

"Same ol' shit, just a different day...."

It was the summer of 2003 and the streets of Toronto were boiling. Not just the actual temperature but the atmosphere of the block was hot. It seemed like every other day a nigga was getting shot and if not, the cops had their handcuffs on another brother. Rakim relished the season without school and spent most of his days and nights in the hood.
It was three months after the incident with Leeco and Rakim had yet to see the gangster anywhere around the ends. Rakim expected as much though. He figured the Yaw'd mon would lay low for a bit, especially with all the heat the hood was now-subjected too. On his way to the Malvern mall, Rakim and his entourage planned to hit up the local beer store. While Tyson and Abdul looked for someone to buy the alcohol, Akiel and Rakim made their way over to the back of the mall. The plan was to find some catties and bring them back to Tyson's mother's apartment. Same ol 'shit, just a different day..., or so he thought.

"Yo, you see any?" Akiel questioned, eyes darting from one face to the next in the busy plaza-like section of the mall.

"Nah," Rakim replied peering into a window of a popular Caribbean grocery store. "I'm tellin' you, we shoulda made Tyson rope in the jubies. Girls just pop up when that nigga's around man."

"Yo, fuck that shit," Akiel retorted. "That light-skinned nigga ain't got shit on me. Bet-chu I bag the baddest bitch of da summer right now."

"Oh really?"

"Yeah, really! I'ma check the parking lot."

"Well okay, I'ma check out Cut Creator and then the Mac's."
As Akiel walked off full of bravado, Rakim could hear his comrade rambling on to himself as he pulled up his baggy pants for the hundredth time. That nigga gets way too emotional, Rakim laughed to himself as he entered the locally renowned barber shop.
Cut Creator was a cornerstone of the Malvern Community. Like most

barbershops/hair salons in any predominantly black community, Cut Creator was the heart of the hood's gossip. Like a bar in a Cheer's episode, it was a place where everybody knew almost everyone's name. Inside wasn't too busy on that day. The shop usually picked up a bulk of its business on Fridays and Saturdays. Seeing that it was only Wednesday, the store wasn't at capacity but still held more than a few patrons.

Hailing up the receptionist and an off-duty barber playing PlayStation 2 at the front desk, Rakim made his way to the men's section of the barbershop, 50 Cent's Get Rich or Die Tryin' could be heard bumping out of a stereo somewhere in the back. There were at least seven people in the men's portion, however, only one was currently getting his hair cut. All seemed to be involved in a heated argument on who won the beef between Nas and Jay-Z.

William T. Brown or Big Will as he liked being called, spearheaded the discussion. His voice was the loudest out of them all and it seemed as if most of the debaters were intimidated by the animated hand gestures of the man who closely resembled Biz Markie in appearance and build.

"Fuck ya'll niggas. Ya'll niggas don't know what cha' ll talkin bout! Nas won that shit, hands down!" Big Will bellowed, "You see Nas is from the streets, nah mean. He spits that real shit. Jay, that lil batty bwoy, all he spits is that blah blah blah, I-got-money commercial shit. That nigga ain't real!"

Rakim shook his head. He heard this argument one too many times. Just as he was turning to leave, Big Will noticed him and beckoned Rakim to join in.

"Prince!" the giant yelled, "you's a smart lil nigga. Let these niggas know what's really good."

Reluctantly Rakim turned back around.

"These niggas don't wanna hear what I gotta say-"

"Yo, Prince stop trippin'. Drop some knowledge on these fools for me please."

Looking around and hailing up those he recognized in the shop, Rakim unenthusiastically inserted himself into the debate.

"Aight, it's like this. Or at least this is how see it. Nas is the better lyricist, hands down. Period. Lyrically he's superior to Jay."

"See, that's what I'm talkin' bout! Told you this lil nigga's smart-" Big Will shouted.

"But," Rakim said cutting back in, "the war these niggas is in is far past the `war of the words' game. This is 'who's-the-better-rapper-game' and wit that brings a whole `nother dimension, ya feel me. Now, we gotta take into account swag, we gotta take into account money, we gotta look at who the `crowds' rooting for and a lot of other things. But when it's all said and done, Jay comes out on top as the better rapper. Probably even the best rapper to ever do it. So, yeah."

No one in the shop said anything for a while. Big Will looked as if he wanted to kill Rakim; the other niggas were just trying to fight back their smiles.

It looked like no one wanted to send Big Will over the edge. Rakim wasn't trippin' though. He knew this nigga, and this nigga was all bark.

"Anyways, I'ma splurt," Rakim said, offering his fist to Big Will for daps. Sucking his teeth, Big Will accepted the gesture and started smiling with the rest of the men, not because he wanted to, but more so because he wanted to save face.

"Shiiit, I thought you was a smart nigga," the fat man said while shaking his head.

Walking around to the lady's section of the barbershop, Rakim could hear the argument pick back up. Apparently, he was no longer of sound mind and might even have been zuked, as told by Big Will to his audience in a bid to regain control of the debate.

Rakim didn't pay any mind to the ramblings of a fool. Searching the lady's section Rakim concluded that all the dimes must had been somewhere else that day, because they were definitely not at the mall.

Counting it as a loss, Rakim exited the shop only to find himself face to face with Jasmine. She had just climbed out of an all white Escalade and as usual, she was dressed to impress. She wore a Boston Celtics jersey that was fashioned into a tight-fitting short one-piece dress. She also had on a pair of all white Uptowns to match the 34 of the Paul Pierce jersey. But what really caught Rakim's eye was the platinum M.O.B. chain dangling from her neck playing seductively against her C-cupped cleavage.

"Oh, it's you." Jasmine said, giving him the once over with her emerald green eyes. "L's lookin' for you."

Stunned by her revelation, Rakim still managed to play it cool.

Returning her gesture by looking her up and down slowly, he responded with an "it's nice to see you too, Jasmine" and a "how're you doing today?"

At that very moment, Akiel walked into the conversation.

"Yo, that's your whip?" Akiel asked in disbelief. "Oh, you ballin' huh?"

"Shut up," Jasmine spat out of annoyance sucking her teeth.

Turning her attention back to Rakim she continued.

"Look, there's a barbeque goin' on in Crow Trail. If you want, I can bring you over. He's there right now. Unless, you're shook or sumthin'."

"Shook?" Rakim countered. "Shit, I ain't never scared."

"Oh, so you're like Bonecrusher now?" Jasmine mocked with a sarcastic smile.

Before Rakim could reply, Abdul and Tyson spotted them and made their way over.

"We got the juice!" Abdul exclaimed triumphantly, Tyson, however, was more focused on the female.

"What's good Jazz? You sayin', you wanna hang wit us?"

"Ahhh, no. Nice try Tyson, your pretty boy shit doesn't work on me. And my name is Jasmine not Jazz. Get it straight."

Once again turning her attention back to Rakim she continued.

"So, what're you sayin' Prince, I'm about to cut."

"Hold on, where you guys going? I'm comin' too," Akiel jumped in not wanting to be left out.

"Hey, if he's reaching then I'm reaching too," Tyson echoed with Abdul, nodding his head in agreement.

"What're you niggas new? There's no way I'm drivin' around Malvern with four black males in a car like that," rebuked Jasmine. "Think I wanna get pulled over? Listen, Prince, what're you saying'?"

Sensing that this was the opportunity he'd been waiting for, Rakim turned to his boys.

"Yo, my niggas, there's something I gotta deal wit right now. I'll explain later. But yo Jasmine," Rakim said turning back to her, "Akiel's rollin' with me, that's my right hand."

"Whatever," Jasmine scoffed, rolling her eyes. "I just gotta get some a pack of Century Sam's and some Pepsi and we're out. If you wanna wait in the truck go ahead, just don't touch anything."

As she sauntered off to the corner store all eyes were glued to her ample backside.

"That girl's thick in all the right places," Rakim commented to no one in particular.

"You're tell in me; whoever's hittin' that is the man fo'real," Tyson concurred.

"What's going on here?" Abdul whined, breaking their trance. "We get the juice but you get the girl? Tell me how that's fair?"

"Yo, it's not even like that," Rakim explained. "Look, remember when I pulled up wit that stoley and picked up Akiel and you niggas wanted to ride but I was like, nah?"

"Yeah?" Abdul replied, not sure he understood where this was going.

"It's kinda like that," Rakim continued "I don't wanna put you or Ty in a position you don't need to be in. Akiel, that nigga's already a fucked up-"

"Oh thanks," Akiel remarked while making himself comfortable in the back seat of the Escalade.

"You niggas know I'll never diss you like that," Rakim finished.

Grudgingly accepting their friend's point of view, Tyson and Abdul agreed to meet up with Akiel and Rakim later on that evening. Taking his place in the front passenger seat, Rakim counted the seconds for the question he knew was coming.

"So who's he and why are we meeting him in Crow Trail?" Akiel inquired from the back seat.

"We're gonna see Leeco," Rakim answered, but before he could say anymore they spotted Jasmine heading back to the car.

"Aight Prince," she said as she climbed into the driver's seat. "You ready?"

*****

Present day

"Yo, Prince, you ready?... Yo...yo?!"
Rakim snapped out of his reverie to find his road dog looking at him strangely.

"Nigga what're you doin', daydreaming? What the fuck's wrong wit you?"

"Yo, do you remember that time we went with Jasmine to that barbeque in Crow trail?" Rakim inquired, ignoring Kilo's rhetorical questions. "How old were we sixteen, seventeen?"

"Man, I don't know. Fuck all that shit, let's go page this yute," his comrade chided before jumping out of the car.

"Yeah, aight," Rakim sighed, regaining his focus. His little brother was laying somewhere in a hospital bed clinging on to dear life.
It was time for him to get some answers.
After retrieving the heat from the stash box, Rakim and Kilo made their way to Cut Creator from a parking lot across the street from the Malvern mall. He was playing it safe. Rakim didn't want any camera's picking up his plates, just in case things popped off.
It was Saturday afternoon and the barbershop was packed with men and women of all ages. Prince winked at the receptionist as he passed her and made his way to Big Will's chair in the men's section of the shop. Drake's latest hit made conversation difficult to hear as it blared out of a boom box near the backroom.
Big Will's back was turned to them as he cut a teenager's hair while talking some foolishness about Kanye West joining the Illuminati. Deja vu, Rakim thought to himself as he acknowledged all those he recognized.
The teen that was getting his haircut by Big Will noticed Prince and Kilo glaring in their direction, and though he didn't know the two gangsters like that, nodded his head out of fear.

"You keep moving like that and you're gonna fuck around and make me cut you-"
Big Will began to rebuke until he followed the young man's gaze to the two wolves eyeing him at a surprisingly close range.
The two gunmen weren't smiling.
This worried the portly barber, so he decided to play it cool.

"Prince, Kilo, wussup, long time no see. You wanna line-up or something? Lil man's almost done."
Rakim smiled back insincerely.
Big Will decided that the smiling worried him even more then the screw face.

"Nah, we're straight," Rakim replied, studying Will's eyes. "We just wanna holla at you for a sec in the back."

Pulling out a brown boy from his pocket, Rakim directed his attention once again to Big Will's customer.

"Yo lil man, you-don't mind if I holla at your barber here for five minutes? Your line-up's on me."

"Nah G, I don't mind," the teen answered, eyeing the hundred-dollar bill in the gangsters' hand. "Take your time, fam."

"Yo, what's goin' on here Prince; everything cool?" repeated Big Will, eyes darting back and forth between Prince and Kilo.

Handing the money over to the kid in the chair, Prince came within two steps of the overweight barber.

Looking him dead in the eye, Rakim could almost smell the fear emanating from the man who years ago he had lost all respect for.

Rakim had always known Big Will as one of Scarborough's best barbers, or at least the most reputed. Upon first impression, everyone adored what seemed to be a gentle giant.

It took Rakim years to see the true snake and con man that hid behind that fleshly smile and the pseudo-compliments. In the underworld of Toronto, the Good, Big Will was a set up artist; the man young stick-up kids would go to for their next move. He rarely got his hands dirty and there were even rumours of him setting up his own cousins to get robbed.

On top of all that, the rumour mill was ablaze with whispers of the fat snake leaking information to rival crews across the city.

As far as Rakim was concerned, this man wasn't to be trusted.

"Let's go talk somewhere more private," Rakim directed, indicating the room in the back of the store with a jerk of his chin.

The realization of his predicament was written all over the barber's face, even though he tried like hell to hide it.

The shit was almost comical to Rakim and if the situation were a bit less serious, he probably would have smiled. However, as things now stood, Rakim was too busy calculating his escape route in a barbershop full of customers, just in case he had to shoot this piece of shit in the back room of a crowded mall.

"Yeah, yeah. No-no problem," Big Will stammered, nodding his double chins as he led the two hoodlums to the barbershop's break room.

Closing the door behind them, Kilo drew the blinds and used his semi-muscular form to block the only exit out. The room was no bigger than a jail cell in the Toronto South Detention Center, yet all three men had their own personal space. It consisted of a love seat against the back wall and a cheap Wal-Mart table on the left. A mini fridge was crudely positioned underneath and seemed to be holding the table up. In turn the table held up a Sony Explode boom box and beside it a medium sized tank, which in turn held in a mean-looking, adolescent python.

"Take a seat man," Rakim ordered Big Will, never once breaking eye contact.
As the barber started to protest, Rakim backed out his strap and repeated his commend, cocking the hammer to add emphasis to his point. The big man quickly found his seat, eyes glued to the gun. Point taken.
"When was the last time you seen my bro?" Rakim quizzed.
"Zu?" the barber replied, "I haven't seen that nigga in over a month."
Will's eyes went from the gun, to Rakim, to Kilo and back to the gun. He raised his hands as if he were being robbed and attempted to smile jovially.
"Do you really need that shit? It's all love in here Prince, you know that."
"He's right," Rakim deadpanned sarcastically looking back at Kilo. "I don't need this shit, it's all love."
Returning a smile that sent chills down Big Will's spine, Rakim walked over to the tank, placing his gat on the table. With his eyes fixed on the snake in the tank, he continued to address the snake on the couch:
"So you say you haven't seen him?-"
"Nah bruh, not for a minute, my word."
"Your word?" Rakim chuckled. "What do you think Keys?"
Kilo sucked his teeth and regarded Big Will with a menacing glare.
"N.F.G."
"N.F.G?-" Big Will began to question.
"No fucking good!" Kilo snapped, cutting him off. "You snake-ass nigga. Your word's no fucking good' round here!"
Big Will held Kilo's stare for all of three seconds before lowering his gaze. At this point, he didn't know who was worse. The unpredictable lunatic who was currently eyeball fucking him, daring him to say something. Or the silence of the calm infamous killer who appeared to be extra fascinated with Clavon the pet snake.
"I heard a ting where you guys put Clavon on a piece of wood- I think it was a two by four or some shit- and he snapped that shit easy. True story?" Rakim inquired eyes still on the tank.
It only took Big Will a moment to adjust to the sudden switch in topic but as he answered, he began to feel more comfortable in the new direction of the conversation.
"Yeah bruh, you shoulda seen it. We brought it out to Blu's annual Barbeque and scared the shit outta them Emprigham kids; it was classic. Yo, I got that shit on video on my phone. You- you wanna see?-"
"Nah, nah it's aight," Rakim said, lifting off the top of the tank.
He reached inside and picked up Clavon, holding his neck and placing his other hand under the snake's belly as he seen the Crocodile Hunter do

countless times as a kid on T.V.

"I think I have a better idea," Rakim revealed, turning back towards Big Will.

"Yo, Prince what're you doin'?-" Big Will began to object, jumping out of his seat.

"Yo, yo what're you dealin' wit my yute?" Kilo hissed backing out his own gun cocking back the hammer.

In an instant, though noticeably conflicted, Big Will decided the gun was more of a threat than the anaconda. He again took a seat, eyes trained on the .357 magnum pointed directly at his chest.

"I don't know what's goin' on here Prince but, yo-yo! Yoo!" Big Will's eyes seemed to bulge out of his head as Rakim wrapped Clavon the pet snake around his plump neck.

"Shhh," Rakim hushed with a soothing tone.

He then proceeded to smack the snake on its head, agitating the reptile, causing it to instinctively wrap itself around the fat man's throat.

"You see, Willie, the funny thing is," Rakim continued to say, "I spoke to broski last week and he left me with the distinct impression that he and Blacks checked you not too long ago. So, since there's nothing but love in here, I'ma give you one more chance at this. When was the last time you seen my bro?"

Sweating profusely now, Big Will began to cave.

"Okay, okay. You're right- you're right I-I seen him last Wednesday. Yeah-yeah, now I remember."

The python was slowly and methodically tightening its body around the frightened barber. Big Will was undoubtedly beginning to feel the building pressure. His hands made a move to dislodge Clavon from his death grip, but as soon as his hands found the slippery texture of the snake's scales, he also felt the cold steel of Kilo's pistol pressed against his temple.

"Uh-ahh, don't taa-ouch," he heard the lunatic sing, detecting the amusement in his voice.

It was at that exact moment Big Will made a pact with himself. If he ever made it out this alive, he swore Kilo would be the first person he killed. (Or at least set up to be killed.)

"So, you heard what happened to my bro then?" Rakim continued to question.

Giving in completely, Big Will began to pour his heart out.

"Yo, I'm sorry Prince, ahh-I didn't, I didn't know shit was gonna go down like that, ahhh- please- please take it off!"

"In a minute, just a few more questions, you'll be aight." Rakim said while he patted the fat man's pockets. Pulling out Big Will's iPhone Rakcontinued his interrogation.

"So, who got at him?"

"I- I don't know exactly who but- but Blacks fucks wit'em-"

Big Will was finding it difficult to breathe and with every passing second, he felt the python was that much closer to snuffing him out or breaking his neck all together.

"Blacks?" Rakim continued seemingly unfazed of the condition of his hostage.

"Where that nigga at? I know you gotta link for him."

"It's in my phone," Big Will gasped, "he said he'll be at the Docks tonight- ahhh please, please Pri- Prince-"

Rakim was going through the barber's phone. Finding what he was looking for, he redirected his attention to his victim. Big Will was starting to blackout.

Rakim didn't feel an ounce worth of pity for the treacherous barber.

"Right," Rakim said peeling the snake off Will's neck.

As soon as the snake was removed, Big Will fell to the floor, gagging and gasping for air. Letting out a final gag, Big Will began to vomit what looked to be the remains of a cheap McDonald's combo. His drink must have been an orange soda.

"Now," Rakim began to say. "If I find out you're playing me, or if you try to set me or my nigga up in any way, Im'a holla at you, zeen. But next time it ain't gonna be no snake," he warned chillingly. "I'm just gonna let the Eagle handle you. Put a hollow tip in ya head, you feel me?"

Big Will didn't look up but nodded his compliance above the puddle of vomit. He couldn't speak just yet. He suspected his vocal cords were damaged.

After putting Big Will's phone in his pocket and retrieving his gun from the table, Prince and Kilo exited the barbershop nodding to all those who dared make eye contact with them on the way out.

Walking back to the car as if it were just another day in the hood, Rakim regarded his comrade with a mischievous smile.

"So, you sayin', you wanna go clubbin?"

CHAPTER 5

"This is my night..."

"Keisha you wouldn't believe this turn out. I never expected so many people in my wildest dreams. I mean- we're almost at capacity!" Alicia gushed to her sister over her cell phone. "I wish you were here... how's he doing?"

"The surgery was successful but he's still in a coma," Keisha replied, sounding tired and frustrated all at the same time. "Kim's here with me but she's starting to get on my nerves...Not to mention Patty. I can't stand that woman Alicia; I'm telling you I can't."

"Just stay away from her Keish. You hear me? Is that Steve-guy still there?"

"No! He left an hour ago. Thank God! I wish I were there with you Alicia. This waiting and waiting is driving me crazy."

Alicia bit her tongue, not wanting to dish out the I-told-you-so's just yet. Instead she said:

"I'll take bare pictures for you and post videos on my Instagram so you can see your big sister's success. Who knows, I might even bring home a doggie bag."

"You're such a bitch!" Keisha joked over the phone.

Alicia always found a way to make her sister smile, no matter the circumstances.

"You still love me though.,." Alicia sang playfully in response. After a pause she added, "You're okay though, right? I mean…, if there's anything I could-?"

"Stop it Alicia. Just shut it down tonight alright. Promise me you'll call when you get home?"

"I promise. I love you."

"I love you too sis. Talk to you later."

"Alright, Keish. Bye."

Pressing end on her Android, Alicia took a deep breath and steadied herself in one of the back rooms of the club. This was it. Her night was finally here. After months of preparation, it seemed as if all of her hard work was finally paying off.

Everything was going better then she had hoped for. It was 11:30pm and already the club was packed. The line-up to get in was massive and if Alicia had a dick, the owners would undoubtedly be on it

The heavy base of the classic Nicki Minaj song "Shitted on'em" bombarded the cramped room which Alicia took cover in, in order to collect her bearings. Outside the makeshift storage room, the club was a mad house. Everyone seemed to be having a good time. Some bottles were already reportedly sold out. Security reported no issues. Everyone respected the dress code, according to her team and the deejays were killing it.

Stepping back out into the ruckus. Alicia made her way to the entrance of the club.

Though it was just a few yards away, getting there was an ordeal. Hundreds of sweaty dressed up bodies swayed and bounced to the music, making it nearly impossible to walk in a straight line. Once she made it through the madness, Alicia immediately spotted Tammy, one of her workers and a childhood friend, chatting it up with one of the security guards by the coat check-in room.

Alicia and Tammy had known each other since grade seven and though it sometimes pained Alicia to admit it, Tammy was one of her best friends. Tammy was one of those white girls who loved black men. In addition, and for some reason that Alicia couldn't explain, the black men loved her back. Jerome had said it was because Tammy had one of the biggest asses in the city, but Alicia wasn't buying it. I mean her face Isn't that pretty, Alicia had thought to herself countless times. Tammy had two kids and two baby-fathers, both black and by the look of things, she was on track for baby-daddy number three.

Walking right up to them, Alicia fixed Tammy with a 'what-the-hell-are-you-doing-you-should- be-working glare, while folding her arms across her chest.

"Hey girl," Tammy shouted over the music, looking at her friend as if she stole something. "This is Premiere. He's the head of security tonight."

"Nice to meet you Premiere, but don't you have a job to do?" Alicia shouted back, getting her boss-woman on.

"Huh, yeah. Uhmm, Tammy, right?" Premiere said once again focusing his attention on the possible D.T.F. "Make sure you find, me afterwards, aight?"

"Aight," Tammy chimed now looking as if she had just found the love of her life.

As Premiere walked away, Tammy's eyes were glued on his departure. It took her a couple of seconds to realize that Alicia was frowning at her disapprovingly.

"What!?" Tammy grinned.

"Nothing," Alicia shouted back, shaking her head. "Girl, just make sure everything's straight tonight, okay? You can get your freak on later."

Tammy sucked her teeth.

"It's not even like that-"

"Oh, it's not?"

"No, it's not...

Both girls regarded each other for a couple of moments before breaking out into a fit of laughter.

"Tammy, you're crazy," Alicia said after the giggling subsided. "But listen, can you please check in on the deejay and his crew and see if they need anything? I'm going to check on the bar and see if we can get some more' bottles in for tonight."

"Yeah, no problem girl," Tammy replied, shooting a fleeting glance at the
entrance.

Going their separate ways, the music changed up as the deejay started to play *"They Shootin!"* by Nas. The club went hysterical.

Despite herself, Alicia started to wonder where Jerome was. She had seen him earlier that night, but he had disappeared with his cousin.

Whatever, Alicia thought to herself I'll catch up with him later.

This is my night.

*****

"This is our night," Rakim stated to the crew of bloodthirsty men. "If anyone gets in your way do what you gotta do. We ain't takin' no check tonight, you feel me?"

All of the men in the parking lot nodded their heads in agreement.

Before making his way Downtown, Rakim decided to round up the troops. He called on only the most trusted men of his platoon. Most of the guys he had known since childhood and if not, he had done a substantial amount of time with them in the Bucket.

There was Gremlin and Ox, two of the grimiest niggas from Scarborough. They hailed from Bay Mills and 400, respectively, and were experts in the game of gunplay. A handful of bodies laid testimony to the fact.

Standing next to the pair was Pyro the Somolian, aka Pyro the Pirate. More times, niggas just called him Warya (pronounced Wo-dee-ya), which was a common nickname for people of his ethnicity. He grew up in Malvern with Rakim and Kilo but now spent most of his time in Dixon, a west end neighborhood that was also known as "Little Somolia". He got the name

Pyro because he was the "hottest nigga on the block". Daytime, crowded mall, it didn't matter. If you were on his hit list, you were halal meat, as he liked to say.

Last, but not least, standing in the semi-circle of thugs was Kilo's dwarf-sized cousin, Smurf. A self-described Crip, out of the six he was probably the craziest. Smurf was a normal kid growing up but when his family moved to Brooklyn something in him had changed. According to Kilo, as the story goes, he just showed up on Kilo's doorstep one day without any explanation. In the same month, every one of Kilo's enemies were either gunned down or shot up. The crew secretly called him Mad Max based off a character in the popular Jamaican movie, `Shottas'.

Rakim and Kilo leaned back against the car as their confidants surrounded them.

"So lemme get this shit straight," Gremlin inquired looking up towards Rakim. "You want us to go up in there, look for that lil nigga Blacks. Hold him. Call you. Then what? Question the faggot about lil man even though we know he had somethin' to do with what went down? What, you getting soft nigga?" the short man joked as he pretended to shadow box with the nigga he would ride for.

"Brother has a point," Ox joined in. "If I see him, I'm probably just gonna girt him myself."

"You don't think I wanna body him on sight?" Rakim asked rhetorically, swatting away Gremlins play punches. "I'm sayin' though, we do that and we get no answers.

"Obviously, there was more than one shooter. I'm tryin' to holla at both them niggas, ya-zee-it?"

Again, everyone nodded just as a group of white girls walked past them, caught up in their own conversation.

"So how we gonna do this?" Pyro asked, eyes following the females until they turned the corner.

"Three niggas in. Three niggas out," Rakim explained, looking into the faces of each man. "We have three whips. So, the three outside will post up; One in the front, two in the back. If shit pops off, the three inside jump in their designated vehicle and fly out.

Apart from that, the man dem on wheels will keep a look out, just in case homeboy tries to make a run for it."

"And you sure homeboy's in there?" Pyro questioned.

"Nothing's a 100%. But on the flipside, he might be in there rollin' deep. That's why the three man dem inside gotta be on point. No drinkin'...No pussy... Just business." Rakim said, eyes falling directly on Pyro.

"Shit I guess I'm on car duty then, Cuz." Pyro half-joked. "You know I'm a recovering alcoholic and a raging nymphomaniac."

"Recovering?" Kilo joked; play punching the Somolian in his arm.

"Aight then, who else is up for car duty?" Rakim asked, looking around the crew.

"Pssht!" Kilo said, sucking his teeth. "Nigga, you know I'm in that bitch, so don't even look at me."

As he said that, a parade of police officers rode past the parking lot on bikes patrolling the party district.

"Smurf, you don't have your license, do you?" Said Rakim as the last police officer exited their line of sight. "I guess you're our third man in. I can't afford the bwoy dem stopping you in the whip with no papers,"

"Fuck!" Ox spat as Gremlin sucked his teeth.

"So, it go," Kilo smiled mockingly at the duo.

"So, how we getting in the club," Smurf asked, patting his waist, indicating that they were all strapped.

"That's the beauty of it," Rakim grinned. "Premiere's runnin' the security tonight at the club with his team. They should know what time it is."

Premiere and Rakim went back, way back. Rakim use to date one of Premiere's sisters in high school and as a result Premiere got close with Rakim and some of his crew. They did favours for each other every now and then.

"Aight, let's do this," Kilo said, anxious to get it in.

"Everyone figure out what position they playin' and who they rollin' with and then we're out," Rakim instructed, handing his car keys over to Pyro.

"And watch out for the bwoy dem."

*****

With the plan in motion, the three men on car detail went to their designated post, as the other three made their way to the club.

The Toronto party district was hectic. The streets were alive with that preliminary energy that accompanied the anticipation of a 'night out on the town'. Rakim observed that some people were already drunk, as two blondes made out with each other as another group of Middle Eastern men watched and cheered. Some cops were watching too. Good, Rakim thought to himself, keep dem pigs distracted for me, mami. The streets were littered with partygoers of all shapes and sizes. The cougars stood apart from the fresh-out-of-high-schoolers. Juiced up Guidos fist pumped to the techno music of parked car sound systems, as tight clothed freshies vied for the attention of big booty divas. Rakim recognized a few girls he knew here and there but kept it moving, avoiding eye contact.

Spotting the club and its ridiculous line up, Rakim and his boys made their way to the giant bouncers guarding the velvet roped entrance.

"Look at this Grizzly-ass nigga gwanin like he's all powerful and shit," Rakim joked mischievously to the larger of the two. "We all 'know all a catty has to do is flash a tit and she'll be all up in there faster than your fat ass can say `I want McDonald's'."

"Oh, you got jokes now?" the giant chuckled. "As-Salaamu Alaykum, brother,"

"Alaykum Salaam, fam," Rakim replied, giving the man daps and a hug.

"P told me to expect ya'll niggas but you ain't the partying-type. What the fuck ya'll niggas doin' here?" The bouncer asked.

"Ahh you know, just passin' through. It ain't nothing," Kilo jumped in with his infamous smile as he greeted the bouncer.

"Yeah?" the mammoth sized bouncer replied, giving Kilo and the rest of the gang a wary look. "Aight. Yo, Teddy let'em in."

"Hey, what the fuck! We've been waiting in this line for over an hour!" A feisty, short West Indian girl screamed, as the trio cut the line and made their way inside.

Smurf wordlessly mocked the already irate woman until Kilo physically pulled him in past the doors.

The sounds of the two bouncers trying to calm the woman down quickly gave way to the roar of music, which engulfed the three men. The security guards inside patting down the patrons recognized Rakim and his crew and nodded, allowing them to pass without the customary pat down or wand search.

"Aight," Rakim said, turning towards his men after they passed security and just before they made their way into the crowd. "This is where we split up. Remember, as soon as you spot homeboy, link my cell then link the next man. We grab him and we're out. Simple'n clean."

His boys nodded in agreement.

As the three descended into the horde, Rakim was immediately hit with a blast of heat that made him wish that he had worn less clothing. Through the crowd of dancing people, Rakim could see Kilo heading for the washrooms. Turning to the right, he could just make out Smurf, with his navy-blue Jays fitted, heading towards the V.I.P.

"Aight. I guess I'll take the bar," he said to himself, adjusting his direction.

The club's crazy tonight, Rakim speculated as he fought against the tide of intoxicated revellers. Nevertheless, despite the volume of people, it was nothing he hadn't seen before. There were the 'I-don't-dance-thugs' that lined the walls of every club, trying their hardest to give off that "don't fuck with me" vibe. Why-such men even bothered to come out was beyond Rakim. Standing a bit to the front of them were the 'two stepping gangsters', bottles in hand, doing everything in their power to attract the opposite sex.

Then came the girls who were too shy to dance or too stush to socialize, screwing up their faces.

Next, deeper in the crowd were the dancers, male and female doing the latest trend. They considered themselves the life of the party and by all means, probably were. A loose circle of people would always form around them, consisting of those who wished they could dance and those who wished they were brave enough. Scattered around were the occasional drunkards, either abandoned by their friends, or just lost in the sauce.

Rakim quickly realized that he and his crew noticeably stood out from the rest of the partygoers. The dress code seemed to be a no-hat, no-hoodie, no-sneakers affair. Rakim and his crew wore an assortment of dark coloured hoodies with matching coloured baseball caps brought down low to their eyebrows.

Ah well, we'll be out of here soon enough, Rakim smiled to himself. Security ain't sayin' nothing. However, as soon as the thought passed, another wedged into his mind as he eyed a group of thugs giving him the once over. I wonder who else is taped up in here? Having a link with security wasn't the only way one could bring weapons inside, Rakim well knew.

He quickly reminded himself that he needed to be more cautious. As he scanned the bar and the surrounding area; he concluded that Blacks was nowhere in sight. He was about to make his way to the other side of the club when he felt a persistent tap on his shoulder.

Turning around rudely, Rakim was stunned to see the beautiful girl he had met earlier in the hospital that morning.

CHAPTER 6

"So you saying I'm ugly?..."

"What the hell! How did you get past security?" Alicia shouted, questioning the tall brother in an all-black hoodie, wearing an infuriating Toronto Raptors snap-back.

"There's a dress code. You know that right?"

The man just stood there smirking at her, making Alicia even more pissed. Something about him seemed familiar but Alicia was too vexed at his smugness to pay her instincts any mind.

"Are you deaf?" Alicia continued to probe, leaning in so she could be heard.

"Alicia, right?" the tall man asked, bringing his own lips to her ears.

"Do I know you?" Alicia asked rudely, continuing the exchange of speaking into one another's eardrums.

"You're Keisha's friend, right?"

"Again, do I know you?"

"We met earlier today at the hospital...Prince...Zulu's brother."

In a flash, Alicia recognized the intruder to be the same man that had invaded her fantasies earlier that day and for a moment, all the heat from the shower rose up to her cheeks. What the hell is he doing here? She thought, becoming momentarily speechless.

Rakim slowly appraised the dime piece in front of him. She wore a black and white one-piece dress with an accessory belt that snugly rested just below her perfectly rounded breasts sitting on top of her voluptuous hips. She wasn't like the rest of the girls in there, with their flash and excessive attempts to look sexy. Dressed simply, yet elegantly, she just was. Gorgeous, Rakim wanted to say but instead he pointed to the clipboard in her hands.

"You work here?"

Regaining control of her tongue, Alicia shook her head as if trying to shake off the remnants of a dream.

"Umm, yeah...I mean-no, I don't work here. I'm just running the event for tonight."

"Oh, this is you? Well, looks like you're doing one hell of a job. It's a zoo in here," Rakim commented, looking around.

"Thanks," Alicia replied, for some reason really enjoying the compliment. "I've been working really hard for this night."

"Well it shows," Rakim said, singing her praise, unable to keep his eyes off her body. "You look good... Beautiful actually."

Rakim then froze. He didn't mean to say that. Girls usually let that kind of thing go straight to their heads.

"Thanks," Alicia replied shyly, hoping to God he didn't notice her blushing. "I wish I could say the same but..." She started pointing at his hat.

"Oww," Rakim mockingly grimaced, holding his hands to his heart as if he had just been stabbed. "You sayin' I'm ugly? How rude-"

"No, I'm not saying you're ugly-"

"Oh, so you're sayin' I'm cute?" Rakim smiled playfully.

"I'm not saying" that either," Alicia lied, giving Prince a light push.

She didn't know what it was about him, but she was beginning to like it. He was the complete opposite of anything she was used to. His eyes were hauntingly piercing. It seemed as if he could see right through her. Even though he was wearing a hoodie, Alicia could tell that he had a nice body underneath it all, He was taller than Jerome and the confidence he conveyed gave him the air of royalty, but in a good way.

"And by the way. I'm Keisha's big sister. Not her friend. Nice to see you were paying attention," Alicia said, now smiling.

"Not paying attention?" Rakim retorted. "You were the one who looked like you was on a different planet!"

"Was not!"

"Oh yeah? What's my real name than?"

Alicia was caught off guard with that one and felt her cheeks burn up even more.

"Uhmm... Tony?" She guessed, knowing damn well that that wasn't his name.

"Tony!?" Rakim repeated, flabbergasted. "You think my name is Tony! As in Tony the Tiger Tony?"

Alicia was laughing now, which brought an even bigger smile to Rakim's face. There was something special about this girl Rakim thought to himself as they laughed and joked together on the dance floor.

"So, what is your real name than?" Alicia asked, after regaining herself.

Before Rakim could answer, his phone began to vibrate. Suddenly, Rakim remembered why he was there and immediately felt guilty for becoming distracted.

"Hold on, hold on," Rakim said to Alicia, reaching for his S10.

Hours later, thinking back to that exact moment, Rakim wondered what came first. The screams or the gunshots.

A series of loud, consistent shots began to ring out somewhere near the V.I.P. section as a chorus of women began screaming, somehow overpowering the music. It took but a second for the club-goers to react.

Mass pandemonium.

Everyone began running to the nearest exit, Rakim backed out his piece and steadied himself against the onslaught of the human stampede. Again, shots began to echo near the V.I.P. but Rakim quickly realized it was of a different caliber.

A shoot-out.

Frantically looking around, Rakim spotted Alicia half submerged in a flood of human bodies that threatened to crush her. Pushing and shoving people out of his path, Rakim grabbed Alicia and led her to safety behind the bar, fighting the current of hysterical people along the way.

Alicia was so confused.

What was happening?

Are those real gunshots? This couldn't be happening. This was supposed to be her night. One minute she was giggling like a schoolgirl on a dance floor with a man she barely knew. The next, she was almost hurled to the floor by a pack of crazed stampeders. Now, she found herself cowering behind a bar with the mysterious man who miraculously saved her and, oh my God, is that a gun in his hand?!? Alicia couldn't believe her eyes.

What the hell was going on?

With the girl safe, Rakim peeked up over the bar into the commotion, trying to sort out friends from foe. Through the madness, he could see Smurf leaning against a wall, holding his shoulder as if he were shot, firing his semi-automatic in the direction towards V.I.P.

Following Smurfs aim, Rakim could just make out a stranger shooting back at his friend with reckless abandonment.

"Stay here!" Rakim shouted to Alicia.

Without waiting for a reply, he jumped over the bar and carefully took aim at the stranger. He stood in what he and his friends called the 'police stance' and, from a distance, fired twice into the stranger's chest, timing his shots carefully, not wanting to hit any innocent bystanders. The bullets found their mark, as they spun the stranger around 180 degrees. Rakim barely had time to relax, as another stranger emerged from behind an up-turned couch in the same V.I.P. booth, letting off his own machine in Rakim's direction. Luckily, for Rakim, the shooter couldn't aim for shit as the bottles behind the bar began to explode around him. Rakim crouched low and continued to fire back. Like a blessing sent from heaven, Rakim could hear the thunderous roars of Kilo's .357 entering the gun battle and with that, the bottles above his head stopped exploding.

Standing now, Rakim took in his surroundings. Two bodies were sprawled out near the floor of the V.I.P.

Premiere and a couple of other bouncers formed a protective circle around Smurf as Premiere, with Smurfs gun in his hand, continued to fire into the section. Someone was still behind there shooting back. Searching towards the direction where he heard Kilo's gun go off Rakim could see his right-hand crouching low, flanking the other side of the booth.

People were still trying desperately to get out of harm's way as the melee continued.

Just as Rakim was about to make his way towards the V.I.P. section the lights above came to life with a mechanical click.

"Drop your weapons!"

"Get the fuck on the floor!"

"Freeze you piece of shit!"

A swarm of yellow jackets fought their way inside the club, weapons drawn, each issuing a string of intimidating commands. For a brief second the place froze, eyes adjusting to the bright lights.

"Yo fuck that shit!" someone yelled, as gunfire resumed, and bullets started to fly in the direction of the police officers. A few of the yellow jackets stood their ground as they fired back into the confusion, but the majority of Toronto's finest ducked and fled for cover. Some even running back outside.

"Fuck!" Rakim muttered forcefully as he realized his plight. Crouching once again, he began firing his .45 at the bwoy dem.

BLAM!

BLAM!

BLAM!

Rakim aimed low, taking out a pig's kneecap. Killing a police officer wasn't something Rakim wanted to add to his résumé; at least not yet.

Kilo's .357 Magnum boomed as it took out another cop sending him flying as if the cop was kicked by the hind legs of a powerful Stallion. Other police officers returned fire from their places of cover. The club was still semi-packed, making it hard for the cops to pinpoint where the shots were coming from precisely.

"Yo!" Rakim yelled catching Kilo's attention.

He signaled for Kilo to make his way across the floor as he provided cover fire. Whoever was in the VIP was now shooting at the cops too, giving the cops an easier target to focus on and distracting them from Kilo as he made his way over to Rakim.

"Yo, these niggas shot my fuckin' cousin!" Kilo shouted over the screams and gunfire.

He was about to fire again at the police when Rakim stopped him.

"Hold up, hold up! Look; they focused on dem yutes there," Rakim said, showing Kilo the play.
Looking back, Rakim could see that Premiere was no longer shooting and that one of his bouncers had put a security jacket on Smurf.
Smart, Rakim nodded and at that moment caught the eyes of Premiere.
"Boogie!" Premiere mouthed to Rakim as he wordlessly indicated that he would look after Smurf.
Rakim nodded that he understood.
Returning his attention once again to the bwoy dem, Rakim's mind was racing, trying to figure out all the possible escape routes.
"We gotta get outta here!" Rakim heard someone yell into his ears.
Turning around, Rakim was shocked to see Alicia crouching down next to Kilo and him.
Gone was the little frightened girl from behind the bar and in her place stood a fierce, yet cautious woman with the determination of survival in her eyes.
"There's a way out the back," the fierce woman yelled. "Follow me!"
The trio ducked and crawled their way out past the multitude into the back portion of the club that was intended for employees only. Making it into a deserted hallway, they ran the rest of the way out of the club.
They found themselves in a back alley with sirens and the sounds of chaos filling the air.
Rakim's phone started to vibrate once again.
"Hello?" Rakim answered out of breath.
"Yo, Aq, you good?" Pyro's voice asked through the phone.
"Smurfs hit. Me and Keys are good though," Rakim began to say.
"Aight yo, listen. I just saw homeboy. He's on foot heading west. I'm following him right now!"
"Yeah?" Rakim said catching his second breath. "Okay. Stay on him. We're fawadin' right now..."

CHAPTER 7

"I don't suppose you can help me out?"

"You okay?" Rakim asked Alicia soothingly, giving her a visual inspection and thanking God that she wasn't hurt.

"What the fuck? What the fuck? What the fuck?!" Alicia gasped in shock as she doubled over, trying in vain to catch her breath.

"Yo Prince, who's this?" Kilo questioned, as his eyes shot to the girl and then back and forth down the alley way. Though it must have been empty, his gun was still drawn.

"Just a friend," Rakim replied. "You gotta moss that though fam, don't make da bwoy dem see it," he warned, indicating Kilo's strap.

"Yeah, what about that?" Kilo shot back pointing to something in Rakim's hand.

Looking down, Rakim was surprised to see that he too still held onto his piece in a death grip.

"Call Ox and Gremlin. See where they are. Maybe they can come pick us up." Rakim said, putting his gun inside his hoodies pocket.

As Kilo made the call, Rakim returned his attention to Alicia. He could see that she was missing a shoe as she was crouched over still trying her best to catch her breath.

"You okay?" he asked her again.

"Do I look like I'm okay?!" Alicia snapped, looking up at Prince. "There's not too many shoot-outs in Ajax...fuck...Fuck!"

"Yo," Kilo interrupted, getting off the phone. "Ox said him and "G" had to fly out. The bwoy dem are tearing the place apart."

"Yeah?" Rakim responded not at all surprised. He could no longer hear any guns going off inside the club but the chaos and the sounds it brought with it were still rampant.

"We gotta get out of here." Turning once again towards Alicia, Rakim crouched low so that his eyes met her own. "We gotta get outta here, okay? he repeated once their eyes locked. "Do you have a car nearby?"

Alicia couldn't believe what was happening. She felt as if she were in a movie. A movie, which almost didn't have a sequel for her. If Prince hadn't saved her, those people in there would've crushed her in their feral attempt to escape.

"Why were those guys shooting at us? What the hell is going on Prince?" she demanded to know, shock giving way to anger.

"I don't know," Rakim replied truthfully, though he had a hunch.
Rakim knew that every second he wasted in the alley way there was a higher chance for Blacks to elude his stalker.

"Alicia, listen to me," he continued. "We gotta get out of here. Do you have a car anywhere near here?"

"Yeah," Alicia managed to reply as she stood up.

"Okay, lead the way," Rakim said taking off his hoodie, exposing the plain white T-Shirt underneath. For the moment, this was the best thing he could come up with in order to change his description. He looked over to Kilo and motioned for him to do the same, bundling his own sweater carefully so that the pistol was not visible. The three made their way into the streets, walking in the direction where Alicia led them to her parked car. The place was in an uproar. People crowded the road and sidewalks, walking in all directions in mass confusion. The police could be heard barking orders to the disoriented crowd, arresting those who didn't comply fast enough. The scene reminded Alicia of the images she had seen on T.V. of the 2010 G20 summit; Sheer madness. Looking around Alicia noticed a woman sitting on the curb, crying and stabbing at her cell phone with bloody fingers. No one seemed to care or even notice her as they walked by. It was at that very moment Alicia realized her party, the party she had been working on for months, her baby, would be remembered for a very long time but for all the wrong reasons.

"This is it," she said as they reached her 2006 Sunfire.

"My boys down the street driving west. We need to catch up with him. Is that cool?" Rakim asked.

"Okay-okay...no- wait," Alicia looked up to Prince and then to his friend. "You guys have gats on you. What happens if the cops pull us over?"
Rakim was fully aware of the risks but there were no other alternatives.

"We'll be fine. Trust me." He assured falsely, looking deep into her hazel eyes.
Alicia didn't know if she could trust him fully. His only saving grace was the fact that he was Zulu's brother. So that must count for something, right?
Traffic out of the chaotic scene was moving at a snail's pace with the police directing the flow. Looking outside, Rakim could see the vibe of the crowd was becoming less tense as everyone got over their initial shock and came into grips with what just happened. Police on horseback directed the crowd,

as the cop's finally regained control. As seconds traversed by, more cops poured in with Alicia and her passengers moving further and further from the crime scene with every traffic light they passed.

Rakim pulled out his cell phone and dialed Pyro.

"Yo, where you at? he questioned into his S10. "A what?...Which one?...Aight... Yeah, yeah I know the one... Okay, make sure. We'll be there in sixty seconds... One."

Disconnecting the call, Rakim turned to Kilo in the backseat.

"We got eyes on. Do you got anymore laces for that shoe there?"

"Nah," Kilo sulked, sucking his teeth.

"Soft. Once we link up with "P" I got extra Jordan's in da whip."

Alicia didn't have a clue of what they were saying. She was the one missing a shoe. Her mind started to drift to the question of where Jerome was during the shooting and if he was okay. If he wasn't hurt Alicia planned on giving him hell for not calling but if he was, well, she didn't want to think about that.

"Make a left here," Rakim directed as the car approached a set of lights.

"There he is right there," Kilo exclaimed from the backseat, pointing to a car parked outside a seedy motel.

"Aight. This is good right here," Rakim said to Alicia, motioning her to stop.

There weren't too many people outside the motel on this street but to Alicia it was a lot compared to what she was used to seeing in Durham for this-time of night. Kilo jumped out of the vehicle before it could even come to a complete stop and ran towards Rakim's waiting car. Rakim himself stayed back with Alicia for a few moments.

"You're okay to get home, right?" he asked, eyes searching her face.

Alicia could see that Prince was genuinely concerned for her well-being and that touched her more than she would have thought. He was so different from Jerome and yet she felt so comfortable with him. Staring into his eyes seemed to slow everything down. They conveyed a sense of security, a calm to the storm raging around them.

"I'll be okay... Really, I'm fine," She answered Shaklee.

Prince looked back at her as if he didn't believe one word. Finally, he asked her where her phone was.

"Excuse me?"

"Take down my number. I want you to call me as soon as you get home."

Startled by his direct approach, Alicia couldn't help but feel nice. After she took down his number, Rakim regarded her for a couple more seconds.

"Make sure you call me, eh. I swear to God I won't sleep until I hear from you, Promise me."

"You're crazy Prince, but yes I promise."

"Okay," Rakim replied hands on the door handle. Jumping out of the car, Rakim jogged to where his boys were parked as Alicia drove off.

Kilo was already in the passenger seat with the stash box compartment wide open. In his hands rested one of Rakim's twin .45s. He skillfully handled the automatic weapon, making sure everything was in order.

"You ready my nigga?" he asked, looking up at Rakim once he was satisfied.

"Yeah, just now. Pyro send your ting, I left mine with the chick."

"What?!" Kilo admonished, as Pyro handed over his 9 mm Browning without question.

"Don't worry. It's safer this way." Rakim rejoined, tucking the gun in his belt and covering it with his T-shirt.

Kilo shook his head as he got out of the car and followed his sometimes-naive friend into the motel. Standing behind the check-in desk stood an oily stump of a man who looked to be of Greek descent. His fake gold chains were in danger of tangling with his overexposed chest hairs as an Adam Sandler movie ran on his mini T.V.

Rakim at once knew exactly how to play it.

"Yo my man, wuddup?" he greeted the clerk with the generic smile he used on all his white crack-head customers.

The man grunted in reply.

Rakim reached into his pocket and fished out a stack of folded $100 bills. This seemed to grab the clerk's attention, as his eyes visually raped the pile of money.

"A friend of mine just came in here a few minutes ago and the schmuck forgot to tell me his room number. Would you believe that? I don't suppose you can help me out?" Rakim inquired, allowing the man to get an eye full of the fist full of cash.

"You know I'm a not suppose to tell you where rooms, rooms," the clerk said in broken English, the greed dancing in his eyes.

Rakim pulled out one of the many bills and pushed it across the counter as a reply. The clerk didn't reach for the money but regarded Rakim with a look that said `you could do much better than that'.

Smirking in disgust, Rakim peeled another brown boy from the stack and laid it on the counter.

"You were saying?"

"Second floor," the clerk said, quickly pocketing the money. "Room 205... Whatever you do; not in hotel room...okay?"

"Alright then," Rakim assented.

The second floor of the Spyros Inn was poorly lit with the unmistakably pungent aroma of urine assaulting the senses of anyone who dare inhale. Rakim and Kilo followed the sign that directed them to where room 205 was supposed to be. However, in the sty that passed for a motel, most of the room numbers were stolen from the doors by suspected crackheads.

"Of course," Kilo whispered looking around them. "So now I guess we gotta knock on every door until we find him?"

Rakim replied. He had an idea. Pulling out Big Will's cell phone, he went through the directory until he came across lament. He pressed send and signaled Kilo to remain silent. Shortly, a cell phone began ringing faintly in the distance. Rakim and Kilo spread out and ran to different rooms, ears pressed against the doors, listening out for the betraying ring tone chiming treacherously on the second floor of the Spyros Inn. Finally, Rakim found the room from which the cell phone rang, just as someone answered the call.

"Hello...Hello?" The voice echoed through the phone and from behind the door at the same time.

Rakim and Kilo looked at each other and smiled.

Bingo!

*****

Knock-knock-knock-knock-knock.
"Who's there?"
"Toronto Police!"
"Yeah? What's going on? the voice asked from behind the closed door.
"There was a robbery just a couple doors down. Can we ask you a few questions?"
Rakim shouted back in his best cop impersonation.
There was a pause and then finally, "ahhh... yeah. Hol- hold on."
Rakim could almost picture Blacks inside the motel room panicking and hiding anything that would connect him to the shooting, a couple blocks away. Including Rakim hoped, his gun. Luckily for Rakim and Kilo, the Spyros Inn was too cheap of an establishment to spring for the doors with the peepholes and in turn left their tenants in the vulnerable position that Blacks now found himself in.
As they heard Blacks fiddling with the locks, Kilo and Rakim backed out their weapons and braced themselves for whatever.
The door swung open and standing in the threshold, stood a horrified, half-dressed Blacks. He wore no shirt, exposing his skinny frame and chest plated tattoo depicting a portrait of the CN Tower and the Toronto city skyline.
"Shit!" Rakim thought he heard Blacks sputter as the skinny gangster futilely tried to slam the door back in their faces.
Kilo used his burly structure to block such an attempt by powerfully shoving the door back into Blacks, sending him flying backwards through the motel room. Before he could have a chance to get up, Kilo and Rakim were on him with a series of vicious kicks and gun-butts to the face and ribs.
"Get him up, get him up," Rakim whispered hoarsely as Kilo delivered a final blow to Blacks who, by now, was curled up in the fetal position.
Once Blacks was on his feet, Rakim jammed the 9mm into his side, nearly bruising his obliques.
"Family, wa gwan!" Rakim sneered. "Let's go for a little a walk. Get some fresh air, huh?" Aggressively manhandling Blacks, Rakim dragged the double-crossing degenerate down the hallway and into the stairwell. Kilo followed closely behind as he nodded his head vigorously and rubbed his hands together, pantomiming his satisfaction in their capture.
The stairwell led them to an alleyway behind the motel. It was dark, - dirty and more importantly, deserted. Aside from the usual debris of garbage, garbage cans and other undesirables littering the immediate surroundings, there, against the greasy wall of the Spyros Inn, stood a dumpster that

helped block the view the streets had of the dreary backstreet. Rakim brought Blacks behind the dumpster, smacking him once more with his steel.

"You dissed brother," Rakim began to say. "You dissed me. You dissed my bro and with that, you dissed yourself. I mean- look at you... all bleedin' and shit. What'd you think was gonna happen?"

"Fuck you!" Blacks barked pushing out his puny chest, acting harder than he felt.

"Fuck me?" Rakim remarked. "Fuck me...0kay!"

CLAP!!

A bullet from the 9mm tore through Blacks' hip and forced him against the dumpster and eventually to the ground where he curled over his wound, groaning in pain.

"Lemme done 'em!" Kilo pleaded, nudging Rakim's shoulder.

"I got this, I got this," said Rakim as he kicked away Blacks' hands and stepped on the recent gunshot wound. -

"Aaaahhhh!! I" Blacks screamed in pain.

"Who was wit you when you got at Zu?...Answer me you lil' piece of shit!"

"Aaaahhh!...It wasn't me!- aaaahh!- Fuck, get off!"

"Wasn't you? Wasn't-nigga? You must take me for a fool or something!" Rakim shot back, pressing the still hot-to-the-touch nozzle up against Blacks' temple.

"I swear, I swear!..." Blacks pled, eyes tightly shut and praying to God Prince didn't pull that trigger again.

"Yo, fuck all that shit!" Kilo yelled from behind them. "Pitch'em man! What're you dealin' wit?"

Rakim knew what he wanted to do, more importantly, what he had to do. But first he needed answers. -

"You're tellin' me you never shot him? You really expect me to believe that?".

"I'm tellin' you Prince! I brought him there, yeah- and I knew what they were going to do, but' didn't shoot him!"

"Then who?" Rakim questioned.

Blacks began to shake his head. "I ain't no snitch."

Out of annoyance, Rakim moved the pistol over Blacks' kneecap.

CLAP!!

"Agrhhhh!"

The pain was excruciating. Blacks was bleeding profusely and in danger of going into shock. This brought a smile to Kilo's face. Rakim however remained stoic as he looked around, searching for any sign of anybody witnessing something they weren't supposed to.

Looking back down at the bleeding mess, he addressed Blacks in a calmer demeanour.

"As you can see, we're not playing. If you ever want to get up again, I suggest you start talking."

"Benny-" Blacks whimpered. "His name is Benny-arghh!"

"Benny?" Rakim echoed. "Not, Bloody Benny?"

"Yeah... that's him... he-he's the one who gave the orders...He sent two niggas-
Kwam and-and S.P. He told 'em to do it!"

Rakim looked back at Kilo in confusion.

He knew the nigga. He did some range time with him in the Toronto East Detention Center & few years back. It made no sense.

"What do you mean 'Benny told' em to do it?" Rakim heard himself say. Blacks started to shake as if he were having a seizure.

"Tsssst! That nigga dead..." Kilo remarked, chuckling to himself.

Rakim bent over and began slapping Blacks in the face. "Yo wake up!...Wake up pussy!"

It was no use. The skinny nigga was already in shock. Rakim straightened back up and stared at the kid he had once considered family doing the Harlem Shake on the ground behind the dumpster of the Spyros Inn. He turned his head to the sky and regarded the stars.

Bloody Benny. Bloody Benny?

Rakim was lost in a cloud of bewilderment that he hadn't anticipated at all. The stars remained silent. He wasn't going to get his answers tonight.

Rakim sighed and looked back at his brethren. Without saying a word, the two communicated all that needed to be said by the simple nod Kilo gave in return to Rakim's determined gaze.

"Let's get outta here," Rakim said, throwing a final glance in Blacks' direction.

As the two made their way out of the alley and back into the streets, Kilo stopped and patted his pockets as if he forgot something.

"Oh shit! Gimme a sec," he exhaled as he jogged back to where Blacks still laid shaking.

Taking out the borrowed .45 once more, Kilo pointed the firearm at Blacks' head.

BLAM!!

CHAPTER 8

"Every man for himself"

"Welcome back to CP24, we have breaking news: Bullets fly in the city's party
district, leaving four dead and over a dozen more injured. Three Toronto police officers
were among those wounded in the early morning melee of what several witnesses describe as a shoot-out between two murderous gangs. There are unconfirmed reports that claim among the four deceased, two were involved in the deadly shooting. Live on scene is our own Shouna Hunt bringing us more coverage. Shouna, what can you tell us about this horrifying event that has left the city of Toronto shaken and its citizens in an uproar?"
"Thank you, Pam, in a word; tragedy. The scene this morning is one of great devastation and sorrow as Toronto police hunt for the callous gunmen responsible for the destruction and horror-"
Click
Alicia couldn't take anymore. Abruptly turning off her flat screen, she closed her eyes tightly, wishing for all of it to go away. Her phone hadn't stopped ringing since she got back to the safety of her abode. After some rigorous convincing, her patients were finally persuaded that she would be fine by herself in her "big lonely apartment" which was "so far away from home". Her friends and her sister, however, seemed less concerned of her vulnerability and were more focused on the passa-passa that had already saturated the gossip circles.

"Girl, I heard it had something to do with Zu and them..." was a constant line, along with: "... did you see Zulu's older brother there?" And of course, there was the "...people are saying' it's a Blood and Crip thing..."
Alicia knew it had nothing to do with Bloods or Crips. Or at least she thought she knew. As for the whole incident being over Zulu, Alicia realty

couldn't answer that. Yes, Prince was there. And yes, he was involved in the shoot-out, but Alicia just couldn't fathom that a nice guy like Prince was deliberately there to raise hell. But then again...

Her phone rang once more, startling her out of her thoughts.

It was Jerome. He was calling to see if she was okay.

Alicia started spewing venom into the phone, questioning him about his absence and lack
of communication until then.

According to Jerome, he and his cousin had seen the whole thing unfold.

"It was fucking crazy Al!" he went on to say. "There we were,. minding our own business, when all of a sudden, this guy- who wasn't abiding by the dress code mind you slapped this other guy with a gun! Before you knew it, a friend of the guy who got slapped in the face pulled out his own gun and started firing..."

Alicia didn't want to hear anymore but she couldn't get a word in edge wise as Jerome continued his narration.

"...So now here's these two guys shooting at each other, and I'm basically caught in the middle, right, and my cousin, well I guess he knows the guy who got slapped in the face and his friend, right. Well, he starts yelling' at them saying how 'the place is surrounded by cops' and that they were all idiots and, well, long story short, we got the hell outta there before things got really hectic with the cops and all that."

"Okay; so, what about me?" Alicia questioned, unable to keep the tears from her eyes.

"What about me Jerome? Why didn't you seek me out? I could've been seriously hurt or worse. You didn't even think about me. What kind of boyfriend are you?"

"It's not like I wasn't thinking about you baby," Jerome back peddled. "But you know...It was like, every man for himself"

With that, Alicia hung up the phone, too disgusted to say anything more. She fought the urge to vomit.

Why am I still with him?

She had asked herself that same exact question countless times before, but now she really couldn't find any answer.

Without warning, her thoughts once again fell on Prince. She admired the way he had taken control of the situation, actually doing what Jerome confessed he couldn't. She picked up her cell phone and scrolled to his number. Butterflies started dancing in her stomach.

She exhaled deeply and pressed dial.

******

Rakim was almost at his destination when his cell phone began to vibrate and then ring on the passenger seat beside him. He had just dropped off Kilo and Pyro with promises of linking back up with them in a few hours after some much-needed rest.

Not being able to recognize the number on the caller I.D. Rakim answered hesitantly.

"...Hello?"

"Hey Prince... It's me, Alicia."

Rakim began to smile at the sound of her voice. He just couldn't help it.

"Alicia; I was beginning to worry."

"I know, I'm sorry. Things have just been so hectic. My phone hasn't stopped ringing since I got in. Tell me, why is it always your family that gives you the most headaches?"

"Yeah...I know the feeling," Rakim sighed, thoughts resting on Blacks and the last images of him bleeding out near a dumpster behind the Spyros Inn. "So, you made it home without any incident?" he questioned.

"Yup, made it back in one piece. Listen, Prince, I just wanted to thank you. I mean, really thank you for what you did tonight. I-"

"Listen, don't watch nothin'. It's soft... What kinda man would I be if I just left a woman by herself in that kind of situation...It's nothing."

"Yeah," Alicia said as she thought about Jerome and how this man was so different from him in comparison_ "I still wanted to thank you."

"Well, I'll tell you what. I left my sweater in your car," Rakim said trying his best to sound as casual as possible. "Uhmm, is it cool if I swing by later on to pick it up?"

Alicia felt a mix of excitement and weariness. On one hand, she really wanted to see him again. There was something about him that made her feel safe and exhilarated all in the same breath.

But on the other hand, she hardly knew him and sensed that he had an ulterior motive in his desires in wanting to see her. Naively she thought it was him just wanting to get inside her pants. And on top of it all he was one of the shooters the news said the cops were 'hunting'.

He was dangerous.

Despite all this, Alicia couldn't stop herself from saying `yes' and that she would text the

directions to her place. Rakim finalized the details of their rendezvous just as he shut off

the ignition to his car.

"Aight, I'll see you then," he said into his phone as he got out of his car. He made his way to the front door of a co-op house located in the heart of Dean Park which was a small mixed-income community that was in many ways controlled by the M.O.B.

Rakim made a mental note to make his morning Salaah as he noticed the sky bearing testimony to the birth of a new day. He knocked on the door and waited. He knew damn well that the occupant inside wasn't asleep.

Opening the door, a moment later and standing in the foyer wearing nothing but a pair of lace-cut panties and her trademark scowl, Jasmine looked as sexy as always. Without a trace of bashfulness, she stood there uninhibited. She fixed Rakim with that exasperating, unreadable gaze.

"Well," she said. "It's about time..."

CHAPTER 9

"Mi like your style big mon..."

Summer of 2003

The barbeque in Crow Trail was like any other. Good food. Good music. A lot of alcohol and even more weed. Everyone knew everyone. Except for the odd cousin or friend of a girl so-and-so met in a club or mall somewhere outside the hood. The vibe was chill. Jokes were told. People were laughing. A middle-aged woman was shamelessly dancing by a speaker the size of a dryer, slowly whining her body to the classic tunes of Beanie Man. Members of the M.O.B. were engaged in a few activities ranging from dominos to dice games. Looking around, Rakim estimated that there was at least eighty-plus people there enjoying themselves that day. Not counting the people inside the house where the barbeque was being held.

"So, this is where all the girls are at..." Rakim heard Akiel say as a group of dimes started laughing in the distance at a joke some Casanova must have said in a one-man performance.

Rakim just nodded his head as he watched Jasmine make her way to the domino table where Leeco sat and played with his back turned to them. Rakim knew it was him by the way Jasmine kissed his cheek and whispered something into his ear, all the while looking deep into Rakim's eyes from across the yard. The look she gave Rakim was almost seductive. Teasing.

Leeco turned around suddenly, catching Rakim off guard. Nodding to himself, Leeco returned to his game, uttering something to Jasmine. Jasmine gave Leeco a final kiss and sauntered back towards Rakim and Akiel.

Looking at Rakim she said; "He told me to say he's gonna holla at you just now and that I should take you in the house to grab some beers."

Turning to Akiel, Jasmine added; "You can stay out here. I think the chickens almost done."

Feeling left out, Akiel quickly got over his sense of rejection when he noticed a Filipino girl with a fat ass, standing by herself, waiting in line for some food by the grill.

"We'll link up later," he said as he made his way to what he hoped was his first "Asian-encounter".

"Let's go," Jasmine said, leading Rakim inside the house.

Walking inside the open doors, Rakim noticed at once that majority of the people inside were of an older generation. The kitchen, which was the first room they entered, was jammed packed with folks who stereotypically resembled the aunts and uncles of a standard, run-of-the-mill, second-generation black family. They were too young and cool to be considered your moms or pops, but they were too old to be deemed as your sister or brother. Guiding Rakim through the kitchen and past the dreads smoking weed in the living room, Jasmine led him down the stairs and into the basement. Rakim remembered it being considerably cooler down there as the atmosphere became eerily calmer compared to the on goings of the upstairs world.

The basement was empty and quiet. The only sounds one could hear was the din of the outside world as the music continued to play. There was a white freezer in the comer humming softly. Rakim guessed that was where the beer was kept but Jasmine made no move towards it. Instead, she took his hand and led him inside a small room adjacent to the stairs. It must have been a laundry room of some sort as Rakim noticed hampers and detergent and everything else related to doing laundry except for, oddly enough, the washer and dryer. Closing the door behind them, Jasmine stood within inches of Rakim, barely pressing her breast against his chest.

"So..." Jasmine breathed seemingly inching closer and closer.

"So..." Rakim echoed, too confused to be stunned but also at the same time, too horny to be confused. Was this really happening? Was the girl of his dreams really coming onto him suddenly unexpectedly? This was like every boy at school's fantasy. He tried like hell to keep his cool. By now, Jasmine could surely feel his excitement, but that didn't deter her from moving in closer and closer still. With both hands clutching at his shirt, Jasmine went on her tiptoes as she placed her moist hot lips lustfully against Rakim's neck, sending shivers down his back and unleashing any inhibitions he might have held on to.

Grabbing her waist and then palming her ass, Rakim pushed her against the wall, urging her on by grinding his erection against the thin fabric of her thong. Her Celtics jersey-dress was pushed up above her hips, exposing a white-laced thong and a tattoo of a butterfly that took up most of her upper left thigh.

Rakim started to finger her sex from behind, reaching below her ass, sending Jasmine into a passionate fury. In return, she started sucking his neck harder, her hands now voraciously trying to unbuckle his belt. Freeing him at last, she dropped down to her knees and pulled his boxers down to the floor. She took him right then and there inside her mouth, working her neck and hands expertly, nearly sending Rakim over the top. She continued her oral assault for what seemed to be hours on end for Rakim. Jasmine as it turned out was an artist at stimulating the head, A prodigy when it came to deep throat.

Rakim was on cloud nine.

As she continued to work on him, Jasmine was simultaneously playing with her own clit, getting herself wetter and wetter by the second. Not wanting to finish this way, Rakim pulled himself out of her mouth and turned her around until she was on all fours, ready to be taken from behind. He went down on his knees and for a moment considered the fact that he was about to 'sex this catty' without any form of protection. Fuck it, he thought as he slid himself into her, causing her to yelp a song of pleasure. His hands were firmly gripped on each ass cheek as he pushed and pulled himself in and out. It didn't take long for him to find his rhythm.

Jasmine tried her best to stifle the moans escaping from her throat as Rakim slammed into her over and over and over again. Finally, she couldn't take it any longer as she let out a cry that held no words, but the meaning was all too clear.

She started to shudder and spasm as she reached her climax.

Rakim wasn't finished yet. He withdrew himself and positioned her on her back. He then lifted her legs over his shoulders, re-inserting himself with a slow rhythm. One of Jasmine's breasts became exposed as the tempo of their lovemaking began to increase as the pleasure started to build up. Jasmine was on a different planet as she rode the waves.

Into yet another orgasm.

Just as he was about to finish, Rakim pulled out and exploded all over Jasmines stomach.

His juices seeped into her naval and ran down her sides.

He collapsed on the floor beside her exhausted and spent.

Jasmine was still trying to catch her breath.

He looked over to her as her chest heaved up and down. She looked back at him as he smiled and said.

"So, what now?"

*****

The barbeque was still in full swing as Jasmine and Rakim made their way back out of the house and towards Akiel. Standing by his side the Filipino girl seemed mesmerized at every word that came out of Akiel's mouth.

Jasmine tapped Rakim's shoulder and indicated that she was going about her way in a different direction. Rakim nodded as he continued onwards towards his friend.

"Look who it is," Akiel bawled as soon as he noticed Rakim's headway, "Where's the beer?"

Rakim smiled slyly and Akiel returned it with a knowing smirk.

"Anyways, this is Mary-Lou. Mary-Lou, this is my brother from another mother, Prince."

Rakim inserted himself into the conversation but played the supporting role to Akiel's production. They laughed and joked for a while as the liquor poured and the food was consumed. Rakim kept an eye out for either Leeco or Jasmine as noon turned to dusk.

Finally emerging out of nowhere, Rakim spotted Leeco walking towards them. His heart began to race as he watched te seasoned killer's approach.

"Wa gwan big mon," Leeco greeted Rakim once he was upon them. "Who's your friends?"

Rakim made the introductions not knowing what else to say.

"Okay, so this is your right hand then?" Leeco asked indicating Akiel.

"Yeah, he's my nigga. He's with me 100%," Rakim confirmed, nodding in his friend's direction.

"Aight," Leeco replied eyeing Akiel. "Akiel huh?...Nah, from now on we g'call you...Kilo...yeah, Kilo."

Akiel smiled, liking the name.

"Kilo," he repeated, trying it out for the first time. "Yeah that'll work."

"But hear wha Kilo," Leeco continued. "Mi and your boy have some business we need to discuss, ya-zee-it? So, you and your lovely empress gwan and enjoy each other's company and we'll link up same ways, zeen?"

"Yeah, yeah no doubt," Kilo agreed, already picturing himself with a M.O.B. chain.

Leeco looked at Rakim and jerked his head.

"Walk wit mi nah?"

Walking away from the barbeque and towards a small elementary school, Leeco and Rakim strolled in silence until they reached the school's playground.

"It took a Jaffa heart doin' wha you did di other day, my yute." Leeco began to say as he climbed the kids ladder and perched himself on top of the winding slide.

"Yeah," Rakim replied, looking up at the gangster who oddly enough

seemed at ease chilling in a park designed for children. "I figured it was just the right thing to do."
Leeco smiled at that and looked up towards the horizon.
The sky was beautiful that day as it exploded with hues of red and purple; casting a heavenly glow over the community known as Malvern.

"So, I trust Jasmine was courteous to you?" Leeco had said, eyes still glued to the painting in the sky.
Rakim froze, finally realizing what had just happened. Leeco must have sent Jasmine to fuck him as a `thank you' or something. He began to fish for the right words.

"Uhh, yeah... she was...cool."
Leeco looked back down at Rakim and smirked.

"Cool, eh?" he began to chuckle. "Mi like your style big mon," Leeco continued to say, turning his attention back to the horizon. "But more importantly, mi like your heart. It's not soft, but pure. Mi need people like that 'round mi. Right now, dere's too much bad minded people corrupting da program, ya-zee-it. And that's not only bad fi business, it's bad fi mi surroundings. Mi reputation. You hear wha mi a say?"

"I hear that," Rakim voiced, wondering what he was getting himself into.

"Do you know about wha mi a do likkle man?...What we do?"
Rakim had an idea but he didn't want to say, afraid the rumours he had heard were just that. Rumours.
As if he could read Rakim's mind, Leeco said;

"It's not wha ya think. Mi mean, we sell drugs, but not like that," Leeco got off his perch and descended from the slide. He looked around as if he expected the cops to be around the corners eavesdropping.

"Extortion," Leeco said lowering his voice. "No crew inna da city can move work pon a level and not expect to pay da fam, ya-zee-it?...Drug dealers can't afford to keep up war. Especially not where dem mek money. If dem no want tings to get outta control, dem pay a fee... A percentage...Now most crew at first gwan wicked and stout but..."
Leeco paused as an evil smile crept to the corners of his lips. "Let's just say dem see tings our way fairly quickly."
Rakim started to smile.

"Shit, I didn't know Malvern ran things like that!..."
"Malvern?" Leeco questioned, eyes gleaming as if he were about to explode with laughter. "Malvern?... You tink it's a 'Malvern-ting'?" Leeco began to shake his head.

"Malvern is just a place where mi rest mi head my yute. Tomorrow it might be Chester or Jane...Nah mon, this hood ting ya yutes a keep up is not wha mi a promote. There may be certain niggas from certain ends I ah wanna fling shots afta but bwoy, it's notta genocide ting mi a keep up wit.

Ya hear wha mi a...say?"

"Yeah," Rakim replied feeling as if he were a kid and an adult had just informed him for the first time that the world didn't revolve around him.

"Hear dis. Mi want you to roll wit mi. F'be mi shadow. Lemme show you wa ah gwan. If we click then yeah, but either one ah we feels this nah work out, well, no misunderstandings... But I got a feeling you're gonna be sumthin' special and mi want you pon di team."

Rakim watched as a man and his dog raced across a nearby field in the growing darkness. He could still faintly hear the music playing in the distance at the barbeque as he thought about Leeco's proposition. He knew that this was a turning point in his life. Few people recognized it for what it really was while it was happening to them. Rakim considered himself blessed for being able to spot the life alternating choice head-on.

Making up his mind, Rakim looked deep into Leeco's eyes and nodded his head.

"Aight, you don't gotta say no more...I'm in."

*****

Present day

Knock!
Knock!
Knock!
"Yo, who that?" came the voice from behind the door.
"Big-Big Will...I-"
"Who?!"
"Big Will ...Uhmm...I got-I-I got some info for Benny."
"Who?'"
"Benny!"

The voice behind the door didn't immediately reply, but Will knew the person was still there because the peephole was still darkened.

Big Will felt awkward just standing there being watched like that. This wasn't his first time in Regent Park. In the past he had always been accompanied by one of the locals or was with an entourage that was familiar with the hood and its hoodlums.

Today, however, he was by himself and regretting his decision to play it solo.

"Yo, who's with you, man?" the voice questioned.
"I'm- It's just me... I'm-I'm alone."
"Yo, da nigga says he's alone, dawg..." Big Will could hear the voice say to somebody else inside the apartment. "I don't know. He a fat nigga though..."

Big Will started to feel self-conscious. Not because he overheard the voice behind the door calling him fat, but because he was alone in a hood that he had no connection with, plus, he was naked. No strap, he didn't even wear a vest. He hoped to God that the information he was willing to share would be enough to see him through.

"Who you say you's lookin' for Blood?" the voice continued to question.
"Benny!"
"And what did you say your name was again?"

Red flags started to flash in Big Will's mind immediately. Something was up. Just as he was contemplating on whether he should leave, the stairwell door opened down the hall and a light skinned man on a cell phone came out and walked straight towards Big Will.

"Yeah, yeah, I see him...Ayo! Ayo big man! What'd you feel like dame" the stranger demanded as he disconnected the call and quickly advanced towards the barber.

"What? - I'm just-" Before Big Will could even finish his sentence the door that he was just knocking on flew open and two men— one black, one white— stood there with a revolver and what looked to be a handheld machine gun pointed directly at his heavyset frame.

Two seconds later the stranger was upon him, brandishing his own firearm. He pressed the barrel to the back of Big Wills head.

"Welcome to the Park nigga...Get your fat-ass inside!"

PART TWO

The Beginning Of the End

CHAPTER 10

"And if the nigga ain't on point..."

"So, how's this gonna end, Prince?"
Rakim didn't reply.
Instead he stood there, staring at Jasmine, wondering to himself what the fuck she was going on about.
End? The shit was just beginning! Not only was his little brother in the hospital, but now one of his main niggas was in there too. And to make things worse, if what he found out was actually true, then a war was brewing, and things were about to get way past ugly.
"Prince...Prince... I'm talking to you!"
"Yeah, yeah I hear you," Rakim began to look around the room for his clothes.
Since that fateful day at the barbeque, Rakim and Jasmine had become friends with benefits. Rakim had quickly realized that Jasmine didn't solely belong to Leeco. In fact, she didn't really belong to anybody. Compared to everyone else, Leeco had the most say in her life now, but Jasmine was her own woman.
A hustler like any other.
An opportunist.
She didn't fuck for money. She fucked for power. And that was why Leeco and so many others favoured her. She was ruthless. More dangerous than most of the men Rakim knew and respected. She once told Rakim that she had long ago found out the weakness of man. Upon hearing this Rakim had been amused.
"And just what is the weakness of man?" he had patronized.
"Pussy," she had stated simply. "And I have one... and with this shit I can make a nigga steal for me...I can make a nigga kill for me... and if a nigga ain't on point...I can make him kill himself for me."
Rakim remembered he had laughed at that, too young and naive to really

understand what she was saying. Later on, though, through the course of things, he began to see.

Through Jasmine he had learned how not to wear his heart on his sleeve and to be cautious of any woman who got too close.

"You know Leeco's not going to like this right?"

"Like what?" Rakim asked, already getting fed up by the truth in Jasmine's disapproval.

"This shit!" Jasmine yelled, pointing to the television. The coverage of the shooting was getting major play on all the news networks, including State-side.

"We're about money Prince. Not some bang-bang shoot 'em up thing. You-"

"Shut the fuck up!" Rakim shouted, cutting her off. "You don't know what the fuck you're talkin about!... You think I'm just fuckin' around here? You think I'm on some cowboy shit? Listen, when Leeco calls, tell him I say I know how the program stay and I remember what he taught me. Tell him I say that I've run across a few knots and I'm just in the process on untangling em. Tell him that he'd understand."

"Yeah?"

"Yeah!"

It was Jasmine who now stood there silent, staring up at Rakim with unmasked condemnation.

Rakim sucked his teeth and slipped on his Air Forces.

"I'm outta here," he said as he unplugged his cell phone from its charger and made his way to the door.

"You're fuckin up the money Ronald!" he heard Jasmine yell as he descended the stairs. She only called him by his gov'y whenever she really wanted to get under his skin. He ignored her as he stepped out into the sunshine. It was well past noon on a hot summer day and Rakim had errands to run.

The first thing on the agenda: Visit Alicia and retrieve his dirty strap.

The second: Initiate the process of the murder of Bloody Benny.

*****

Big Will's wrists were starting to itch from the nylon pink skipping rope tied painfully around his hands and feet. He had lost track of time, though he figured a few hours must have passed by since he had been abducted. They had stripped him of his clothes and left him butt naked in a tiny bathroom, hog-tied and made to lie in a dirty bathtub.

Just outside the bathroom doors, Big Will could hear his kidnappers laugh and carry on as Mobb Deep bumped in the background. If one were to ask Big Will on any other day if he had believed in God or his angels, the overweight barber would have bellowed and laughed until tears ran from his eyes.

Today however, cold, bleeding and wearing nothing but his birthday suit, Big Will prayed and he prayed hard. He found himself making promises to the once jested Deity that he would attend church or the mosque or wherever it took to please the Merciful Lord in exchange for a miracle that would see him to safety. As he frantically searched his mind for the once memorized *"Lord's Prayer"*, the music outside the doors came to a halt and a new voice could be heard in addition to his captors.

Big Will froze and held his ragged breathing, straining to hear what was being said. What were they going to do with him? That was the question plaguing Big Will's mind. Maybe, just maybe, if I could get my hands from behind my back, put one of 'em in a chokehold before the others get wind and take his gun from him.

Maybe I could escape or kill' em all in a gunfight.

Yeah! Then we'll see what's up then you stupid motherfuck-

The door to the bathroom suddenly burst open, disrupting Big Will's fanciful thoughts. Standing in the threshold, wearing a pair of black True Religion jeans and a solid red button up shirt with a white collar and the matching cuffs stood a man who one might describe as "mulatto". His hair was freshly cut into a one level fade with waves and his chinstrap was wide and pronounced. Big Will always noticed the grooming styles of all those he met. It was like an unconscious tick for him. The man stood there studying the tied-up fat man for a few seconds.

Big Will held his breathe.

Finally, the man spoke;

"You know me nigga?"

No, Big Will didn't know the light-skinned brother in front of him. He was not one of the men who had abducted him. He didn't look familiar at all. But before Big Will could even voice this, the mixed nigga continued his questioning.

"Do I know you? I mean-You're walkin' up in here like you know me...screamin' my name and shit... So, what up nigga? You a cop or something'?"

"No, no I ain't- I ain't no cop!" Big Will managed to stammer.

"So then what nigga?"

"Blacks!"

"Blacks?"

"I-I know Blacks," Big Will began to stutter fretfully. "You're- you're Bloody Benny, right? Well me and- me and Blacks are family."

"Family? Yo, where you from nigga?

"Malvern-"

"Oh word?" Benny said, pulling out a gun that was tucked in the front of his True Religions. "And you came here?... What're you, new nigga?"

"No-no," Big Will pled straining against the bathtub, speaking rapidly. "You see what happened last night? I know the niggas from my hood that was involved. I know where they stay!"

Benny paused for just a moment as he analyzed the big piece-of-shit, shivering in his nigga's bathtub.

"`You tryin' to set me up or sumthin"?"

"Nah man, I swear!" the large man pleaded. "I hate dem niggas! I want them dead. All of em!"

"What about Zu?" Benny inquired. "You know that nigga?"

"Yeah-yeah, fuck him too! If he makes it outta da hospital, I'll show you where he rests his head; my word!"

Bloody Benny started to nod to himself, his mind going a hundred miles per second.

"Okay fat boy," Benny finally began to say after a moment's reflection. "Let's talk....

CHAPTER 11

"It's better to be caught with it than without..."

"So, where's he at?" Rakim inquired about Smurf into his cell phone, as he barreled down the freeway.

"St Michael's," Premiere replied from the other side of the city. "Yeah man, they saying they might release him today. The slug went through and through, so you done know, no major damage. Plus, the cops think he's apart of the security team so it's all good."

Rakim nodded to himself as he exited off the 401 and onto Salem. So now, he had two niggas in the hospital over this shit. Well, at least there was a little bit of good news, he thought to himself. Now if only his little brother could wake up and make it out of there, maybe then all of this would become clear.

"You see all the media coverage this shit's getting?" Premiere asked through the phone. "There's mad feds around the hospital. They're questioning the shit outta everyone who got touched."

"Oh yeah?" Rakim replied, as he switched the call over to speakerphone in order to get the directions for Alicia's crib. "What that look like?"

"I don't know. It's too early to tell if anyone's singin'. But me and my team are going around to everyone we could and tellin 'em to stay solid on the D.L., you know, but shit's getting hot out here man, fo'real."

"Aight fam, do me a favour," Rakim said trying to figure out a way to distance himself from the brewing shit storm while at the same time, finish what had to be done.

"Go check on my brother while you're there and let my peoples know I ain't gonna forward around until things cool off or until Zu wakes up, zeen?"

"Yeah yeah, I got you. If you need anything else holla at me. I'm ridin'."

"Aight family, you done know. One," Rakim said disconnecting the call and squinting up at the address on the building that the directions had led him to.

Rakim found himself in downtown, Ajax outside the buildings next to the

local hospital.
He looked back down at his phone and began texting.

-I'm downstairs. Do u want me 2 come up or r u going 2 meet me down here?
- P
-I'll meet u in the parking lot. Give me a sec ok?
- Alicia

She messaged back. It didn't take any longer than five minutes for Rakim to spot the sexy mocha skin coloured girl exiting the building. Rakim shook his head as soon as he seen her. Alicia looked even more banging than he had remembered. How the fuck is that possible? He thought to himself as he got out of his car and called out her name. I gotta watch it around this girl. Something about her just throws me off focus.

"Hey," Alicia purred as she walked up to him.

"Hey back," Rakim replied giving her the once over then nodding towards the building she just came from. "So, you live here by yourself? Where's your boyfriend at?"

"Smooth," Alicia chuckled. "If you want to know if I have a man or not, you know you could just ask."

Rakim smiled and cocked his head to the side.

"Some things are just safe to assume baby-girl. There's no way a dime like you is ridin' solo."

"Yeah, well," Alicia said looking down, subconsciously trying to hide her smile.

"It's just me. And as for my boyfriend...well, he, isn't here right now."

Rakim noticed how the smile on her face disappeared at the mere mention of her man.

"My cars parked over there," she said, pointing off into the distance.

"So ...is everything okay? I mean- you're watching the news, right?" Alicia continued to say as they walked towards her car.

"Yeah... Don't watch that," Rakim said hesitantly. "All that... all that was just a misunderstanding, you know?"

Alicia paused in mid-stride and scoffed, causing Rakim to stop and look back at her.

"A misunderstanding?" she repeated; eyebrows raised. "Boy, if that was a misunderstanding then you need to work on your communication skills."

Rakim smirked as he took a step closer to her, causing something in Alicia to stir. Something that she desperately tried to ignore.

"Ma, don't even paint me with that brush. You seen me...I was just there tryin' to have a good time like everybody else.

"With a gun on your waist? ... Riiight," Alicia sneered, giving him a sceptical look.

"That's just for protection.," Rakim started to say as they continued walking. "As you can see, things could pop off at any second in this fucked up city... all that was just... preservation."

"Preservation, huh?" Alicia scoffed again as they reached her car. "Its that kind of preservation that's gonna put you in jail or worse... I bet that's the same preservation that has your brother laid up in a hospital-' Alicia stopped herself as she caught the look on Prince's face when she brought up his sibling.

"Sorry."

"Nah, nah don't worry about it," Rakim said, shaking his head and waving her off. "I hear you. It's just..., where I'm from... it 's better to be caught with it than without, you know?"

"Yeah," Alicia lied as she unlocked her car's door; she opened it and allowed Rakim to retrieve what she thought was only his sweater. Rakim looked under the passenger seat where he left his burner and grabbed the hoodie in such a way where the gun was concealed from Alicia's view.

"Thanks," Rakim said awkwardly. He instinctively looked around the parking lot, watching out for any pigs in sheep's clothing.

"So..." Alicia said feeling awkward herself "Do you know how Zulu's doing?"

"He's the same last time I checked... How's Keisha?" he asked once again focusing back on her.

"She's coping." Alicia replied as her thoughts started to picture her sister sitting in the hospital's ICU waiting room,

"Good," Rakim nodded as he felt his cell phone vibrate. He pulled it out and read the text message.

-Yo I'm wit K. We're at da spot. Where u at?
-Pyro

Rakim quickly typed **"soon come"** and looked back up at Alicia to find her smirking at him.

"What?" Rakim asked.

"Is that your girlfriend?" she chimed teasingly.

"Smooth..." Rakim smiled, mocking her. "If you want to know if I have a girlfriend, you know you could just ask...But nah, I'm single right now."

"Bullshit!" Alicia exclaimed. "You're probably like some type of player with like ten different girls on his roster," she teased.

She was trying her best to sound playful and as if she wasn't fishing for information, even though in reality she really was.

"Nah," Rakim lied as he subconsciously started to think about all the chicken-heads on his phone. "I'm too busy for all that right now."

"Whatever you say Prince," Alicia deadpanned.

She didn't know why, or maybe she did, but just didn't want to admit it; but she hoped against logic that Prince was telling the truth. There was something about him that intrigued her. He wasn't like any other guy she

had met before, and he definitely wasn't anything like Jerome. Prince with his sexy, disarming smile. The way he made her feel dredged up a sense of guilt that was only matched in intensity with the raw attraction she experienced whenever she was around him. Alicia tried her best to swallow her feelings.
They started walking back towards Rakim's car.
"So, when are you going back to the hospital?" she asked, casting him a shy glance.
Rakim shrugged his shoulders.
"Don't know," he said in response. "Maybe when things die down a bit; I'm not tryin' to bump into the bwoy dem right now for obvious reasons, nah mean?
At that very moment, Alicia froze, she urgently grabbed his hand and squeezed,
"Speak of the devil," she whispered fearfully, eyes wide-in shock.
Rakim followed her gaze to the Durham police cruiser pulling into the building's parking lot.
His heart sank.
"Shit!" he spat under his breath.
Suddenly, the handgun concealed in his sweater wasn't so inconspicuous and seemed to grow even heavier. Why the fuck're the cops here, Rakim thought to himself as he awkwardly adjusted the way he carried the bundled-up sweater.
Alicia froze as her heart did summersaults in her chest.
"What do we do?" she whispered.
Rakim had to think fast.
Was this a coincidence or were they somehow here for him; he couldn't tell. The police cruiser steadily made its way towards them.
Rakim quickly made up his mind. He turned until he was face to face with Alicia and looked deep into her eyes.
"Just go with it," he said urgently as he leaned into a kiss.
The unexpected feeling of Prince's lips on her own caught Alicia completely off guard. Though she was surprised, she didn't pull back but instead found herself naturally melting into his warm embrace. His soft, full lips sent shivers down her spine, nearly stealing her breath away.
Sliding his hand onto her lower back, Rakim gently brought Alicia's body closer to his as the police cruiser drove past them. The sweet taste of Alicia's lips almost knocked Rakim off his game.
Almost but not quite.
Slowly breaking their embrace, he covertly watched the police cruiser park itself by the only entrance of the building's parking lot.
Alicia, still halfway in the spell of the kiss, reluctantly pulled back.
"Is anyone up in your crib right now?" Rakim asked, maintaining a

plastered smile for the cops' benefit.

Alicia shook her head no, too afraid that her voice might betray how excited the kiss had made her feel. Rakim looked back into her eyes.

"Do you mind if I chill out a while until the cops leave? I'm not tryin' to get pulled over right now."

Still speechless, Alicia nodded her head and as nonchalantly as she could, led him through the parking lot and into her building's main lobby. As soon as they were in the elevator and the metal doors closed, Rakim let out a sigh of relief. He held the bundled-up sweater uneasily, wondering to himself if Alicia had caught the play. He desperately wanted to dispose of the gun discreetly. His mind ran through all his available options.

Alicia, however, was in her own whirlwind of emotions. Aside from Jerome and some of their mutual friends, she had never let another man up into her apartment. She was both terrified and excited. Was this a good idea? She thought to herself in the silence of the ascending elevator. Would Prince make a move on her? He did seem to have an ulterior motive in his request to meet up... but was it sex? The question was reasonable, but it wasn't her major dilemma. The problem Alicia had difficulty answering was; if Prince did come onto her, would she reject him or give into her growing desires? She honestly couldn't answer.

The elevator doors chimed open and Alicia nervously led Rakim down the hallway and into her home.

She didn't plan on having any guests, so her tiny apartment wasn't as tidy as she now wished it was. Unfolded laundry decorated her living room couch with a few of its items rebelliously taking refuge on the nearby floor. On the coffee table by the couch, a lone bowl with the remnants of milk and Fruit Loops told the story of what she had for breakfast that morning. In the kitchen, dishes shamelessly littered the sink, affirming Alicia's scorn for the simple chore. Alicia prayed that Prince didn't notice the chaos, reasoning to herself that boys were, by nature, messier than their female counterparts. She was wrong. Rakim did notice how untidy her apartment was but paid it no mind. In his experience, girls were much messier than guys. Instead, he surveyed his surroundings for any clues as to who her boyfriend was and if he'd be back anytime soon. There weren't any pictures of any guys on her walls and from as far as he could tell, there weren't any men's clothing mixed into the heap of laundry on her couch.

All good signs.

An unnecessary altercation with a jealous boyfriend was the last thing Rakim needed.

"Sorry for the mess," Alicia apologized as she closed the door behind Prince.

"Soft," Rakim replied. "Can I use your washroom real quick?"

"Sure," she answered while taking off her shoes.

"It's down the hall and to your left."

Rakim removed his Air Forces and made his way down the hallway with the bundled-up sweater.

As soon as Prince was in her bathroom, Alicia quickly rushed over to the couch. She swiftly gathered up her clothes and unceremoniously threw them back into its hamper, taking special care to hide any bras or panties from view.

Meanwhile, Rakim unbundled the handgun from his sweater and inspected it quickly. Satisfied, he looked around the washroom for any possible hiding spots. He opened the bathroom cabinet beneath the sink and stashed the burner behind a bucket of cleaning products, reasoning to himself that he would come back for it as soon as the cruiser outside drove away.

Heading back into the living room, Rakim caught Alicia scurrying around the apartment, briskly tidying up whatever she could. She hadn't noticed him yet and was in the process of wiping down her coffee table and organizing the magazines on its glass surface. The sight of her form captivated Rakim as he watched her as she bent over to retrieve the remote control that had fallen on the floor next to the table. Her body is bangin', he again thought to himself as he admired the way her curves defied the bagginess of her sweatpants.

Not wanting to seem like a creep, Rakim cleared his throat, announcing his presence.

"You need some help?" he inquired, startling Alicia from her household chores. Straightening up, Alicia looked back over at him and smiled self-consciously.

"No, no, its okay, I got it... Thank you though."

Rakim nodded his head and headed towards the kitchen. Completely ignoring her, he went over to the sink and began to do the dishes.

Embarrassed, Alicia hurried in behind him and tried to stop him.

"No, no Prince, you don't need to do that. It's okay. Really-"

"So how long've you been with your man?" Rakim asked, once again ignoring Alicia's unneeded modesty.

Alicia was stunned over Prince's stubbornness; Jerome had never helped her with the dishes or any other small chores around the apartment. Prince was proving to her that he was cut from a different cloth. It was kind of sexy. Most men didn't offer to do the dishes if they only wanted sex, she reasoned to herself. Maybe Prince really didn't have any ulterior motives. Giving into his obstinacy and picking up a dishrag, Alicia began working in tandem with Prince, drying the dishes off as soon he was finished washing them.

"Six years," she answered without looking at him. "We've been together since high school."

"What's his name?" he asked.

"Jerome..."

Rakim scrolled through his mental index trying to put a face to the name but came up empty.

"Where's he from, if you don't mind me asking?" he continued to investigate casually.

"Pickering...I don't think you'd know him, though. He's not... uhmm-"

"A gangster?" Rakim helpfully filled in the blank.

Alicia blushed at his bluntness.

"Yeah, I'm sorry. I didn't want to offend you."

"Why would I be offended?" Rakim asked. "I know what I am... Or at least, I know how the world perceives me. I might regret some of the things I've done, but I'm not ashamed of who I am. I'm a product of my own choices."

"But why would anybody choose to sell drugs or a carry gun?" Alicia probed, genuinely confused. "I mean, you seem like a smart guy; what's wrong with finding a job and living a peaceful life?"

"There's nothing wrong with it. It's just..." Rakim paused, struggling to find the right words. "It's just not for me. Now, I ain't tryin' to diss your man or anything, but to be honest, living a square life is boring as fuck in my eyes. It's the safe route. It's the kind of life you'd live if you were content on being average. I ain't an average nigga and I'm not one for taking the safe route. You only live once. Why waste it on a merry-go-round when you could spend it on a rollercoaster?"

"Because at least on a merry-go-round, you'd get to live a longer life without the ever-looming threat of jail," she said pointedly. "Your brother's in the hospital suffering from gunshot wounds, Prince. If that doesn't do anything to jar your perspective on things than I don't know what will."

"I think my perspective is just fine, thanks."

"You really think that?" Alicia questioned.

"Yeah, I do. Not everybody gets to grow up in the suburbs," he replied in a much harsher tone than he had intended.

After a few moments of awkward silence, Rakim handed Alicia the last dish to be dried and then turned, staring at her intently.

"What?" she asked with a hint of attitude.

"I think you got some hood in you," he answered with levity, hoping to lighten the mood.

"Excuse me?"

Rakim took a step toward her, playing as if he were examining her soul.

"Yeah, yeah, I see it now," he said, smiling while still searching her eyes. "It's right there; right in that corner in your left eye."

Alicia fought back a smile. "You're an idiot."

"Only when I'm around you," he replied honestly.

They were standing only inches apart. Alicia's heart began to flutter as

Prince continued to look deeply into her eyes.

The attraction he felt for her was obvious. Alicia on the other hand tried her best to suppress her own feelings but was unsuccessful. Her mind kept going back to the kiss they had shared in the parking lot only minutes earlier.

Rakim took another step closer, increasing the budding sexual tension between them.

"So, what're you saying?" he asked with his eyes still penetrating her own. "You ready to jump on that rollercoaster, or are you still stuck on a merry-go-round?"

They were so close to each other now that their noses were almost touching. At that very moment Alicia should have been thinking about her man and how kissing Prince in her kitchen would be a very shady thing to do. However, unfortunately for Jerome, those sobering thoughts were far from Alicia's mind as Prince slipped his hand onto her waist, snaking it around her lower back, drawing her even closer. Their lips were so close now that she could feel his breath tickling the bottom of her nose.

Their bodies practically pressed against each other. Rakim was still staring into her eyes, slowly inching closer and closer, daring her to pull away. Sex was far from the reason why he was there but something about Alicia had him a ways. He just couldn't help himself. Finally, their lips touched. They embraced slowly at first, tentatively probing and tasting each other but soon their kiss grew passionate.

*****

Alicia lost herself in the heat of the moment, her hands dancing along the hardened, well defined muscles beneath Prince's black and white Crooks and Castles t-shirt. She could feel herself getting wet as he slid his hands from her lower back down to her ass, kneading her butt cheeks through her sweatpants. She urgently pressed herself against his body, wanting to feel even more of him. What she felt was the hard outline of his desire, straining against her stomach to be unleashed. Without thinking, she reached for Prince's waist and unbuckled his belt, pulling his jeans downwards.
He moaned slightly as Alicia wrapped her hand around his member, slowly stroking the shaft up and down as they continued to embrace. Any questions of how far this was going to go was erased from the lover's mind as Rakim in turn slid down Alicia's sweatpants, exposing a sheer red thong. Alicia stepped out of her pants with one foot at a time as Prince effortlessly lifted her onto the kitchen counter, never once breaking from their kiss.
Alicia's mind was ablaze. Is this really happening? She thought to herself in a brief moment of clarity. Was she really about to cheat on Jerome? She knew what she was doing was wrong, but she couldn't stop herself now. She was so far gone, addicted to the taste of Prince's lips. She continued to massage the erect, velvety muscle in her hand, working it up and down. Usually at this point, Jerome would have lost control and skipped the much-needed foreplay, jamming himself into Alicia with a reckless abandon. Prince, however, is different. He doesn't appear to be in any rush. Instead, he deliberately takes his time as he begins to kiss her neck and earlobe, driving Alicia crazy. In the end, its Alicia who loses control, no longer satisfied with him being anywhere else but inside her. She gradually guides Prince in, inch by inch, savouring the feel of him. It's at this very moment where Prince takes control, thrusting himself into her and then out.
Steadily, he increases the tempo, causing tiny moans to escape from somewhere deep inside. Alicia could feel something building up from deep within. The way Prince was stroking it had her seeing stars. She reached around him and gripped his bare butt cheeks, urging him to continue the rhythm that was driving her wild.
Suddenly, Prince lifted her off the counter and began fucking her standing up. The unexpected change in position pushed Alicia off edge, causing her to climax violently all over Prince's member as he continued to pump her up and down. She wrapped her legs around him almost naturally and rode the tidal waves of pleasure. This was the very first time Alicia had ever experienced an orgasm. Jerome had never been able to bring her to this point. She marveled at Prince's endurance as he continued to bounce her up

and down, threatening her of the possibility of a second orgasm. Ultimately, she felt Prince shudder, signaling the moment where he too found ecstasy. He held her suspended in his arms as he spilled his seed, both mildly aware that he had finished inside of her without a condom.

Gently, after a few seconds of cooling down, he lowered Alicia off him. The pregnant silence that followed was full of Uncertainty. They both pulled up their pants as they struggled to figure out what to do or say next. Alicia was ashamed of herself. She couldn't believe that she had just done that. Not only was she now a certified cheater, she figured Prince, from that point on, would forever look at her as if she was just a commonplace ho. She kept her eyes downcast, emotionally kicking herself for her lapse in judgement. Prince softly lifted her chin with the tip of his finger until their eyes locked onto one another. He smiled reassuringly, melting any insecurity she felt, as he looked deep into her eyes. How does he do that? She wondered to herself as butterflies began to dance, and twirl in the base of her stomach. He brought his face close and kissed her lightly on the lips.

"There's something special about you, Alicia," he whispered against her lips almost as if it were a confession.

"I know you got a man and all that, but I doubt homey's aware of the fact. I don't wanna make it seem like I'ma hit it and quit it on you, but I gotta bounce right now. If that cop is gone I gotta take advantage and dip before they decide to show up again...

"When all this shit blows over, do you wanna link up and maybe see where all this goes? Or am I reading all this wrong?"

Alicia wanted to scream and shout that she too felt the same way about him; That she was finished with Jerome and was ready for something new. Something more.

Instead, she replied with a much calmer, "Sure, we can see where this goes," suppressing the urge to jump into his arms and hug him over how excited she was. After they made their way back to the living room, where Prince spied on the parking lot below, confirming the police cruiser was indeed gone; he retreated to the bathroom where Alicia assumed, he washed himself up. Before he left, he kissed her again and instructed her to text him later that night. Closing the door behind him, Alicia exhaled and took stock of herself with her forehead pressed against its wood. She felt a mix of emotions ranging from extreme happiness to the hollowing pangs of a guilty conscience. She was in the process of weighing her feelings when suddenly the door vibrated with somebody knocking on the other side. Who the hell? Was Prince back already? Maybe he forgot something, Alicia reasoned to herself as she reopened the door. She couldn't help herself from feeling excited; thinking that Prince had decided to forgo everything and just spend the rest of the day with her. She began to blush and smile at the prospect of spending even just a few more minutes with him. However, the person standing on the other side of the door wasn't Prince. In fact, he was far from Prince Charming.

Jerome regarded Alicia with a questioning glare.

"Yo, why aren't you answering your phone?" he demanded, wiping the smile off her face. "And who was that nigga in the hallway just now? Did you just have somebody up here?"

Alicia's heart skipped a beat, knowing that Prince and Jerome had just crossed paths. Still, she played the dummy,

"I don't know who you're talking about Jerome," she lied with a straight poker face. "Listen, we need to talk..."

CHAPTER 12

"When I grow up I wanna be just like you niggas..."

"So, what's the deal wit this Benny yute?" Pyro asked sitting back down to roll his blunt after giving Rakim daps. "Keys says he was like your celly or something in the burg?... What's up wit that?"

"He wasn't my celly man, we were just on the same range for a minute," said Rakim as he took a seat at the kitchen table. They were mossed-out in Pyro's twin sister's basement apartment, the spot where they usually kicked it at when Pyro was in town. Pyro was seated on the couch of the surprisingly spacious apartment and looked up at his nigga perplexed.

"So, what the fuck's da difference? You was still livin', wit da nigga, nigga!"

"There's a difference man, stop this." Rakim said, un-wrapping his sweater on the ratable inspecting the semiautomatic.

"Shit, stop playin' nigga," Kilo joined in, learning against the fridge with his arms crossed over his massive chest. "Word is, is that you and da nigga were like best friends in there yo. A real batty and bench!"

All three of them started laughing. Rakim shook his head and offered his middle finger to his homeboy clowning him.

"But on the real though," Pyro said as the laughter died down, putting the final touches on his backwood. "Tell me about this nigga. Is he a problem or what?"

Rakim started to think back to the time he met Bloody Benny. It had been about two years-after that fateful day at the barbeque with Leeco.

Rakim had become Leeco's prodigy. His heir of sorts. The gangster had shown the young Prince the ins and outs of the game. The money flowed in, but with the cash came the coffins, and with the coffins came the cops.

It was the beginning of the winter of 2005 and the year had already been pegged as the year of the gun by the media. Michael Steinbach, Rakim's newly acquired lawyer but long-time counsel and associate of the M.O.B., warned Leeco that the recently fashioned Guns & Gangs Task Force were rumoured to be very interested in the activities of the "Fam" and its high-ranking members.

"But how does he know that?" Rakim had questioned his mentor upon hearing the cautionary report "Dude's just a lawyer."

Leeco shook his head, dismissing his pupil's inexperience. He explained that Steinbach had friends in high places, and that he had never once led them astray. As a result, Leeco had decided it was best to play the "back-burner", allowing Rakim and a few other youngins a chance to step up. They were instructed to play it cool and not to add anymore unnecessary heat to the already scrutinized clan. To achieve this it was decided, for the time being, that the M.O.B. would not engage in any new "ventures" but only collect from their more than lucrative pool of existing "clients". However, at the time, this tactic did not sit well with Rakim and his pack of hungry wolves. They wanted more.

The plan was simple, they were to run up on an underworld gambling spot that doubled as a Caribbean take-out restaurant, located somewhere in Rexdale, and rob all the big timers for their loot.

"What could possibly go wrong?" Kilo had said smiling his trademark bad boy smile from ear to ear with his fellow gangsters. There were four of them in Kilo's Filipino baby mother's basement that day. Sitting on the couch nearest to Kilo was Harlem, a flashy loud-mouthed nigga that knew Kilo from their T.Y.A.C. days. The Toronto Youth Assessment Center was a juvie detention lock-up with a reputation for breeding monsters. Harlem was no exception. He was a loose cannon, a statistic. He was headed to either an early grave or a mandatory life sentence. Seated on a Laz-E boy directly across from them sat the Dread, a Rastafarian gangster who loved to preach the teachings of Marcus Garvey. No one really took him seriously though because the boy loved his pork. He also ate other things normal Rasta's dashed fire upon; namely pussy.

Rakim that day was anxiously pacing the length of the pinched basement. He felt something in his gut. Maybe they should've listened to Leeco and the others he was thinking to himself. What if things did go wrong? But it was too late for Rakim to back out. He couldn't afford to look soft in front of his niggas. Besides, since they were so far down the totem pole in the M.O.B., the share of the gwop they received during those watchful days did nothing to satisfy the hunger of the young hoodlums. It was time to get paid.

Rakim and his crew found themselves in the parking lot of the popular Caribbean restaurant. It was just past 2 a.m., which meant the poker games were well on their way and the pot was ripe for the taking. Ski-masked up, Kilo, Harlem and Rakim crept to the back of the store while the Dread played the Getaway. There were two men smoking cigarettes by the back door.

The trio ran up on them, guns drawn and had them on their knees in a matter of seconds.

So far so good, Rakim thought to himself as they disarmed the assumed guards and made their way inside.

Laughter and chitchat could be heard coming from behind the door of a room at the end of the darkened hallway the threesome had found themselves in. Kilo quickly stormed the room, kicking the door open, waving his Blue Steel Lama from one side to the next, Rakim and Harlem were right behind him, brandishing their own pistols at everyone in the room.

"Nobody fuckin' move! You already know what this is!" yelled Kilo with a hint of amusement in his eyes. "We're here for the loot, not your lives. So, I don't wanna see no fuckin' heroes' tonight, aight!"

There were about twelve men in the smoke-filled room. Five of them were sitting down at the poker table, hands raised in the air. The others were either at the makeshift bar or by the wall where a dice game was being held. Money, jewelry and what appeared to be a key of cocaine was piled on the middle of the table. Hundreds and fifty-dollar bills littered the floor where the men played dice. Harlem went straight for the table and picked up the packaged yayo.

"Oh, so ya'll niggas is bran'!" he exclaimed, as he shoved the drugs into his trash bag, smiling behind his ski mask. "When I grow up I wanna be just like ya'll niggas, fo'real!"

"Yo, lemme see ya hands, nigga. Lemme see your hands!"

Rakim shouted as he ran up on one of the men at the bar who looked like he wanted to do a ling. He smacked the Coolie yute in his face with his burner, causing teeth and blood to fly out of his mouth upon impact, Rakim pressed his barrel to the back of the man's head and searched his waist with his free hand.

"Fuckin' Braveheart, huh?" Rakim spat as he pulled out the man's gun from his belt. "Anyone else feelin' fuckin' brave tonight?!" Rakim shouted, now pointing two guns at the group of men.

Harlem and Kilo went around the room and stuffed everything that looked valuable into their bags. Within sixty seconds, the three raiders were sprinting across the parking lot to their awaiting getaway vehicle.

"Drive, drive, drive, drive!"

Harlem commanded the Dread as he laughed in victory over their success. All four men were amped. They did it! They got away! They felt invincible. Who could fuck with them? They were on top of the world. But shortly after they got onto the on-ramp to the 427, sirens accompanied the red and blue lights illuminating the rear-view mirror of the Dread's four door Honda. A chorus of "Shits!" and "Fucks!" could be heard inside the car as the men did a 180 from triumph to despair.

"Don't stop, don't stop!" Rakim urged the Dread as he looked back and weighed his options. Nothing looked good.

Four black men in a car full of guns, drugs and money was the sure-shot recipe for a couple of summers in jail. All Rakim could think of was the warnings Leeco had given him and how stupid he was for not taking heed as the car charged down the nearly deserted west end highway. The Dread maneuvered his Honda with frightening speed as if he were a seasoned NASCAR driver. They passed the exits for Rexdale Blvd and then Martin Grove in record time. There were at least three Toronto police cruisers behind them. When the Dread made a sharp turn onto Weston Rd the patrol car closest to them couldn't keep up, skidding his squad car into a full-on roll-over.

"Yeah, take that- take that!" The Dread cheered exuberantly as Kilo and Harlem voiced their approval by mimicking gunshot noises. Rakim was too busy fidgeting with his seat belt.

Though he tried his best to shake the cops, the Dread eventually lost control as the car smashed through a bus shelter and into a near-by tree, killing the Dread instantly and seriously injuring the others.

Rakim, Harlem and Kilo found themselves in 23 Division that night, The Dread found himself in the morgue.

After their first appearance, the three co-accused were separated and placed in different detention centres. Rakim was placed in the East, Kilo in the West and Harlem landed in the Don Jail. After spending eight weeks on the medical range, Rakim was finally let out into population. He landed on 4B west with half of his chest still bandaged like a mummy under his orange jump suit. As soon as he walked onto the range and took a seat at the end table, a group of niggas approached him.

"Yo, where you from nigga?" The leader of the pack questioned.

Rakim looked him up and down and stated simply;

"Malvern. Who're you?"

The light-skinned nigga smiled and cocked his head to the side.

"These lil niggas call me boss but you; you can call me Bloody Benny..."

*****

Growing up in the hood Rakim had always heard vivid horror stories about being in jail. The vicious beat downs by rival crews. The malicious oppression of the guards. The months one can spend in solitary confinement.

And granted, when he got there, he had seen it all, but the real horror; the one thing that truly got under his skin, was the inanity of the whole system. It was senseless. They locked you up as a deterrent to crime, but they locked you up with criminals; thus thrusting one even further down the path of the lawless. There was no correction in the correctional system. Rakim had learned much more behind bars than he had done on the streets and none of it had to do with being transformed into a "productive, law-abiding citizen."

The Toronto Fast Detention Centre was the hub for the city's most recent casualties of the TPS's gang raids; consequently, making it one of the most violent lockups in the province of Ontario. Rakim felt right at home.

Amidst the jailhouse politicians, the two-faced gangsters and the crack-addicted fiends, Rakim made a name for himself. He masterminded ways of capturing drug laden packages that were en route to other ranges and then, turning around, he'd sell it right back to the intended receiver. What he didn't sell he ended up sharing amongst the men on his range. This made him very popular. Those who dabbled in the drug game behind bars incurred almost a celebrity status amongst incarcerated criminals.

Needless to say, Bloody Benny became one of Rakim's biggest fans. The fake love was comical to Rakim, but he embraced it, playing his part as he was supposed to. There was no beef between the two therefore there was no threat. They lived together peacefully sharing the coveted serving duties and controlling their own individual phones.

While on range, Rakim had observed Benny's behaviour and movements. Bloody Benny was a complicated man to say the least. Someone had once quipped that he suffered from the light skin syndrome, which basically meant he thought that he was naturally better than many of the darker niggas around him. It appeared to Rakim that Bloody Benny craved to be the centre of attention. He often told incriminating stories about himself to help bolster his reputation as a boss in his hood.

Rakim didn't believe half of the shit he said but the power Bloody Benny exerted over his followers led the young gangster to respect him. However, there was just something about him. Rakim could never quite put his finger on it; he just felt it. There was just something off about the way Bloody Benny carried himself, something weird.

One day on the range, it was established that a box-thief had gone around stealing pill from the man dem while they were out at yard. The suspects were few on the small range of twenty men, so it didn't take long to discover that a black meth-head was the feebleminded culprit. The meth-head had been Benny's cellmate for weeks until one of Benny's soldiers landed on the block, kicking the fiend out into a less sought-after cell. The victims of the theft and a few others viciously attacked the pitiable drug addict accordingly, leaving him broken and battered at the back of the jailhouse range. But be that as it may, Bloody Benny still wasn't satisfied He kept pacing back and forth, uttering to no one in particular that 'the bitch was gonna talk...the bitch -was gonna talk'. No one on range really believed the meth-head was the snitching-type but hey, who could really tell.

A day later, Bloody Benny had ordered an over-zealous underling to run up into the lacerated man's cell and to administer a "few pokes", A few pokes ended up turning into the East Detention's first homicide since the early 90's, landing the misguided subordinate a mandatory life sentence. The youth, before the incident, use to take pride in being a part of Bloody Benny's gang. A real "dick rider" Rakim used to privately joke to himself. Bloody Benny and the youth even went as far as to calling themselves cousins and who knows, they probably were. But one day, after everything was returned to normal, Rakim had inquired about the youth while playing Bid Wiz with Bloody Benny and a few others.

Bloody Benny had looked up from his cards and scoffed.

"Fuck that kid," he spat, flicking his wrists as if the gesture alone would discard the youth's image from his memory. "That nigga was a waste yute."

"But I thought he was your fam though?" Rakim mocked while he continued to play his hand.

Bloody Benny looked up and smiled at Rakim crookedly.

"Yeah...well, fuck family!"

"That's some cold shit," Pyro exhaled as he snubbed out his roach into the ashtray on the coffee table. "Sounds like this Benny-yute gots no honour, yo."

Rakim just shrugged his shoulders as he looked down and inspected his work. During his narrative, he had been dismantling his gun with plans of discarding the pieces separately throughout the day.

Kilo now sat at the table with Rakim, drinking a beer and fantasizing to himself on how good it will feel to finally catch the light-skinned faggot and put a barrel down his throat, blowing him to smithereens. Rakim looked at his best friend and knew exactly what was on his mind by the look in his eyes.

"We'll get him my nigga. Have patience."

"Yeah?" Kilo replied shaking his head as if awakening from a trance. "So, what's your plans? How you wanna do this?"

Rakim didn't answer right away. As he sat in silence, he tried to remember when exactly he had become the leader of heartless killers. When exactly did his life change? Was it at the barbeque that day with Leeco? Or maybe his life had changed even before that.

Was he the reason why his kid brother was laid up in a hospital?

Maybe Alicia was right.

Maybe his perspective was off. Maybe if he had become a lawyer, Zulu would have followed suit. Maybe if his moms didn't die, he wouldn't have rebelled...Maybe I should slow down, Rakim began to think to himself, second guessing his lifestyle.

With all of his sins on his conscience and all the dirt he had done, Rakim, for the first time in his life, was beginning to have doubts.

He looked across the table and into his best friend's waiting eyes. Suddenly, he realized that he still hadn't answered his nigga's question. Swallowing the seedlings of doubt, Rakim buried any feelings that distracted him from the current situation. He smiled crookedly, looking over at Pyro and then back to Kilo.

"The plan is simple," he said. "We start by hitting homeboy where it hurts...Mount up!"

CHAPTER 13

"... the smallest things."

Inside the confines of Alicia's one-bedroom apartment, the tension in the air was almost tangible. The once self-described unbreakable couple was finally doing the impossible. They were breaking up.
The argument itself lasted for hours but in truth had been ongoing for years. They had become different people, headed in different directions. Staying together could no longer be justified for the mere sake of comfort It was time for them to go their separate ways.
Yet this simple truth, though never actually spoken aloud, was easier said then done. Jerome just couldn't let her go. It wasn't because he loved her; those feelings had long since passed. It was more so the idea of him losing. Jerome never lost. He was a winner.
There was no way he would allow Alicia the satisfaction of telling their friends that she had indeed broken up with him. He and only he would dictate when it was over. Now, according to Jerome, was not the time, So the bickering continued.
Alicia was tired. She was tired of the fighting. She was tired of the "back and forths". She was tired of wondering night after night if there was someone better for her out there. She refused to allow herself to be drawn in by the manipulative reasoning of the man who now caused her more pain than joy.
But reason he did and after hours of arguing, Alicia now found herself stranded on her queen-sized pillow-top, head resting in her hands, eyes tightly shut, waiting for a break in Jerome's tyrannical monologue.
"...You're just upset that your little project ended up on the six o'clock news rather than being featured in today's Life Style section of the Toronto Star," he was in the middle of saying.
"This has nothing to do with' me. This has nothing to do with me! You're just being a drama-queen! As usual! Blowing up the smallest things-"
"Small things?" Alicia snapped, unable to listen to his bullshit any longer.
"You call me almost getting killed a 'small thing?'... You're not a man.

You're a bitch!"

Through the tears and the anger, Alicia couldn't believe that she had gone that far but damn it felt good. She wished that she could freeze the look on Jerome's face right now.

It was priceless.

"Bitch?" Jerome repeated almost to himself, as if tasting the word for the first time.

"Yeah, a bitch, a coward! You're not a real man," Alicia continued, not allowing Jerome the opportunity to dominate the conversation again. A real man protects the women around him. A real man takes charge of situations..."

"Oh, and I'm not a real man?"

"Apparently not...You're a bitch!"

Alicia fell in love with the word and decided to use it more freely when describing her soon-to-be-ex.

"Compared to who?" he questioned, heatedly.

The look on Alicia's face sent red flags flashing in Jerome's mind.

"Wait a minute...Compared to who Alicia?" he asked again.

Unrestrained images of Prince leapt before Alicia's eyes; Prince pulling her out of harms way; the look of concern written on Prince's face just before he asked her for her number; and then finally Prince smiling and kissing her...

She tried to hide her intimate thoughts from Jerome's prying eyes.

"It doesn't matter," she whispered quickly, almost in a hushed tone, looking away.

All the spunk that had filled her up with power by simply calling Jerome a "bitch" quickly evaporated out of her body.

It was way too early for Jerome to even suspect that she might be interested in another man. She herself still didn't even know how she felt about Prince. Now was definitely not the time for Jerome to know anything about her secret lover. She desperately tried to change the subject.

"The point, Jerome, is that you left me, and to tell you the truth, I haven't been happy in this relationship for a very long time. Last night was just the breaking point"

"Screw all that!" Jerome shouted, visibly upset. "Are you seeing someone else?"

Alicia shook her head out of exhaustion.

"Just go home Jerome, okay? Just-just go..."

Jerome felt as if he had just been punched in the gut.

If Alicia were cheating on him, the embarrassment alone would ruin him. There was no way he would let this shit get a one up on him. He needed to get to the bottom of it.

However, the look on Alicia's face informed him that he would not get anything out of her tonight. So, though difficult, Jerome swallowed his words and headed out the door. He had never killed anyone before. The thought had never even crossed his mind. But as he descended with the elevator, he promised himself that if he couldn't have Alicia then no other man could.

CHAPTER 14

"You get the picture?"

    Big Will was finally permitted to put back on his clothes after hours of being imprisoned in the scummy and stained bathtub. He now currently sat with his tormentors in an unkempt living room that was infested with spliff roaches, beer cans and what appeared to be the remains of an ancient Chinese food take-out dinner. The air was peppered with the fetid stench of stale tobacco, dirty laundry and rotten egg rolls. To Big Will's astonishment, this didn't seem to bother his captors in the slightest. Very much like garbage collectors sifting through the morning trash, the hoodlums carried on as if the stench were as common placed as the pungent aroma of coffee in a downtown office breakroom.

The conversation they held, if listened to by the Crown Attorney, would have been enough to charge and convict them for conspiracy to commit murder.

During the course of the discussion, Big Will had been able to learn the names of his kidnapers. Besides Bloody Benny, there were three other men. One was black, the other was white and the last was mixed.

The black kid was named Shells and would have been the easiest man to identify in a police line-up. Half of Shells' face had been blown off in some consequential disagreement, reminding Big Will of a character he had once seen on HBO's *Boardwalk Empire*. The barber was having a hard time trying not to stare at the gaping hole in the side of the man's face.

Mouse was the name given to the white kid with the shaggy, hippy-style hair. Big Will assumed he had gotten the moniker from his small stature and skinny frame. Mouse also had a long and narrow face which made him look even more like a rodent but without the whiskers and fur.

The third man, the "light-skinned yute", was the infamous Scotian's Pride, or S.P. for short. Big Will had heard stories of this one from all the way across the city. To put it simply: he was a problem.

S.P. hailed from Nova Scotia, which was where the Underground Railroad deposited its shipments of escaped American black slaves. The black community that now thrived in the east coast province was renowned across Canada as a batch of strong willed, close-knitted families. S.P. was a descendent of the infamous Downey Clan. It was rumoured that a child psychologist had once described him as being a sadist. Next to Bloody Benny, he was probably the most dangerous person in the room. What freaked Big Will out the most was the way S.P.'s eyes would always shift back to him, with what seemed to be a murderous intent.

To say Big Will was uneasy at that particular moment would be the understatement of the year.

He was trying so very desperately to satisfy his captors with the information he was more than willing to share. He told them about the M.O.B. and where they were known to congregate. He told them about Price and Kilo. Hell, he even told them about Leeco and what they should expect from him after they bodied "P" and "K".

He told them everything.

After his tutorial, Bloody Benny asked all the questions.

"So, you're sayin' Zulu is Prince's lil brother?"

"Yeah… They're half-brothers or-or stepbrothers, or some shit…" Big Will replied, quick to please.

Benny sat back and continued to take pulls off his DuMaurier, absorbing the new information like a *bounty-quilted* paper-towel. He remembered Prince back from his days in the East Detention Centre and was fascinated by how small the world was. When he had put the word out for Zulu to get *got,* he didn't anticipate any real retaliatory action from the streets. So the other night, when Blacks had come running to him in the club, crying about some Scarborough chumps looking for him, Bloody Benny didn't even give it a second thought. He had ordered one of his little soldiers to roll with Blacks throughout the crowd and to "slap out" whoever he had pointed to. Those commands resulted in a bloody shoot-out that claimed three of his followers and earned him the privilege of being hunted by half of the city's police force.

Bloody Benny loved it.

He thrived in the spotlight. Everything was about him. Everyone else were just pawns; *Small fish*. He didn't give a fuck if one *goof* was related to the next. If he decided that someone had to go, then *gone* they would be; *Fuck everyone else! He was the Boss!*

As Bloody Benny continued to float around in his thoughts, lost in his own tyranny, Big Will now faced a dilemma. He couldn't figure out where exactly to rest his eyes. He refused to look at S.P. His shifting glances had now turned into a full-blown "Michael-Myers-Stare", which more than unsettled the cowardly barber. Looking at Shells was also out of the question. The gaping hole, if gazed upon for too long, seemed to grow with every passing second. It made Big Will sick to his oversized stomach.

Mouse was now somewhere behind him, dealing with various people who came in and out of the apartment. Which caused Big Will to suspect that the establishment was actually the neighbourhood crack house. At one point, he vaguely wondered that if were to try to signal for help, would one of the visitors respond to his pleas or would they ignore him and leave him to his plight?

Big Will knew the answer and wearily decided to keep his eyes on his wrist where the pain was still rampant.

With any luck, he would soon be allowed to leave the dreadful apartment and make his way back to the safety of his side of the city, where he could watch the demise of Kilo and Prince in peace.

As Big Will waited and waited, marveling at how he could still faintly see the red marks left by the nylon pink skipping rope on his dark brown skin, Bloody Benny finally spoke.

"This is what I want you to do…they like you in your hood right?" Big Will was slightly caught off guard by the question.

"Yeah," he lied, wondering what exactly this maniac had in mind.

"I wanna get them all in one spot-"

"What, the entire M.O.B.? … How the hell am I supposed to do that?" Big Will yelled in trepidation. He was close to some of the M.O.B. niggas but not that close.

"You'll find a way," Bloody Benny countered, blowing smoke into the already poisoned air.

"Cause if you don't," he continued to say. "I'll kidnap your fat-ass again, but this time I ain't gonna tie you up in no bathtub…Nah, I'ma tie you up on my pool table, fuck you wit a pool stick and make you suck on my *40 cal* until it bust…You get the picture?"

Big Will's mouth went bone dry as he pictured the scene vividly. He looked up and found S.P. still staring at him with that hard, menacing glare.

"Whadda you lookin' at bitch?" the Scotian hissed threateningly. Bloody Benny had asked without even knowing how he would do it. All Big Will could really focus n was getting out of that apartment.

Bloody Benny took the fat man's wallet and promised to visit the address on the driver's license if he didn't hear what he wanted to hear in the next 24 hours.

After what seemed like a month to the cowardly barber, Big Will was finally back in his S.U.V. But before he could turn on his ignition, he quickly re-opened his door and vomited on the curb for what seemed like an eternity.

*****

Jasmine was still fuming from the little disagreement she had had with Prince earlier on that day. Why couldn't he just see things her way? And why were men so *stupid?* It was as if their minds were stuck in some rudimentary stage of development. Even, Jasmine thought to herself resentfully, the "smart ones". *Fuckin animals!*
The entire episode had only further cemented in Jasmine's mind, the belief that all men were merely created to be manipulated by women like her. The Queen Bee. *The Queen Bitch.*
As a little girl, Jasmine had witnessed her frail mother, forfeit her power to her *weak-ass* husband. It would have been an understatement to call Jasmine's father a no-good piece of shit. For as long as she could remember, her father had been an abusive man. In Cairo, it wasn't uncommon for women to be treated as second-class citizens but even after they had immigrated to Canada, the ill-treatment they had experienced in Egypt continued.
As Women, they had been forbidden to leave the house without his permission.
He had claimed it was Sharia Law. Funny thing though, Sharia Law had never prevented him from consuming alcohol. Nor did it prevent him from climbing into Jasmine's bed whenever he was in one of his many drunken states. Jasmine could still feel his hot, sour breath on her neck; His massive weight crushing her tiny frame. She hated the bastard with every fiber of her being. Yet still, she didn't blame him; It was her mother she blamed. Her mother was the one who had failed her. Her mother was the one should have protected her. Her mother was weak, where Jasmine vowed to be strong.
At a very early age, Jasmine had promised herself that she would never allow herself to become the victim of a man again. Thus, growing up, she had learned to become ruthless. Instead of letting the men in her life control and twist her mind, she had quickly learned how to maneuver them into doing things she had wanted them to do. First, she started small, convincing the boys around the neighbourhood into stealing this and that. Gradually, she moved her way up into making the teens rob and beat down whomsoever she willed.
Eventually, she learned how to make the love-struck men kill for her.
Her father had become her first victim.
It was surprising what teenage boys would do for a little bit of pussy.
If only Prince were that easy to manipulate, Jasmine mused to herself as she bit her lower lip and gazed down at the nigga licking her clit as if it were butter scotched ice cream. The fool was a young drug dealer from the ends

who she had met at a barbeque a few months ago. He had claimed to be a hustler, which had initially piqued Jasmine's interest She needed a new sugar daddy. However, it turned out, that the only thing the *fool* was good for was giving head. The little nigga had no *real money*.

Normally, Jasmine would have sent the loser packing but then she had discovered his connections to the hood. Coincidentally, the little nigga was related to Leeco. His nephew to be exact. In light of this, Jasmine had sensed opportunity in the young thug and continued to string him along. She knew his kind. He was the type that was eager to please. Give him a gun and whisper a few promises into his ear and Jasmine was sure she could "soldier" him out for at least two bodies.

That kind of power went a long way on the streets.

Damn he's good, Jasmine thought to herself s her stomach started to tighten, and her climax approached. After Jasmine found her way back down from cloud nine, she allowed her "Mr. Fool" the entry that he so eagerly desired. She hopped onto his hood and began to ride him, grinding her freshly trimmed flesh slowly.

For Jasmine, it was all about control.

As she rode him, her mind started to drift back onto prince. While he was sleeping, she had gone through his phone, checked his recent call log and had noticed the new entry.

Alicia? Who the fuck is Alicia? She had thought.

Jasmine was far from being the jealous type and it wasn't as if Prince and she were exclusive or anything like that, but the feelings she got when she had seen Alicia's name gave her a bad vibe. And Jasmine had always been one to follow her gut. She decided that when she was finished with Mr. Fool she would investigate and see what more she could find out about this Alicia-bitch. *Maybe this bitch could be the key to finally controlling Prince*, she conspired as she increased the speed of her rhythm. Mr. Fool's breathing started to intensify, indicating that he was almost ready.

"I love you- I love you…" He moaned as he reached up and cupped Jasmine's breasts.

Jasmine pushed away his hands, commanding him to "shut up".

If she were able to control Prince, like she controlled Mr. Fool and others like him, then she would be more in the position of controlling the M.O.B. She had tried and failed with Leeco. But Leeco was the past; Prince was the future.

A second orgasm was building in Jasmine and sensing this, Mr. Fool desperately held onto his own, aiming to please his exotic mistress.

That afternoon, Mr. Fool had foolishly believed that his sexual prowess had alone brought his lover to her peak. He had no idea of the thoughts of grandeur and power racing through Jasmine's mind, propelling her to ecstasy.

CHAPTER 15

"This is what I fuckin' do!"

The harsh incandescent lights that blared in Pyros sister's washroom did nothing to hide the exhaustion written just below Rakim's eyes. Every time Rakim looked into the mirror, he had always seen someone different staring right back. Sometimes it was a friend, gloating with him in his accomplishments. At other times, it had been the boy he used to be. Some days, Rakim thought he could see the man that he was becoming, and at times didn't know if this image pleased or scared him.

However, more often than not, like today, Rakim glared at his enemy, the one person in his life who caused him the most pain. The only person, Rakim thought grimly, who ever really could. He hated not knowing, and the man in the mirror only taunted Rakim for his lack of knowledge. As he stared into his own eyes a thousand questions reeled through his mind, but one in particular kept resurfacing to the forefront: Why?

Why did Bloody Benny order a hit out on his brother?

Moreover, why didn't Zulu tell him that there might have been some sort of beef with the downtown gangster? Rakim couldn't make any sense out of it. He needed Zulu to wake up. He needed answers. However, to wait for his brother to make it out of the hospital would be to break one of Leeco's golden rules of war.

"He who hesitates has lost..."

Rakim could still hear the Jamaican's accented words resonate through his mind:

"You hear me young bwoy; Shoot first'n axe questions lass..."

The man in the mirror shook-his head as if he could shake away the cerebral cobwebs shrouding his mind and turned on the water stained faucet Rakim splashed cold water onto his face, hoping the frigid liquid would somehow jolt some sort of clarity back into his senses. He needed more sleep.

The knock at the door did more to annoy Rakim than it did to notify him of someone's presence.

"Yo?" Rakim answered over his shoulder.

"You're holdin' up the flex man. What're doin in there; jerkin off?"

Rakim dried his face with the navy-blue bandana that was neatly folded in his left back pocket and told Kilo to "chill the fuck out!"

A final glance in the mirror revealed a resolute killer with only one thing on his mind.

Rakim knew this man well.

"You're startin' to scare me, man," Kilo said, giving Rakim a sideways glance as Rakim walked back into the room. "You gwanin' like you don't wanna put in that work."

"Yeah?" Rakim replied, fixing Kilo with a hard stare. "And you're gwanin' like this is my first fuckin' war; what up!"

"What up?" Kilo retorted, refusing to back down. Taking a few steps forward, he got up in Rakim's face. "This is what's up nigga... You were about to let that bitch-ass nigga Blacks slide. What the fucks up wit that? And-and let's not forget about that little daydreamin' episode in the car before we paged that fuckin' Will-yute... You gwanin' like you don't wanna do this!"

"Don't wanna do what? - This? Nigga this is what I fuckin' do! Don't forget who put you onto this shit nigga-"

"Put me on?" Kilo cut in, temper rising. "Oh, so-so you put me on, did you?... Nah fan, I ain't you. Leeco didn't make me nigga. I'm self-made-"

Kilo's reaction time wasn't up to par to stop the right hook that caught him just below his left ear.

Though Rakim was quick with his hands, the blow that he dealt his best friend wasn't strong enough to knock him out. Kilo stumbled, but quickly regained his footing as he delivered a whopping punch to Rakim's gut.

As Rakim doubled-over, Kilo latched onto his neck, throwing Rakim into a vice-gripped headlock.

"Sucker-punch me nigga? You-"

However, he didn't have time to finish his sentence as Rakim surprised him by picking him up and slamming him back down into the hard part of the couches' armrest.

Kilo had to let go of Rakim, as he grimaced in pain. Rakim rolled away and sat up against the wall, fighting hard to catch his breath.

If this had been anybody else, Rakim thought to himself as he kept his eyes fixed on Kilo, he would have pulled out the gun he had borrowed from Pyro arid put two into the man's dome. This nigga's lucky got so much love for him.

Kilo had trouble getting up, so he too decided, to sit on the floor with his back against the couch, eyes trained on Rakim.

"No homo nigga, but if I didn't love you so much, I'd probably would've bodied you a long time ago..." Kilo said with his teeth clenched, as he massaged his back.

Rakim started laughing out loud.

Kilo didn't get the joke.

"What's so funny?"

Rakim had to wait for the fit of laughter to subside before he could answer.

"You see,"-Rakim finally paid, still finding it hard to breath. "That's why I love you... I was just thinkin' the exact same thing..."

Kilo smiled his bad boy smile and shoot his head. "So, you sayin'; Great minds think alike."

Before Rakim could reply, they were interrupted by a lone set of applause being clapped in the nearby kitchen. Pyro had been watching the whole thing and though he had seen it before, he had been thoroughly entertained.

"You nigga's gonna fuck now or what?" he mocked, eyes going back and forth between the two.

Neither of the two thought it was even worth their breath to answer the Somolian clowning them from his perch on the kitchen table.

"No," Pyro continued. "Aight then, let's do this... We gotta couple'a stops we need to make, a lie?"

CHAPTER 16

"City's on fire..."

The sensational news of the downtown club shooting had spread through the streets of the GTA like wildfire. Everybody and their momma were gossiping about the ill-famed shoot out that was now being described as the city's worst shooting ever.

No doubt feeling the political pressure from the Premiere of Ontario and of course the opposition, the Mayor had the police doing back flips, impelling them to apprehend the gunmen as quickly as possible. So, in turn, the police swarmed the streets like angry hornets in search of the culprits who disturbed the proverbial nest. Those with any sense knew what time it was. Someone was bound to get stung. Mother's urged their sons to stay off the roads, fearing the police would stop any black male caught driving in the city. C.I.'s were probed by their detectives for whatever information they could give. Outgoing jailhouse calls were monitored meticulously. The amount of homicides that had been solved by intercepted prison phone calls was staggering.

Enter the still incarcerated Harlem.

Unlike his counterparts, Harlem never made it back to the streets after that robbery in Rexdale. Landing in the Don Jail, Harlem continued to foster his reputation as a wild child. Stomping out or stabbing anyone who got in his way. Harlem aimed to be the man behind bars. If you didn't respect him, he made damn sure that you feared him. There was nothing more important than his name. He could never understand how some men could rat or "pussy-out', sacrificing everything that their name stood for. Consequently, it was that same twisted sense of pride that earned Harlem a much lengthier stay than he had first envisioned. Nothing could have prepared the poor man who idiotically called Harlem a "goof' in front of an entire range. When the correctional officers finally discovered the body on a routine walk, in their reports they stated that the victim had appeared to have been stabbed over a hundred times in the face and neck areas, flooding the tiny cell with a menacing pool of blood. Realizing that there was no way to beat the charge, Harlem pled guilty to manslaughter. Two months later, he freed-up his coey's by claiming that all of the drugs and guns found in the car that night in Rexdale belonged to him. The Crown was less than pleased to make the deal, but they had figured that they would catch Prince and Kilo on future charges.

Harlem's prison stay didn't stop him from still being connected to the streets, however.

He had made it a habit of calling Kilo and a few others every other week to check in and see what was what. If there was something going down in the city, Harlem was always one of the first inside to know. Harlem had awoken sore that morning after the shooting. The previous night's workout was intense. After completing his ritual of doing one hundred push-ups and then one hundred sit-ups, Harlem made a bowl of oatmeal and turned on the 15-inch television in his 6 by 9 cell. The news channels held Harlem captive, his eyes refusing to leave the screen. No one could ever really say why gangsters loved to watch the body counts rise on their local news network. Maybe they felt justified watching other people's murderous actions, rationalizing in their own little minds that if people were still killing people out there, then what they had done was all that could have been expected of them.

Or maybe they just wanted to see somebody else fall as they once fell, feeding into the saying: misery loves company. Or maybe it was more basic than that. Something like dogs staring at other dogs on a television screen. Whatever the reason, Harlem was glued to his T.V. set until his steel door buzzed open. The first thing Harlem did was head, straight for the phones. Seeing that it was only seven something in the morning, the chances of Kilo answering his cell were slim to none. So, Harlem waited until well into the afternoon. Kilo picked up on the third ring.

"Yo," he answered.

Harlem could hear that Kilo was out doing something due to all of the noise in the background.

"Yo, family!" Harlem saluted through the phone. "What's good out there, dawg?"

"Ah shit, my nigga- yo, yo its Harlem...turn that shit down..." Kilo said into his cell phone and then to whoever he was with. "Yo family; we just out here man. Same old, same old."

"Oh yeah?... Well I'm hearin' a lotta other shit here on this news channel, dawg. They saying' da city's on fire right now fam."

The sounds of hip-hop music being turned down and men talking blended into the background on Kilo's side of the phone call.

"Man, you better off watching the Space Channel and shit, bro... You know dem fools be lyin' on that T.V. screen..."

Harlem shook his head. He wasn't satisfied with that answer.

He knew damn well that Kilo knew something about the shooting. If he hadn't, Harlem knew Kilo would have said something like, "... Never mind all that. That shit don't involve us..." But the fact that he didn't made Harlem probe even more.

"Yo, I just wanna make sure niggas are safe out there, dawg," Harlem prodded.

"You know I'll catch another body up in here if I ever found out one of my niggas got hit."

"Nah man, we straight You ain't gotta worry about that my nigga," Kilo said, purposely withholding the fact that his cousin was somewhere in a hospital for a gunshot wound for that exact same reason. He knew Harlem could be a hothead at times.

"Aight," Harlem replied still probing. "Just let me know if there's someone in here that needs to get touched."

Kilo started laughing and then repeated what Harlem just said to whomever he was with. More laughter could be heard in the background.

"Yo, Prince says to chill on that, fam. We got this."

"Aight," said Harlem, now knowing for sure that his niggas were behind the shooting. "Anyone I should look out for in here though?"

"Yeah," Kilo's tone changed to a more serious note. "Look out for dem Park niggas... You hear what I'm sayin'?"

"Uh-huh, no doubt-no doubt. Say no more," Harlem said, nodding into the phone,

"Tell Prince I say wuddup. I'ma holla at you niggas later on tonight, aight?"

"Yeah, yeah; you do that," Kilo agreed. "Prince hails you up too. He's askin' how the funds are lookin'?"

"Tell him I'm straight for now and much love on that box he sent down a month ago...Aight then my nigga... You done know. Love."

As the phone call ended, Harlem went back to his cell for the dinnertime count. Back in Toronto, the police officer listening in on the wire ran to his supervisor.

CHAPTER 17

"All we wanna do is say hello..."

After he got off the call, Kilo checked his inbox for the text message he had received while on the phone with Harlem. Some shorty from around the way that had once given him head, was now inquiring about some party being thrown at a popular Scarborough nightclub called Caddies. Supposedly, all of the members of the M.O.B. were rumoured to be attending.

"Yo," he said, getting Princes and Pyro's attention. "Do you guys know anything about some party being held at Caddies for the mandem tonight?" Both of his niggas shook their head.

"Well," Kilo continued to say. "Apparently we're all going...Bitch says the entire M.O.B. supposed to be there..."

Rakim waved it off as he parked outside of a self-storage compound. "Fuck all that," was his only reply. Turning off the engine, he got out of the car with his boys following closely behind, he then proceeded to his storage unit at the back of the site and stopped in front of the orange garage door. He opened it and all three men made their way inside, closing the door behind them. After a moment of darkness, Rakim clicked on the portable lamp to reveal two twin silver cabinets, standing six feet high, against the back wall. He unlocked both of the padlocks guarding his hidden treasure...

Inside the steel boxes was a collection of firearms ranging from handguns to assault rifles. Beretta's to AK's. Different types of ammunition decorated the cabinet's floor. The gangster stood back and admired the arsenal of guns for all of thirty seconds.

"Aight," Rakim said proudly, glancing from one homie to the next. "Let's do this..."

*****

Kato didn't even hear them come in.
He was too busy slapping up the pussy to pay the sounds of someone

creeping up the stairs any mind. Usually, in situations like this, he was on point. Rarely did he ever miss an opportunity to brag to his "people" on how milli he moved when first meeting up with "bitches" off the Internet. But this girl was so damn fine, Kato swore to himself that she looked even better than her profile pic. As soon as she had opened up that door, Kato was on it.

Her name was Maria and it had taken Kato no longer than three weeks of sweet talk to arrange the booty call. Plentyoffish.com was a kennel full of "horny-ass bitches" and Kato was the "motherfuckin' top dog." The girls seemed to go crazy for his male-stripper like abs and his hazel coloured eyes. Maria was by far the best "ting" he had ever scooped off of the site. She was a five-foot-something, curvy-as-hell Latina with the juiciest set of dick-sucking lips Kato had ever laid eyes upon. Her only flaw, as far as Kato was concerned, was the fact that she had a kid; which meant, somewhere in the world, she had a baby-father. Nevertheless, like the creaking emanating from the intruders on the stairs, Maria's baby's father was the furthest thing from Kato's mind.

His back was to her bedroom door, as her legs were on his shoulders. This was Kato's second most favourite position. He loved to place his girls on the edge of a couch or a bed with their legs propped up on his shoulders and his knees on the floor. There was something about watching his hood slide in and out of the girl's sex that made him feel like a man's man.

"Aye! ... Aye! ... Aye! ..." seemed to be all that Maria could moan, as Kato rammed into her, making what was once pink a scarlet red.

Maria's eyes were closed in pleasure as she tried to take the dick like a champ, but Kato wasn't having it.

"Open ya eyes!" he commanded. "Look at me!"

"Aye! ... Aye! … Aye! ..." was Maria's only reply.

The bitch seemed to grow louder and louder by the second, Kato thought to himself, well pleased. The way the pussy's tight, it's like she never had a good piece a dick in a while. He decided to continue torturing her.

"Open...Your...Eyes!" he grunted once more. Thrusting harder with each word for emphasis.

As Maria's breasts bounced to their rhythm, she slowly started to open her eyes. At first, with a cat-like smile, she gazed into her lover's face, but then something just behind him stole her attention.

"AHHHH!!!" she screamed at the top of her lungs, nearly shattering Kato's eardrums.

Like an idiot, Kato misidentified Maria's blood curdling scream for a climatic ending. However, after hearing a strange new voice in the room, followed by the feeling of a cold barrel violently shoved to the back of his head, things started to make a little bit more sense.

"Aight lova-boy... Ease outta that pussy nice' n slow. Playtime's over."

"What the fuck!" Kato gasped, as his hands flew up in the air thinking he was being robbed.

He slowly obeyed the stranger's command as he withdrew himself from Maria and heedfully stood up, the hard, cold menacing metal never once left the back of his head.

"Bitch, you set me up?" he accused Maria, glaring at her as she pathetically tried to cover-up her nakedness.

"Set you up?" a second voice questioned from behind him. "Why nigga, you got sumthin' we want?"

Kato could hear the belt buckle on his pants chime, as whoever it was behind him rummaged through his belongings.

"Listen partna; if its money ya'll niggas is lookin' for-"

"Brother," yet another voice cut in, interrupting Kato. "This is probably the ideal time for you to shut the fuck up."

Kato noticed that this third voice was much calmer than the first two. This one was obviously the leader. Kato didn't give a fuck though. He wasn't about to go out like some punk.

"Y'all niggas don't know who y'all fuckin with!" he yelled, mustering up bravado.

"Do you know where I'm from, nigga?"

Chuckling could now be heard from behind him as Maria silently broke into tears.

"Nah brother, why don't you tell us," the third voice answered, seemingly closer than before.

"South Side Jane partna...Best believe I'ma ride for dis shit!"

"Oh yeah?" voice number three replied.

However, before he could say anymore, Kato spun on the nigga with the gun to his head, catching voice number one off guard. A shot rang out as the firearm discharged its burden into the pillow, inches away from Maria's face, sending feathers and more of Maria's blood curdling cries into the air.

As the naked Kato struggled with the gunman, voice number three ordered voice number two to "shut the bitch up," as number three calmly walked up to the fighting two-some and shot Kato in the hip.

CLAP!!

Kato landed on the hardwood floor with a THUD! And grunted in pain.

"Yo, I said shut that bitch up!" voice number three yelled as Maria thrashed and screamed as the masked bandit tried to cover her mouth. Voice number two pulled out his

burner and cocked it back, placing the barrel against Maria's crotch.

"Shhh," he gestured with his left index finger against his bandana-covered mouth.

Maria instantly lost her voice.

Rakim nodded to Pyro and then looked over to Kilo, who was currently

Beckham-kicking the shit out of the curled-up Kato.

"You! Stupid! Mutha! Fucka!" he shouted with every kick.

Rakim, with the gun still smoking in his hand, went to the window and peeked out. He wondered to himself if anyone had heard the shots. Closing the blinds, he walked back to Kato and signaled for Kilo to stop.

"Brother," Rakim began to say. "I know niggas from the Jane-strip and they're some of the realest niggas I know, but you..." Rakim shook his head. "You gots to be the dumbest motherfucker I have ever met...We're not even here for you, you dumb fuck. And now look at this..." Rakim pointed to Kilo's unmasked face. His bandana was torn off in the struggle. You seen our faces...You know we can't "take that chance..."

Sighing, Rakim pointed the Beretta at Kato's chest.

"Yo cuz," Rakim said to Kilo. "Pass me that pillow."

Kilo picked up the un-shot cushion off Maria's bed and handed it to his nigga.

Rakim placed the pillow on the side of Kato's head and then placed the nozzle of the gun on top of the pillow.

WHAP!!

WHAP!!

He fired two nuzzled shots into Kato's temple, prompting Maria to whimper and cry even harder. Rakim tilted his head to her and stared at the sexy mamacita trembling naked in her bed.

"You must be Maria," he said after a moment of silence. "Your baby-father's Bloody Benny, right?"

Maria shook her head with tears streaming down her face. Rakim cocked his eyebrow and took off his bandana.

"Don't lie to me now, beautiful," he sang, taking a step closer to the bed. "Yo family, let her put on her clothes." Rakim said to Pyro, once again heading for the window and peeking out.

Once fully dressed, Maria had calmed down enough to speak.

"So-so, this is about...Benny?" she managed to say. "Are you- are you going to kill me?"

"Nah," Rakim said, taking a seat on her dresser. "Not if you do the right thing."

Pyro was leaning against the wall, as Kilo kept six by the window.

"I-I don't know what you want from me," Maria sniffled, eyes locked on Kato's dead body.

"All we want is your baby-father," Rakim reassured softly. "That's all we want."

Maria shook her head and closed her eyes from the sight of Kato's blood pooling around his head.

"I don't even talk to him anymore. We broke up like, a long time ago..."

"But you still know how to get a hold of him, right? ... All we wanna do is say hello..."

Maria knew damn well that the killer inside her bedroom was lying. Rakim knew that she knew that he was lying. It didn't matter. Fear was a wonderful thing to control if wielded correctly.
Bloody Benny was as good as dead.

CHAPTER 18

"I told you not all gangsters were bad..."

After hitting ignore on an invite for some M.O.B. party being thrown in Scarborough, Jasmine continued her search online for the mysterious "Alicia-bitch". Scouring the popular social networks, Jasmine found herself on Facebook, invading her friend's "friends list" for a hit. Searching for information on somebody in the city was easy, provided you had the right amount and mixture of friends. All one would really have to do was type the person's name inside the search box and viola, information at your fingertips. People really do underestimate the power of social networking, Jasmine ruminated as she scanned the list of all the Alicia's her friends knew.
It didn't take long for Jasmine to find what she was looking for. One of the "Alicia's" statuses caught her-attention. It read: At St. Mike's w/ sis. Zulu my prayers are for you and everyone who went to my party last night ® T-Dot stop the violence!
 "This has to be her," Jasmine whispered to herself as she clicked on Alicia's public page.
The profile picture depicted a beautiful, wide-eyed, light-skinned girl, smiling cheerfully into the camera. So, this is the bitch Prince's fuckin'... She ain't all that, Jasmine thought to herself as she browsed through the different photo albums. Jasmine spent the better part of an hour studying every last photo and every single posting on Alicia's wall until she was satisfied. Once she had her fill, Jasmine got dressed and grabbed her Guess purse, which Consisted of tampons, credit cards, lip-gloss and a pearl-handled .22 calibre handgun. With a final glance into the mirror, she headed out the door.
Time to see what this "Alicia-bitch" is all about.

*****

"Who the fuck're you callin' a bitch?!" Keisha yelled in the defense of her older sister.

Some knuckle-headed scrub had tried to pick up Alicia with a cheesy generic one-liner. They were in the Tim Horton's coffee shop on the first floor of the St. Michael's hospital. The place was packed with some of the partygoers from the previous night. Alicia was stunned and left feeling a little guilty after seeing some of the disheveled people still waiting in the hospital, all because they'd decided to go to her party.

She had tried to let the scrub down easy when he had approached her in his dirty clothes that reeked of stale liquor and fresh B.O. However, the boy wasn't taking the no with a grain of salt, especially not in front of his "mans 'n dem". He had attempted to salvage whatever piece of pride Alicia had wounded with her rejection, by unleashing a string of profanities that were sure to make his friends laugh. However, the only thing that was unleashed was the fiery attitude of Alicia's younger sister. As Keisha's neck rolled from side to side like some sort of Hollywood dancer, she called the regretful scrub every name under the sun. It took Alicia more than sixty seconds to pry her sister away from the unnecessary drama that was becoming the primary focus in the crowded coffee shop.

"You need to calm your ass down," Alicia began to admonish her sister afterwards, as they waited for the elevator. "I'm a big girl. I can fight my own battles. I don't know why you always feel like you need to make a scene, when all you need to do is walk away."

"Oh, well fuck you too," Keisha cut in, not understanding why she was being yelled at "I wasn't just gonna stand there and let some waste nigga call you a bitch! The kid's lucky I didn't smack him across the face... Why the hell are you getting mad at me?"

Alicia just shook her head. In truth, she really didn't know why she was coming down so hard on her sister. Between the break-up with Jerome and again coming face to face with the aftermath of the previous night, maybe all of the frustration was finally starting to leak out. Keisha didn't deserve that.

"I'm sorry," Alicia said after a moment's reflection. "I'm just so stressed out...I broke up with Jerome this afternoon."

"You what!?!" Keisha shrieked, startling an elderly lady who was walking nearby. "You finally ditched the asshole? I'm so proud of you Al. Why the hell are you stressin' over that? You should be jumping for joy."

"I'm not stressing over him. It's... all this..." Alicia said pointing to the crowd of young people milling about in the hospital. "This is all my fault...None of these people would even be here if it wasn't for my stupid party... Four people died last night Keisha.... Four! The news is calling it the worst shooting ever in the city's history...I mean, I wanted to make history, but not like this..."

"The shooting had nothing to do with you Al," Keisha said soothingly as they entered the elevator. "If anyone's to blame its Prince and whoever he was aiming at."

"No, you're wrong. You can't blame Prince. I was there with him when the shooting started Keish. He was just...protecting himself."

Keisha paused in the elevator, staring at her sister in disbelief.

"Protecting himself? This is coming from you? You hate gangsters... and now all of the sudden you understand them? Nah-uh, what's going on Alicia? Do you have a thing for Zulu's brother?"

"NO!" Alicia cried out, trying her best to sound offended.

The skeptical look on Keisha's face advised Alicia that her little sister wasn't buying it.

Alicia started to blush despite herself.

"O.M.F'n.G.!... You like my boyfriend's older brother."

"No, I don't... well, it's not that I don't like him, it's just-"

"Isn't this kinda like incest?" Keisha questioned with confusion knitted into her eyebrows.

"You're not even married to Zulu! How the hell can this be called incest?-"

"Ha, ha; gotcha!" Keisha giggled. "You do like him!"

Alicia froze with pure mortification painted onto her face. She wasn't even sure she had any real feelings for Prince. Just because she got butterflies in her stomach whenever she thought of him or the fact that she thought he was the sexiest man she had ever met didn't necessarily mean that she was in love with him.

Did it?

Obviously, Keisha thought there was something there and usually her sister was good at reading Alicia's emotions. Alicia didn't know what to think. If you were to ask her two months ago if she would ever consider dating a gangster, Alicia would have for sure laughed in your face.

But now things were different.

Jerome was fading out of the picture and now for the first time in a long time, Alicia was having thoughts of being with another man.

So why was it so hard for her to admit it to her little sister?

Why was it so hard for her to admit it to herself?

"I told you not all gangsters were bad," Keisha said, breaking into Alicia's thoughts.

Alicia just shook her head again and remained silent as they walked into the familiar I.C.U. waiting room. To Alicia's dismay, Patty was still there. Thank God, Alicia thought. Steve was no where in sight. Sitting beside Patty, however, were two overweight black women who Alicia assumed were Patty's friends.

As Keisha and Alicia walked into the waiting area, the three elder women had ceased their conversation and were openly staring at the two sisters.

Alicia would have felt self-conscious if she wasn't so offended by their glares.

"What the hell is their problem?" she questioned Keisha as they sat as far away from them as possible.

Kim, Keisha's best friend, was already there waiting for her girl to return from meeting up with her sister. Kim was your typical around-the-way-black-girl. Her single parent household was not as successful as her best friend's, so she was notorious for using her five-finger discount at all of the over-priced stores. She was Keisha's one and only ride or die best friend.

"Don't mind them," Kim said to Alicia as she glared back at the older women.

"They've been acting tough all day. But trust me girl; those heifers don't want it."

"Do you see what I'm dealing with?" Keisha added, purposely ignoring the laughs that were now cackling between the three Witches. "Zulu needs to hurry and wake the fuck up before I knock out his Mom."

Alicia didn't bother getting involved in the conversation her sister and Kim were having on how "whack" the older women dressed. Instead, pulling out her cell phone, she contemplated on whether or not she should text Prince. Maybe he would like to know that she was at the hospital, waiting on his brother, she rationalized to herself as an excuse to contact him.

As she sent the text message, the butterflies came back in full force. This is ridiculous, Alicia's inner voice remarked. I'm not falling for this guy, am I? Maybe I shouldn't have texted him...

Alicia quickly pushed her cell phone back inside her purse, promising herself that she wouldn't check it every "two seconds" to see if Prince had answered back. Just as she glanced up, Steve had walked into the waiting room followed by the audible sighs of her younger sister. Right behind Steve was an exotic young woman.

The two were clearly not together, as Steve made his way over to Patty and the girl who resembled a Kardashian, sat elsewhere. However, what made Alicia notice the woman, was not her stunning looks, but the way the exotic looking beauty had looked at her. It was almost as if she had recognized her.

Weird, Alicia thought to herself as she absentmindedly pulled out her cell phone and checked for text messages.

*****

The miniature thunderous sounds emitting out of Big Will's gut was somehow communicating with his pet rottweiler Tyson. Every time his stomach would rumble, the one-year-old Tyson would softly growl, eyeing his master's massive belly cautiously as if he expected a tiny alien to burst out Big Will was becoming annoyed with the mutt. If the "fuckin dog" didn't "shut up" with it's "fuckin growling", in the next two seconds, Big Will swore that he would smash his computer screen across its face.

The irritable barber had been slaving away at his desktop for the past four hours. Or had it been five? The barber had lost track of time as he mercilessly attacked every social network he could think of. Setting up a party in Scarborough in one day was easily summed up in one word: Difficult.

Yet, despite his mood and his apparent hunger, everything was coming along as planned.

There was already a buzz online over the so-called "Mob party". Big Will had to use all of his connects and call in most of his favours in order to get the RSVP turn out that he desired. It was quite simple: If people didn't show up to the party, then the chances of the M.O.B. niggas attending would be slim. Big Will needed to gather as much of those niggas there as possible if he intended on never seeing the business end of Bloody Benny's gun again.

So far, it seemed to be working. Through the grapevine, he had heard that more than a few of "dem boys" were talking about "stopping by the joint if nothing else was gwanin".

Unfortunately, however, much to Big Will's disappointment, no one could either confirm or deny the fact if Prince and Kilo would indeed make an appearance.

The barber kept his fingers crossed.

After viciously kicking away his puppy, Big Will logged off his computer, deciding for himself that there was nothing more left to do but wait.

Setting niggas up was nothing new to the disloyal barber. It was almost as if he had an innate talent for the art. The waiting part was the easiest of the whole process. Through the years, the treacherous barber had even developed a ritual while awaiting the fruits of his labour, Big Will had made it a habit of ordering a family-sized meal from Swiss Chalet It was sort of like a celebratory feast.

The minutes dragged by slowly as Big Will's stomach continued to speak to him in tongues.

The Canadian news networks were having a field day with all of the shootings and murders popping up around Toronto. A photograph of Blacks accompanied the footage of police officials carting away a body from an alley way of a downtown motel.

Big Will was hardly moved. At this point, he held more feelings toward the whereabouts of his deliveryman than the apparent murder of his once called brethren. Just as he was about to pick up the phone and call the restaurant to investigate the mystery of his delayed take-out-food, a knock at the door prompted Tyson into a barking frenzy.

"Finally," Big Will wheezed, as he hoisted himself off his second-hand leather couch and hurried to the front door.

Without looking through the peephole of his two-bedroom apartment, Big Will hastily swung open his door, fully planning on giving the unpunctual delivery man a piece of his mind. However, standing there in the hallway wasn't the familiar greeting of the smell of roasted chicken: Nor was there the face of the acne-scarred teenager who served as the regular deliveryman for Big Will's favourite restaurant.

Smiling maliciously, and accompanied by Mouse, Shells and another unknown goon, stood something out of the fat barber's newly acquired nightmares.

"Well, aren't you gonna let us in?" S.P. asked mockingly, as he glared at the fat man who was About to shit himself.

"I-I...uhm..." Big Will was at a loss for words.

The four men pushed their way inside Big Will's sanctuary just as the Swiss Chalet deliveryman finally made his way to the stricken barber's apartment.

The acne scarred teenaged delivery boy was left in a state of confusion as he glanced upon the face-of the overweight man closing the door.

If he didn't know any better, he could have sworn that the obese black man was mouthing the words: "Help me..."

*****

The Sisters of St. Joseph, who operated Notre Dame des Anges, a boarding house for working women, established the St. Michael's hospital in Toronto in 1892. Their founding goal was to take care of the sick and the poor of the inner city in a new, sprawling metropolis. The hospital first opened its doors with a staff of six doctors, four graduate nurses and a bed capacity of twenty-six.

By the late 1960's, with on-going physical expansions, the original twenty-six bed facility had increased to a high of 900 plus beds. The downtown adult trauma centre had been affectionately dubbed as the city's Urban Angel. It was here where victims of downtown street violence amassed, hoping for a miracle.

Nurse Sandra Bronson was making her normal rounds the evening after the dreadful shooting at the Docks nightclub that had the city on high alert for its ever-growing gang infestation. She and her best friend Cecilia. Downey had walked the renowned hallways of St. Michael's for almost thirteen years. They had both seen their fair share of the aftermath of urban warfare, but never on a scale like this. It had seemed as if the city was going to hell in a hand basket with all of the shootings, stabbings and murders popping up around the GTA.

Making their way past an unusually high number of young adults milling about the hospital's cafeteria, Nurse Sandra shook her head in disbelief and sorrow.

"La'hd Jesus, wha gwan in a di world today? Too many a we young black son dem a dead...A wha do dem so?"

"I'll tell you what a do dem so;" Cecilia answered as they made their way to the ICU. "If s all those damn rap videos. It's corrupting their heads! And I'll tell you what, if we as, strong black women had half a mind, we would come together and put a stop to all that nonsense stinking up the airwaves and rotting out our television sets. And don't even get me started on that YouTube crap, girl."

Nurse Sandra glanced over at her colleague and shook her head. She didn't agree that YouTube was the main reason why young black males in Toronto were becoming an endangered species. Back home in St. Vincent, the Bute den? were killing off each other at the same rate and everyone knew that it had nothing to do with the latest rap or dancehall song.

"No, I don't tink that a wha a do it Me tink is more a de poverty ting that a push dem to pick up gun." Sandra said as she inspected the life-supporting machine that was hooked tip to somebody's poor child. She picked up the chart and read the name on the clipboard aloud.

"Anthony Mark-Zulu Anderson...Zulu?...You tink dis a one ya is an African bwoy?"

Cecilia made her way over to the bed where Sandra was standing after she checked the
I.V,'s of a woman suffering from first and second-degree bums.

"He doesn't look African," Cecilia said after a while of studying what she could discern of his face under the multitude of bandages. Cecilia sighed and then continued her rounds, checking the vitals and I. V.'s of all her patients in the intensive care unit.

"I don't think you can blame poverty on all the gangs infesting this city," Cecilia continued to say. "I mean, look at the poor white kids... Hey don't you roll your eyes at me, there is such a thing as, poor white kids, Sandra...Look at them; they're not killin' off each other like our kids."
Sandra put down the clipboard and began to checking the I.V.'s of Mr. "Zulu" Anderson.

"Black and white is two different tings-" she began to retort but before she could finish her thought, her charge started to moan, sending Nurse Sandra into a Panic.

"Waa! l ...Dis one a wake up... Cecilia! Come-come quick-come quick!" Nurse Cecilia ran over and was as shocked as her colleague was.

"I'm going to go get a doctor. Stay with him I" Cecilia, yelped excitedly as she ran out of the ward.
Sandra grasped onto Zulu's hand as if he were her own boy and began patting it soothingly.

"Don't worry child. Every ting will be alright Just hol'on. Hol'on child!"

PART THREE
This changes everything...

CHAPTER 19

"How many more bodies..."

Apart from the sounds of traffic, the silence was almost deafening inside of Rakim's 740 BMW. All four occupants were each caught up in their own thoughts. As they made their way down the 401 in the direction of Bloody Benny's supposed hide-out, Maria, the Hispanic beauty turned captive, couldn't stop herself from shaking. She wondered to herself endlessly over whether or not she was indeed doing the right thing.
The "three evil men" who had invaded her home and who had murdered Kato had promised her that she and her son would remain safe if she could in truth lead them to her baby's daddy.
Benny was a deadbeat father. He rarely visited his first-born son and Maria would've had an easier time squeezing water out of a rock than getting a single loonie from her ex-boyfriend.
The decision between her and her son's wellbeing and giving the murderous thugs Benny's whereabouts had been arc easy one to make. Yet, as she sat in the backseat of the killer's BMW with a crazy Somolian pointing a gun at her, Maria was beginning to experience the pangs of a guilty conscience.
As the questions of betrayal were weighed in Maria's mind, Pyro continued to play sentry.
He watched Maria as the tears silently rolled down her cheeks. Now a normal man would I have probably felt some sort of pity or sympathy for the young woman crying softly in the backseat of his nigga's whip. But Pyro considered himself a soldier. A bad mot. This bitch was connected to the nigga who had brought war against his team. Her tears meant nothing to him. In fact, the only thought Pyro had in his head was the memory of Maria's naked body and how he quickly wanted to get back to the West End to incur the favours of a hood-rat everyone called "Hanna-Hand-Job."
Kilo was in the front passenger seat smoking a cigarette. He too was thinking of Maria.
However, unlike his brethren, his thoughts were not of her flesh but of her

blood. She had witnessed a homicide. She had seen their faces. She had to go. He exhaled a stream of smoke out of the open passenger side window and turned his head, regarding his Right Hand Man. His nigga had said nothing since they had left Bloody Benny's baby-mother's house.

Rakim's own mind was reeling with over a hundred thoughts. Too many things had played out in the span of the last twenty-four hours. Pictures of Zulu, Blacks, Big Will and Bloody Benny eddied in Rakim's mind like the waves of water in a whirlpool. How many more bodies would he have to catch before this was all over?

Hopefully just one other, he thought joylessly to himself as he glanced into his rear-view, mirror and caught the sight of Maria's tears.

Honour thy brother.

Leeco had spoken those last words to the young gangster before he had been deported.

Rakim began to think back onto those last days with his mentor. It had been just a few months after Rakim and Kilo were released from jail in the wake of Harlem's convictions.

Touching road for the first time after being incarcerated was an experience onto itself for I the young Prince. Everything seemed so different. The people who Rakim thought he had known had changed. The places where the "crowd' use to congregate had now shifted.

Even the dress code of the once popular baggy attire had somehow morphed into the tight, form-fitting apparel he had once mocked. He was only away for twenty-one months but the world had taken on a new shine in the eyes of Rakim. The only thing that had seemed to remain the same was the money and the man Rakim had grown to look up to.

Leeco was still moving cautiously as if the warnings of Michael Steinbach were still fresh in his mind.

According to the Jamaican gangster, a raid the size of Project Impact* was headed their way. Rakim, being fresh out of jail, was anxious to get back into the game of eating niggas food and extortion. But Leeco wouldn't have it. He ordered Rakim to lay low by slyly reminding him of his folly when he chose not to heed the advice of his teacher.

Unbeknownst to Rakim, Leeco was conditioning his young protégé for the leadership of the M.O.B., sensing his own time behind bars was imminent.

The night Leeco's predictions came true were forever imprinted in Rakim's mind...

" Project Impact was a high risked take down of one of Toronto city's most notoriously violent street gangs. In 2003, armed with approximately one hundred various arrest warrants, the TPS carried out early morning raids, which led to the historical disbandment of the "Malvern Crew."

CHAPTER 20

"I thought you niggas was rollin together?"

June 2007

Rakim had just finished getting head from a Section 6 hood rat when his phone started to vibrate.

"Yo," he answered into the flip phone as he balanced the mobile between his head and his shoulder, leisurely buckling up the belt on his jeans.

"Yo where you at?" Leeco inquired in his thick Jamaican accent over the phone.

"Around the way. Wa gwan?"

"Me need fi you.to go by Sheppard and McCowan, zeen. Deadus is in di Harvey's parkin lot. Him need fi somebody to pick him up, ASAP. Ya understand wha me a say?"

"Yeah yeah, I got you," Rakim replied into the phone as he glanced back at the hood rat who was now furiously texting a message into her own mobile device. "But I thought my boy was supposed to be with the fat yute takin' care of sumthin'?"

Leeco had sucked his teeth out of frustration.

"My bwoy; jus go draw fi di yute, zeen. Bring him back over here sa. And don't mek him talk up-talk up inna ya ear 'bout he wants to be dropped off someplace. I need' im here and nowhere else, zeen?"

Rakim hated it when Leeco tried to act like more of a boss than a mentor. He was of the right mind to just hang up the phone and deal with the Jamaican's reproach on a later that, but the young gangster had sensed something was afoot.

"Yeah, yeah, I hear you. I'm on my way," he had replied instead.

"Ayo Prince," Leeco beckoned before Rakim could hang up the phone, "Mek sure nuttin' no inna di trunk when you a link up wit my bwoy, zeen."

"Yeah, I hear you, was all Rakim had said into the phone before hanging up.

The hood rat had finished typing Whatever she had been texting and had just put back on her bra after cleaning the mess Rakim had made on her chin and neck.

"Okay, you have to go," she had said, eyeing Rakim anxiously. "My baby-father's gonna be here any minute."

Rakim smirked and shook his head. He wanted to feel sorry for all of the men who impregnated scallies in the city but the "thug" in him just wouldn't allow it.

If a nigga was stupid, enough to entangle himself for life with a slewgie, then it was only right that he should endure the consequences. Plus, everyone knew that you couldn't turn a ho into a housewife. Those types of girls were never meant to be saved.

"Cool," Rakim answered indifferently, "I gotta bounce anyways."

He headed for the front door, but before he exited the apartment, he turned back around and pointed to a string of white semen in her hair. "Oh yeah; you missed a spot," he said smiling before letting himself out.

It took no less than fifteen minutes for Rakim to navigate through the evening traffic.

Scarborough was a beautiful place if one had the eye for it. Rakim marvelled how on any given night, the city came to life. It's roads swelling with vehicles driven by people as different from one another as the diversity of wildlife at a watering pool in the Savannah.

Predators mixed with prey, well aware of each other, yet restrained by the commonality of their environment. It was then Rakim had realized that he had somehow made the transition from being a lamb to a lion. He smiled at the thought. Pulling up in his rented Nissan Altima, he scanned the Harvey's parking lot before finally discovering Deadus near the dumpster, parked in his own rented Honda Accord with its back window apparently shot out Rakim drove over slowly, instantly becoming alert, realizing that things had gone horribly wrong for whatever Deadus and his homeboy had been up to. Deadus was sitting on the curb next to his rental, alone, smoking a cigarette.

"It took you long enough, star," the elder hoodlum had said, standing up to greet the youngster.

"The big mon said you might need a ride," Rakim answered, ignoring Deadus' criticism as if he hadn't said anything at all.

Deadus had been in the game for a long time. He had just been released from the Pen for doing almost six years for his role in a botched bank robbery that had occurred way back before Rakim's time. The niggas in the hood regarded him as an O.G. and respected him as such. Leeco however, barely treated Deadus as an equal, which prompted Rakim and a few others to regard the O.G. as a lame duck of sorts. If Deadus knew of the position he held in his associates minds he showed no ill will over it. Rakim however, didn't trust him at all and preferred to deal with the O.G. at an anus length.

"Where's Small-up at? I thought you niggas was rollin' together?" Rakim continued.

Deadus sucked his teeth before taking a final deep pull of his cancer stick.

"He didn't make it," was all Deadus said, as he ousted the spent cigarette on the floor by stomping on its still glowing filter.

Rakim looked down and noticed almost a pack's worth of butts decorating the pavement around Deadus' Timberland's. He looked back into the 0.G.'s eyes and knew that no further words would be broken on the subject.

Rakim nodded tacitly. "Right, say no more. Let's get the fuck outta here."

"Not so fast youngin'. Go pop your trunk," Deadus instructed, as he himself made his way to do the same with his own rental.

When Rakim got back to Deadus' car and peeked at what was inside, his jaw dropped, and his eyes shot open even wider. Jam packed inside of Deadus' trunk, were duffel bags on top of duffel bags of what appeared to be keys of cocaine and bricks of marijuana. The bags were so full of narcotic wealth that it seemed as if they couldn't even be zipped up all the way.

This wasn't Rakim's first time seeing a brick of weed or even a key of coke, but never in all his life had he ever seen so much in one spot.

"Whoa," was all Rakim managed to say before falling completely speechless.

"Yeah," Deadus deadpanned.

The drive to Leeco's place was shared in strained silence.

Deadus was starting to become paranoid of his young, hungry companion and wondered silently to himself if he was being set up. It wasn't a stretch in his mind to imagine Leeco sending one of his soldiers to do his dirty work. The treasure in the trunk had already proven to be worth one man's life, Deadus was beginning to speculate if it was indeed worth two. He shook his head at the thought and clandestinely gripped his dagger. If the little man tried anything stupid, Deadus was confident that he could stab the yute in his neck way before he even had a chance to reach for his gun. He started to feel more relaxed in his self-assurance.

Rakim was oblivious to the O.G. 's suspicions but still felt overtly anxious to get the scorching hot merchandise and the shady O.G. out of his car as quickly as possible.

Leeco was waiting outside of his two-storey home as Rakim and Deadus pulled up. The Yaw 'di proceeded to help his two visitors unload their cargo into his basement through the backyard. Once the precious burden was piled on high in the middle of Leeco's hardwood floor, the Jamaican just stood there and admired the collection of duffel bags.

Rakim found a seat on a leather couch and studied his mentor in his reverence. Leeco looked as if he were a priest standing at the altar, giving thanks for a manifest miracle. It seemed almost sacrilegious to speak aloud at that particular moment, so Rakim had just kept silent, eyes falling on the prize that almost anyone Ile knew would kill for.

It was impossible to stop the desires that seeped into his mind at the sight of such a fortune. A man's life would be set with that kind of-wealth, Rakim thought to himself.

There wouldn't be any need for robberies or extortions...no more need of pimping and scheming. No more gun trading or dealings of various drugs...0kay; maybe at least one more drug deal, Rakim mused silently as he turned his attention over to Deadus. The O.G.'s eyes, unlike his counterparts, were not on the assembly of duffel bags, Rakim uncomfortably noticed, but locked on the still entranced Leeco. Something about the look in the O.G.'s eyes made Rakim subconsciously move his hand to the bulge the .45 made in the front of his jeans.

At that moment, Deadus cleared his throat, breaking the trance the duffel bags had over Leeco. The smile that had flirted with the Jamaican's lips with the arrival of the duffel bags had faded as Ile addressed the elephant in the room.

"Wa gwan wit Small-Up," he questioned Deadus as he made his way to the home bar located next to the red velveted pool table.

"He didn't make it," Deadus replied in a much softer tone than he had first used with Rakim when asked the exact same question.

Behind the bar, Leeco only nodded his head as he poured himself a glass of Hennessey.

Rakim wondered silently if Deadus was aware of the Baby-Nine Leeco kept hidden from view behind the tin of ice.

Deadus didn't appear to be at all worried, but still Rakim had noticed how after five long minutes, the O.G. had yet to find himself a seat.

The silence that had filled the room as Leeco slowly took swigs from his beverage was disquieting.

Rakim inched his hand closer to his waist.

"You're gonna hava gimme a lico more detail den dat, rude bwoy," Leeco said, while calmly refilling his cup.

"We went to the spot you told us to go," Deadus replied. "Everything was going as planned-"

"How many of dem yutes dere was inna di house?" Leeco cut in.

"Just the two... Just like you had said," Deadus answered unperturbed. "You were right; security was lacking. The two slant-eyed boys they left to guard the stash were waste yutes. They couldn't even pop off right-"

"So, what da fuck happened?!" Leeco roared, once again cutting Deadus off.

The room was draped in silence as the young Rakim watched and waited for the roof to come crashing down.

Deadus continued his narrative with a much more cautious tone:

"We tied up the Chins dem. Small-Up held dem at bay, while I filled the bags. Everything was plug-in. We start loadin' the shit in the trunk, but just before we're about to peel out, a couple shots rang off. They miss me and hit up the whip. I start bussin' back but... but that's when I realize Small-Up's hit. Homeboy's on his back but the fat-fuck's still buckin'," Deadus paused a moment as he chuckled at the memory.

"So, we clappin' it out," he went on to say: "I think I clipped one of dem yutes but the fuckin' Chins are still bussin' back-"

"These're the same bwoy ya done tied up?" Leeco interrogated.

"Nah, these were the neighbours," Deadus said almost distastefully. "It was like they owned the whole fuckin' block 'cause next thing you know, they're runnin' out from all different directions, comin' out of all these fuckin' houses... All a dem're buckin' at us. It was like fuckin' World War III!.

"I jump in the whip and yell for Small-Up to drag himself in... But it was too late. Half his forehead was gone... just clean gone...I peeled out and drove like I Was Vin Diesel in Fast'n Furious...That's when I called you."

Rakim was still on the couch, picturing the story in his mind with his brows knitted in confusion. Something didn't add up.

He glanced over at Leeco and was surprised to find his mentor staring back at him.

Before Rakim could say anything, Leeco spoke up:

"Armshouse ting," he said, sucking his teeth, addressing Deadus. "Someone fi hava tell Small Up's brudda.... Prince," Leeco said turning to Rakim, "take a bag fi Big- Up'n tell him wa gwan. Be easy when you speak to him, zeen. Break tings down gently. Tell' im I say fi chill and to take di bag fi di fomily. I'll link up wit'im when everyting sort out."

Rakim stood up hesitantly.

"What?" Deadus objected, taking a step closer to the duffel bags, "Nah man, think we should count and divide the shit up first before we start dishin' out shares...".

Leeco just stood there and stared at the O. G. silently.

"Gwan bring two bags fi di yute," he repeated to Rakim after moments past. He held his eyes on Deadus. It was a blatant challenge the O.G. didn't dare to take up.

Rakim went along and picked up two duffel bags as the two men continued to grill each other from opposite sides of the basement, the stockpile of narcotic wealth hanging precariously in the middle. Outside, Rakim once again loaded the drugs into the trunk of his rental. With all the tension building up in that basement, he half wondered to himself if the next thing to be loaded up in his trunk would be Deadus' body...

*****

Present Day

"Exit here," a timid voice said cutting through Rakim's reminiscence.
Looking in the rear-view mirror, Rakim noted Maria pointing to the exit ramp that would bring him one-step closer to Bloody Benny. He had also noticed Kilo watching him through the corner of his eye. Maybe his nigga was right. Maybe there was a chance that he wasn't acting like himself Rakim pondered. He had been losing focus excessively often and that in itself was way out of Rakim's character. Perhaps it was because the bloodshed had found its wry so close to home with his little brother getting shot. Whatever it was, Rakim knew he had to get his head back into the game.
The occupants of the BMW found themselves minutes away from the infamously derelict buildings of downtown's Regent Park. As Rakim embraced the familiar rush of increased adrenalin that only comes with the thrill of "putting in work", his phone started to vibrate.
It was an in-coming text from Alicia.
Rakim smiled to himself.
This was already the second text in the span of twenty minutes. The girl's dick-whipped already, he mused as he opened the inbox. Almost swerving and hitting a pedestrian, Rakim had to slow down and re-read the text message digitally printed on his cell phone.

"Yo, what's up?" Kilo asked as he caught the expression on his nigga's face.
A smile that signaled relief was plastered on Rakim's mug as he turned to his Right Hand Man.

"My little brother... He just woke up from his coma..."

CHAPTER 21

"Only fools get caught..."

Tears of joy and the sounds of laughter could be seen and heard in the intermissions of the doctor's report as he addressed Zulu's family in the waiting room of St Mike's hospital. He wouldn't have called it a miracle, but the sudden improvements of Mr. Anderson's condition were "stunningly optimistic." If things were to progress in the same fashion, a full-on recovery was "almost certainly imminent."

"So, what you're saying' is-is that my baby's gonna make it?" Patty beseeched with tears streaking her recently applied mascara.

The doctor nodded his head triumphantly, cherishing the rare moments like this where he could deliver the type of news his patient's families prayed for.

The two elder women who had accompanied Patty repeatedly shouted a call to anyone who was listening to "Praise the Lord" Though not overtly religious, Alicia couldn't help but feel some sort of gratitude to whatever unseen force that may, (or may not) have played a role in Zulu's speedy recovery. The smile on Keisha's face was priceless and contagious as she shrieked and hugged her best friend Kim and then her big sister. It was as if a weight had been lifted off their shoulders; the once sombre ICU waiting room now a bright, spacious chamber of hope where the burdens of the world seemed less dismal.

For a brief second, it almost appeared as if Patty and Keisha were on the verge of hugging, but the moment quickly passed as both women held onto their pride; arrogance overcoming humility.

"So, can we see him?" Keisha inquired, leaving Alicia mildly surprised. Though the news was positive, Alicia was sure that Zulu still looked as he did the last time the sisters had seen him.

The doctor explained that he wanted to run a few more tests but once they were completed, he would have no problem in approving a regular timeframe of visits for Mr. Anderson. With the good news delivered, the doctor retreated to his duties leaving the group in a sense of relief and euphoria. Patty and her bevy of friends found their seats on the other side of the waiting room as Keisha, Alicia and Kim receded to theirs.

Alicia had noted that Steve hadn't even budged from his seat when the doctor had entered the room with the good news. He was apparently too bewitched with an episode of Teen Mom on MTV as it ran on the waiting room's flat screen television. Though Alicia didn't really know Steve, she somehow wasn't surprised at his lack of empathy. She was however confused on why it had appeared as if the woman who had resembled a Kardashian had seemed to be so interested in what the doctor had come to say.

She had caught the woman on several different occasions rubbernecking the group, What had also seemed weird to Alicia was the fact that whenever she had noticed the woman eavesdropping, it had always seemed as if the woman was watching her. Or was it all in her mind, Alicia questioned herself as her phone started to vibrate with an in-coming text.

It was from Prince:

   -Have u seen him yet? Can he talk?

Alicia typed back that she hadn't but paraphrased what the doctor had said only moments earlier.

Prince's response was almost instantaneous:

   -I'm on my way

The butterflies that had infested Alicia's stomach had made their return with the thoughts of seeing Prince once again so soon.

   -Okay. I'll he here: She typed back unable to contain a bashful smile.

"Why're you blushing?" Keisha inquired as she examined her sister's face.

Alicia rolled her eyes and ignored her little sister, annoyed at how easy it was for Keisha to read her emotions.

"Its Prince isn't it?" Keisha continued to question relentlessly. "Did you tell him the good news? Is he coming back?"

Alicia sucked her teeth, exasperated.

"Yes, yes and yes," she answered, swiftly stuffing her cell phone into her purse.

She stood up then.

"I'm going to the washroom; I'll be right back," she announced.

She had been waiting in the hospital for a couple of hours now and though she wasn't the type to fret over her appearance, there was still no way in hell she was going to let Prince see her looking as tired as she did. As Alicia made her way out of the waiting room, she purposely ignored the mysterious woman; chalking up her suspicions as paranoia brought on by stress and exhaustion. I need sleep, she mumbled to herself silently as she walked in the direction of the nearest washrooms. As she searched her purse for her lip-gloss and her portable make-up kit, Alicia failed to notice the mysterious woman following ten paces behind.

Jerome had run into a problem. He was almost one hundred percent certain that Alicia was in fact seeing another man. Though he was okay with losing her, or so he told himself over and over again; he wasn't too fond of the idea of someone else claiming that they had fucked her while she had still been with him. To Jerome it was a matter of pride; it was a matter of honour. And no one fucked with Jerome's honour and lived, or so he vowed to himself the minute he exited Alicia's building.

Finding out who the other pot was wasn't the issue. All Jerome really had to do was wait and watch Alicia to see who she was messing with. And actually killing the guy when he found him wasn't a concern either. Though he hadn't killed anyone before, Jerome was fairly confident that he could get the job done. Shit, he had seen it on T.V. a bunch of times. It couldn't be all that hard. Only fools get caught; he had told himself.

His only problem was the fact that he didn't own a gun, He had ruled out the idea of stabbing or bludgeoning the pry to death as being way too messy. A nice little handgun would solve most of his problems with a twitch of a finger. But where could he find one?

It was in moments like this where Jerome had wished he had lived in the States. There one could simply pick up a gat at his local Wal-Mart. However, since Canada's gun laws were a bit more stringent, Jerome settled on the fact that he would have to rely on the underworld of Toronto's subculture.

He scrolled through his phone's directory for his cousin's cell phone number. His aunt's son was the only real gangster he really knew, and if anyone could get him a gun, it would be him. Luckily, Jerome had kept their relationship alive throughout the years. In fact, this was the same cousin he was with on the night of Alicia's party. The way his cousin had taken control of the situation told Jerome that his aunt's son was no low-level thug.

I wonder how he's gonna react when I tell him I'm calling for a gun? Jerome mused to himself as he found his cousin's number. Smiling, yet holding his breath, Jerome pressed dial on Bloody Benny's Cell.

CHAPTER 22

"I come in peace..."

With the news of Zulu's speedy recovery, Rakim's plans of running up into Bloody Benny's spot were momentarily put on hold. Family came first where Prince and his niggas were from, so seeing his kid brother make it out of the hospital topic priority over everything. With Zulu now awake, every one of Rakim's questions could now be answered. Knowledge was power and Rakim wanted every single drop of it going against the self-ascribed "Boss of Regent Park".

After committing to memory the location of Bloody Benny's supposed apartment- the same spot Maria had directed him to- Rakim, along with his entourage plus one, made his way over to St. Michael's. The police presence around the hospital wasn't as heavy as Rakim had first envisioned but nonetheless two or three patrol cars peppered the streets.

Also, in a noticeable contrast from when Rakim had first visited the previous morning, an increased number of young adults roamed about; exiled partygoers of the night's past.

"So, what about the girl?" Kilo questioned, as Rakim drove pass an unmarked police cruiser.

Rakim knew he couldn't run the risk of getting caught up with the girl in the backseat.

Looking in his rear-view mirror, he could see Pyro force Maria's head down onto his lap and away from the tinted yet revealing windows as a precaution.

"I'ma run up in there and see what's good," Rakim answered, indicating the hospital and ignoring Maria's protests. "You and P chill wit da catty until I forward back. Drive her somewhere dead; somewhere where there's not too many people around."

Kilo fumed to himself silently. His nigga was making yet another mistake, Between Rakim leaving his strap in the bitch's ride the other night, not finishing Blacks off and now hesitating with disposing of their hostage, who was actually a witness to a homicide, Kilo was seriously beginning to lose faith in his best friend's judgement. However, he kept his silence, deciding for himself that now was the time for him to finally take charge.

Rakim pulled into a side street a couple of blocks away from St. Michael's. He had circled the hospital twice before parking. Playing it cautiously, Rakim swore to himself that the bwoy dem would never catch him slipping around there again.

Before hopping out of the whip, Kilo and Prince automatically scanned their surroundings for any signs of unwanted on-lookers. With the coast clear, Rakim turned to Pyro in the backseat arid padded his head.

"Soon come," he said to his nigga, But the meaning behind the words was much deeper than that.

Unspoken between the two was the understanding that Pyro was responsible for the girl until Rakim returned. In addition, there was the underlying question of whether or not Pyro was indeed up for the task. Wordlessly Pyro nodded his head, giving his nigga the reassurance, he needed. Outside of the car, Kilo made his way over to the driver's side where Prince was waiting with further instructions.

"Yo text me if anything pops off, zeen. And make sure you niggas stay low key."

Kilo just nodded his head; avoiding eye contact with the nigga he had mown since elementary. By his actions and demeanour, Rakim knew his best friend didn't agree with his tactics. Soft tings, Rakim thought to himself as he turned his head, subconsciously masking the tiny annoyance he felt at that particular moment. He would deal with his nigga's concerns when he got back.

Nodding his head, Rakim gave Kilo an open-handed daps before making his way back to the hospital where his kid brother was laid up. The answers to the questions that had been plaguing Rakim's mind were just around the comer.

*****

Alicia was staring into the mirror, applying lip-gloss with her thoughts on Prince when the door to the lady's room creaked open. Through the reflection of the Windex, scented mirror, Alicia observed, with increased anxiety, the Kardashian-look-alike from the waiting room make her way inside. She walked over to the sink, just two sinks away from where Alicia stood. This is just a coincidence; Alicia's inner voice assured itself in a bid to pacify her racing heartbeat. The woman from the waiting room rummaged through her purse as Alicia continued on about her business, trying her hardest to act normal and unconcerned.

"Uhmm, excuse me," the Kardashian-look-alike smiled, apparently defeated in her search. "You wouldn't happen to have, like, an extra tampon by any chance? I must've left mine's in my other purse."

The commonality of the question almost made Alicia break out into laughter as the last traces of her fears subsided. I told you, you were making a big deal out of nothing, the voice in Alicia's mind chided as she smiled a smile of relief.

"Uhmm...yeah, I think I might have one somewhere in here," Alicia chuckled in a friendly manner, indicating the ample size of here own purse. The two women shared a knowing giggle in the ladies' room, as Alicia began to rifle through her bag.

Jasmine continued to smile deceitfully. This bitch is so clueless, she thought to herself as Alicia found a tampon at the bottom of her Guess purse.

"Here you go," she said, handing if over.

"Thanks," Jasmine replied.

Alicia turned back to her reflection in the mirror and began to apply mascara: but something wasn't right. The Kardashian-look-alike wasn't making any head way towards the bathroom stalls. In fact, she was just standing there, staring at Alicia through the mirror, biting her inner lip in contemplation.

"Okay," Alicia said, finally fed up. "Now I'm officially freaked out Do I know you or something?"

The Kardashian continued to stare at Alicia as a guilty smile tugged at the corners of her strawberry flavoured glossed lips.

"No... I'm Sorry. I know you must totally think I'm, like, a weirdo or something,"

Jasmine replied in her best privileged-girl impersonation. "But I couldn't help but overhear that you were here for Zulu."

Alicia slowly turned from the mirror to face the source of its smiling reflection.

"You know Zulu?" she asked incredulously.

Jasmine shyly nodded.

"Well, I sort of know him. I'm more, like, his brother's friend," she clarified with an even shier Smile. "Do you know Prince?" she asked innocently.

Alicia immediately jumped into defence-mode.

Who was this girl?

And was Prince lying to her this entire time?

Could this beautiful woman actually be his girlfriend?

And if so, was she there to confront Alicia over her growing feelings?

Of course not! Alicia rebuked herself inwardly. Don't be ridiculous. She's not a mind reader.

Get a grip, Alicia. Outwardly, she replied with a mere "Yes. I've met him a few times."

But it was too late. Jasmine had already seen the conflicting emotions behind Alicia's eyes. The bitch flicked him. She was sure of it.

Jasmine continued to smile the smile of perfected deception as she secretly seethed inside.

"Well I guess I can say the exact same thing for Zulu," Jasmine continued the conversation. "I've only met him, like, a couple of times. I mean- I don't even know what I'm' really doing here to tell you the truth. I guess I just wanted to offer, like, some support to his family and I guess I thought Prince would be here, but-"

"He's not here," Alicia said, finishing her sentence for her.

"Exactly!" Jasmine sighed, exasperated.

"So, are you his girlfriend or something?" Alicia inquired tentatively. Jasmine scoffed.

"No! Me and Prince are like brother and sister. I could never see him in, like, that kinda light...I mean- its just so- eww!

"But don't get me wrong," Jasmine continued to say hurriedly after seeing tire expression on Alicia's face. "He's super-sexy...It's just that me and him're more like family, you know?"

"I get it, I get it," Alicia nodded, trying to mask her relief. "So, I take it you know Patty then?"

"Patty?"

"Zulu's mother."

"No," Jasmine answered honestly. In reality, she really didn't know much about Prince's younger brother. Prince had always kept that side of his life separate. She wasn't lying when she had said that she had only met Zulu a few times. Rookie gangsters rarely appeared on her radar.

"Okay, well why don't you come back and sit with us in the waiting room? I'm Alicia, Zulu's girlfriend's older sister. My advice: Stay away from Zulu's mother. I'm pretty sure she's borderline psycho," Alicia said, smiling conspiratorially.

"Okay, thank you," Jasmine giggled in response. "I'm Jennifer," she lied. "Do you know when Prince's suppose to show up because-?"

"Yeah, yeah," Alicia cut in. "He should be here any minute now. We texted him and told him that Zulu's awake from his coma, so I'm pretty sure he's on his way."

Jasmine smiled and nodded.

Prince was in for a surprise.

*****

Cautiously avoiding police detection, Rakim made his way down the exact same hospital corridors he had visited the day before. Even though it was messed up on so many levels, he was grateful for the shooting that had rocked the city. If it wasn't for the events of the previous night, Rakim wouldn't have been able to blend in so well with the throng of disheveled partygoers.

Toronto police constables and resident staff security guards patrolled the crowded hallways as nurses and detectives moved about from patient to patient.

The nurses were busy sifting through injuries.

The detectives were busy sifting through information.

Rakim walked with his head down low, aiming to remain inconspicuous. Successfully dodging the harassment of the local authority, Rakim stood outside the entrance that was marked Intensive Care Unit.

Testing the waters, Rakim cracked the doors open just enough to stick his head through as he surveyed the ward. Aside from alone nurse and six occupied beds, the room was empty. Not a police officer in sight. Rakim quietly slipped in.

With a slow swivel of his head, he silently took stock of each patient until his eyes landed on Zulu. Rakim's heart began to race as his blood boiled over at the sight of his shot-up brother. His presence continued to go unnoticed by the lone nurse as she hovered over her ailing charge, going about her duties. The way she attended to his brother put Rakim at ease. She was so gentle in the way she handled him.' She moved as if he were her own child.

Humming Amazing Grace to herself, Nurse Sandra didn't even realize that there was somebody else standing in the room until Rakim cleared his throat from behind her.

"Lah'd Jesus!" she cried out in shock, hand clutching her chest. "Bwoy, you frightened me! Where you come from?" she questioned, glaring at the stranger suspiciously.

Rakim smiled disarmingly and put his hands up in mock surrender.

"Whoa, whoa, whoa," he said in a playful manner, hoping to calm the nurse's nerves. "I come in peace, I'm just here to check on my kid brother."

Nurse Sandra eyed the stranger cautiously. Baseball cap worn down low. A diamond studded earring; expensive running shoes decorating the feet. Right off, the bat she could tell that he was trouble; probably a drug dealer or worse.

"Ah dis your brother?" she asked with her Caribbean accent, indicating Zulu. The smile vanished from Rakim's lips as his eyes fell on his kin. He nodded his head solemnly.

"I heard he's awake now... Can he- is he able to speak?"

Nurse Sandi-a's heart softened a little at the grief that shone through the bad boy's eyes.

It was obvious that there was a genuine connection there.

"Your brother's not much of a talker," she replied in a milder tone. "But yes, he's awake."

They both stood there for a moment, watching over Zulu as the heart monitor continued to sing its mechanicalized song of life.

"Di doctor dem haven't yet approved any visits for your brother, so technically you're not supposed to be here," Nurse Sandra began to say to Rakim with her eyes still on her charge.

"But I can tell you di type to break di rule demon a regular so..." she smiled as she turned to the bad boy. "Me nah say nuttin' if you don't."

Rakim looked at her and smiled crookedly.

"You done know," he replied, nodding his head in appreciation as the nurse walked out of the room, giving him his privacy.

As the door shut, he turned his attention back to his brother. The smile that played on Rakim's lips was bittersweet. He was happy to see his brother alive and breathing, but with the bond that brother's share, he acutely felt his pain. Rakim would burn down the entire world just to see his brother survive. He'd go to any lengths. Cross any boundaries.

Seeing his brother in such a state sparked something dangerous inside of him. Something Rakim wasn't sure he could control. His trigger finger was itching as his heart bled for Bloody Benny and whoever else was responsible for his brother's condition.

Rakim took Zulu's hand inside of his own and squeezed. He wouldn't have considered himself an affectionate type of nigga, but at that moment, Rakim's emotions were all out of whack. The blood-stained bandages that covered up half of Zulu's face was a token of how ruthless the streets could be.

Rakim squeezed his brother's hand once more, causing Zulu to stir out of his chemically induced slumber.

"Wa gwan, lil bro," Rakim greeted softly as Zulu's eyes groggily opened.

It took a few seconds for Zulu to focus on his big brother's face, but once he had recognized who his visitor was, his eyes conveyed the smile that his bandaged jaw was unable to. Rakim's heart swelled.

"Yeah man, its good to see you too," he said smiling for the both of them. "Can you talk or..." The words died in his throat as Rakim's eyes rested on Zulu's battered jaw. The pain in Zulu's eyes was evident, as he shook his head "no".

Whatever answers Rakim came for wouldn't be gained that day; or at least not verbally. Rakim reached into his pocket and pulled out his S10.

"Do your fingers still work?" he asked sarcastically as he placed the cell phone in his brother's hand. "I need to know what happened...I need to know everything."

*****

Kilo knew what he had to do. The rules of the game were clear. Standing just outside of Rakim's car, he inhaled the calming fumes of his cigarette as he watched Maria sob quietly to herself in the back seat. Pyro sat next to her, discreetly pressing his gun to her side.

Why couldn't Prince see what was so obvious, Kilo thought to himself. Just like how playing a game of chess wasn't intended for the blind; running the streets wasn't intended for the weak-hearted. They were parked a few blocks away from the hospital in an empty school parking lot.

Kilo glanced at his gold-plated Rolex. Prince had been gone for ten minutes now and Kilo estimated that he'd probably be gone for ten more. That left Kilo with more than enough time to do what he had deliberated to do. Flicking away the spent cigarette, he hopped into the driver's seat and started the engine.

"My man call?" Pyro inquired from the backseat, referring to Prince.

Glancing in the rear view, Kilo shook his head and started to drive away. "Nah, he didn't call," he replied without elaborating any further.

Pyro held his tongue against the onslaught of questions that strained against his lips. Something was up. Kilo was known for being impulsive and reckless, so wherever he was headed, Pyro was sure, it definitely wasn't apart of the plans.

"Excuse me?" Maria squeaked timidly; cutting into the tension-filled silence.

"Can I please, please leave now? I did everything you asked of me...I told you everything I know...I swear to God I won't go to the police...I just...I just want to go home..."

Outside, the downtown landscape unsympathetically whizzed by as Maria's heartfelt plea went unanswered. Kilo was focused on what he had to do. His mind was made up. For him, there was no point in any further dialogue. Apprehensively, Maria tried again; this time, aiming her supplications at the skinny Somalian who held the looming pistol to her side.

"Please mister...I have a little boy at home who needs me. I don't care about Benny. Just let me go and I promise you I won't say anything...please!"

Pyro reluctantly acknowledged his charge. In all honesty, if it were up to him, he would've let her go from the jump. Nevertheless, the man dem had other plans and he couldn't go against his niggas. If Prince was there, there would've been at least a 50% chance that she would survive: But with Kilo...Pyro just shook his head.

"Just chill mon, everything'll be alright" he lied, as he caught Kilo glancing at him through the rear-view mirror. . .

Even though he wasn't the one in any danger, Pyro felt a chill run through his spine as the day slowly turned to night. Thing's were about to turn ugly. Really, really ugly.

CHAPTER 23

"Can a nigga eat or what?"

As the minutes slowly inched by, Zulu laboriously typed out the beginnings of the conflict between him and Bloody Benny on his big brother's cell phone. The hospital's staff remained absent and Rakim silently thanked the little, black nurse who he believed was partially responsible for his temporary alone time. Maybe hospitals weren't all that bad he contemplated to himself as he considered his brother's condition and the staff that had helped him to survive. The place, however, in Rakim's opinion, still reeked of death mixed with sanitizers and the doctors were still regarded as overpaid quacks in their silly white coats. Nevertheless, forgetting about his annoyances, he continued to wait patiently by his brother's bedside, eyes drawn to the blood-stained bandage skillfully wrapped around Zulu's face. The image reminded him of the bloodstain that had formed on the bed sheet wrapped around Deadus' head and body just a few years back...

*****

June 2007

A young Rakim readied himself by the entrance of Leeco's crib by ensuring his .45 was off safety. He wasn't about to take any chances with the situation being so tense between Deadus and Leeco. He had just returned from dropping off the duffel bags full of pirated narcotics to Small-Up's older brother. Breaking the news to Big-Up went as he had expected. Biggs, as he-was dubbed for short, didn't take the news well and the duffel bags had done nothing to ease the pain of learning his kid brother was the city's latest homicide. Rakim had done his best to soothe the heartache of his mentor's comrade, but words had always seemed to fail in the face of those mourning their love ones. The young Prince was forced to leave Biggs amidst his unrefined sorrow and mounting rage. Standing by the back door to Leeco's crib, Rakim struggled to decipher any sign that the argument was still ongoing inside. In the warm summer night, all Rakim could hear was silence. He tentatively ventured inside.

Even though Leeco was regarded as a bad breed who could, without a doubt, hold his own in the roughest environments, his home was actually located in what a lot of people considered to be the good part of Scarborough. Around here, the houses were bigger, and the neighbours were, as wittingly described by real estate agents, blonder. Along with better schools and the close proximity of the city's local bus service, the TTC; real estate agents also boasted of the very low crime rate the neighbourhood held when compared to other areas of the GTA.

"Never shit where you sleep," Leeco had advised his protégé on more than one occasion.

Doing any type of dirt was never to be done where one lived. It was just common sense; an unwritten rule. So, as Rakim slowly made his way through the spacious, open-concept basement, Leeco's words ricocheted through his mind.

"Never shit where you sleep. Never shit where you sleep..." Rakim quietly

repeated to himself almost as a mantra, as he cautiously scanned the darkened, apparently vacant basement. Surely, Leeco wouldn't have bumped off Deadus in his own crib. The thought alone was ludicrous. Rakim noticed that the duffel bags remained where he had dropped them. The only thing that had changed since he had left was the absence of the two O.G.'s and the lighting. The basement was bathed in darkness. The only sources of light emanated from the commercials playing on the muted flat screen and from the cracks of the nearby bathroom door. The tension that had filled the basement before was replaced by a cold and eerie stillness. Rakim paused as he heard the scratches of a lighter being ignited in the occupied bathroom that was situated just to the right of the home bar. He made his way over and paused at the door. Based off the odor, he could tell that somebody was sparking up a spliff inside. Rakim hesitantly knocked twice, announcing his presence.

"Yo?" Came the response from behind the door.

"Leeco, it's me, wa gwan?" Rakim replied loud enough to be heard. "Is everything bless?"

There was a pause.

Rakim wanted to believe that Leeco was merely using the john, but the whole vibe of the situation suggested otherwise.

"Yo, forward," Leeco, summoned Rakim, as the marijuana fumes grew more pungent.

Rakim entered slowly.

The blood was the first thing he had remembered seeing.

There was just so much of it.

In the bright incandescent lights of the basement's bathroom, the blood that had seemed to fill the bathtub was prominent. The second thing Rakim had remembered noticing was the absence of Deadus' face. All that remained of his scowl was a jumble of shot up flesh and even more blood. Leeco must have emptied his clip in homeboy's forehead; Rakim surmised, shaking his head in wonder.

Deadus' body was twisted, as it lay awkwardly in Leeco's shower. Leeco himself was seated on the toilet, puffing away on his L. The spliffs amber glowed brilliantly as Leeco inhaled on its intoxicating fumes.

Rakim took in the entire scene without stepping one foot inside.

Leeco appeared to be as calm as ever. He sat as if he wasn't just inches away from a dead body, who Rakim assumed, he had been mainly responsible for. He looked up at the young Prince and exhaled a thick stream of grey smoke.

"You gave dat to my boy?" he inquired, ignoring the questions dancing in Rakim's eyes. Rakim nodded his head and then once again took in the sight of Deadus' crumpled up remains. He slightly wondered to himself if Leeco had shot the O.G. in the bathroom or if he had caught him slipping outside and then dragged his body into the tub? Noting the lack of any blood trails, Rakim concluded that the shady O.G. must have met his demise in the room where his mentor took his morning piss. What a shitty way to die, Rakim mused silently. He refocused on Leeco.

"So, wa gwan with him?" Rakim finally questioned, indicating Deadus with a jerk of his chin.

Leeco looked over at the dead body with disdain.

"Fuck'im," was his only reply, as he continued to take pulls off his spliff. Whatever had happened between Leeco and the shady O.G. would remain in the category of topics left unspoken...

First-degree murder, even amongst friends, was always considered a touchy subject. Rakim tilted his head as a thought occurred. "Well, since he's a dead issue, all pun intended, wa gwan with his share of the take? Niggas is hungry out here, man. Can a nigga eat or what?"

Leeco smiled and then barked out in laughter.

"Yeah man, you done know I'ma feed da wolves dem," the Jamaican answered between chuckles, "Just help me wrap up the fool before he starts stinkin' up mi tings, zeen. We can dash him away outside while it's still dark."

"Cool," Rakim replied smiling, even though nothing about the situation was funny.

They wrapped up what was left of Deadus in one of the spare bed sheets Leeco had kept in a spare room and mopped up every drop of blood that they could find.

Leeco offhandedly remarked to himself that he would have to flood the small bathroom with bleach in order to "erase away" what was left of his "sins".

Rakim remained silent as he tried to detach himself from the moment, He forced himself to daydream of what a dead man's share of a botched robbery could net him. There was a certain BMW for sale that he had had his eyes on for quite some time. Nearly an hour later, using the cover of night, they carried the veiled remains of the shady O.G. outside and crudely stuffed him inside the trunk of Rakim's rental as if he were just cheap luggage.

Rakim was new to the whole disposing-of-a-dead-body-thing. In his experience, when business was handled, the shooter would simply just leave the body where it lay. He relied on Leeco's guidance to show him the next step before driving off.

"Where to?" he asked as they took their seats in the rental.

Leeco was scanning his neighbourhood, looking out for any nosy neighbours witnessing something that they weren't supposed to.

"Malton," Leeco answered, throwing Rakim completely off guard.

"Malton? Why the fuck do you wanna fly all the way out there? What happens if the bwoy dem stop us along the way? What happens if they wanna search the whip? Nah man, fuck that shit! Let's just dump him off somewhere close and avoid the risk."

Leeco sucked his teeth. "Listen, Mr. Know-it-all," he exasperatedly explained.

"When di bodies dem pop up around here, it's ah we who da bwoy dem a pree, ah lie?

When di body dem pop up elsewhere, were further down the suspect list, ya zee it"

Rakim thought about it for a second and as much as he hated to admit it, the logic of his mentor made absolute sense.

They headed West, both praying in his own way that they wouldn't bump heads with any trouble-seeking, late night cruisers. Those who are superstitious consider it bad luck to cross the path of a black cat. However, the niggas from the hood knew better. They knew it was a pig's path one should be wary of.

Luckily, their prayers were answered that night as they made it to their destination safely. They discarded the remains of the shady O.G. in a littered ditch on a side road in Malton. Leeco called Biggs, and speaking in code, updated him with the news. Even though Rakim could only hear one side of the conversation, he still could tell that the update did nothing to alleviate Biggs' sorrow.

They made it back to Leeco's crib a couple of hours before dawn. It took them until sunrise to weigh up and divide the stolen drugs. Rakim, that night, garnered six keys of cocaine, three bricks of marijuana and the black steel Tanta dagger Deadus had on him at the time of his untimely demise.

By piecing together little tidbits of information from Leeco, Rakim also gained a slight insight on why Deadus was laid out, face down in a ditch somewhere in Malton. If Rakim was reading between the lines correctly, Deadus was a snake, as told by his mentor. As inconspicuously indicated by Leeco, Deadus was the reason why Small-Up was killed. The details would forever remain unclear to the young Prince but nevertheless the lesson was learned. Greed and deception weren't to be tolerated within The Family.

The Jamaican that morning was all about "brotherhood". He lectured the young Prince about the importance of it and even quoted scriptures from the Bible to support his message.

"Honour thy brother," Leeco had preached, warning his young protégé that those who went against the saying were destined for an early grave. Rakim took heed.

That fateful morning would be the last time Rakim and Leeco would see each other face to face. Later on, that day, Leeco's house was raided by the Guns and Gangs task force and the remainder of the stolen drugs were found and confiscated. Project Mayhem, as it was coined by the police, was the same gang raid Leeco's lawyer, Michael Steinbach, had cautioned him about months earlier. The majority of the top-ranking members of the M.O.B. were rounded up and slapped with "O.C.", (organized crime) charges.

Even with the prompt warnings of his lawyer, Leeco had been caught slipping. He was charged and then subsequently convicted for a series of gun and drug related offences. In addition, he was labelled as a gang leader and was successfully ordered to be deported from Canada. The old M.O.B. was effectively dismantled that year, thanks to wiretaps and juries who were fed up with the growing 'gun culture "plaguing" their city. Unfortunately, in its place a newer, more ruthless M.O.B. with younger and more ruthless members took root and thus, the cycle continued.

Leeco was deported to Jamaica after serving four years behind Canadian bars. Upon his homecoming to his native country, the Jamaican police officials arrested him on the spot in the airport He was charged for a murder that had occurred years before and was thrown into a detention center that resembled a murky dungeon when compared to the relatively new prisons he had just been deported from. Luckily for Leeco, the jailhouse guards on the poverty-stricken Caribbean island were not too proud to take a bribe. According to official documents, Carlito Mannings, aka.Leeco the Deportee, escaped lawful custody and was thought to have fled the island. It was added that there were no known contacts attributed to the escaped con.

Despite this fact, Rakim and a select few had him on speed dial. The now older Prince had kept in touch with his mentor throughout the years. In fact, it was Leeco who was now calling Rakim's cell phone as Zulu typed out his explanation on why he was currently beefing a downtown gangster.

"Ignore it and finish typing," Rakim instructed his little brother as the minutes continued to inch by slowly; Whoever was calling could wait, Rakim decided callously. The bloodstain that was inscribed on his kid brother's bandage continued to hold his attention; It seemed to spell out one word: Revenge.

CHAPTER 24

"So, this is what a dead man sounds like..."

Bloody Benny's cell phone began ringing as he made his way up the DVP northbound. He was en-route to meet up with S.P. and the rest of his goons who had taken over Big Will's apartment in Scarborough. If the city had thought the little shooting at the club was something special, Bloody Benny couldn't wait to demonstrate how he really got down when it came to gunplay. Tonight, he was planning on unleashing hell.

"Yo?" He said, answering his cell phone without checking the caller I.D.

"Yo, what's up Cuz? What's crackin'?"

"Cuz?... What's crackin?" Bloody Benny echoed sarcastically into his handheld.

"What the fu-; who's this?"

"It's-me... Jerome," the voice on the other end replied, sounding a bit dejected that he, a blood relative, wasn't recognized right away. This was the third time Jerome had dialed his cousin's number within the hour. He didn't want to come off as a pest but he desperately needed access to weapons and his auntie's son, Benny, was his only option.

"What do you want Jerome? You've been ringin' off my cell all day." Jerome wanted a gun. He just didn't know how to work it into a conversation without triggering Benny to interrogate him with over a hundred questions. He tried his hand at creating small talk.

"How's Aunt Pain? I heard she was sick last week-"

"Nigga, did you really just call me to see how my mom's doin'? Call her your damn self and stop being a bug. I'm busy right now, man," Bloody Benny replied on the verge of hanging up.

"I'm not being a bye Jerome quickly shot back before his hotheaded cousin could disconnect the call. "I wanted to ask you for a favour-"

"I don't do favours," Bloody Benny answered tersely.

"Yo, just hear me out I need some..." Jerome paused briefly to find the least incriminating word. "Hardware... You understand what I'm saying?"

"Yo, who's this?" Bloody Benny asked again, this time decking the caller ID.

"What the fuck do you mean you need hardware?"

"I need a tool...A sheen...A gat-"

"Nigga, I know what you mean!" Bloody Benny snapped, yelling into the phone.

"Stop hotting up my fuckin' line, you fool... I mean, why do you need something like that? You ain't bangin', nigga. You ain't bout this life."

"I need to handle something quick-fast," Jerome pleaded. "I got the money for one, I just need the link. You got me?"

Bloody Benny sucked his teeth out of annoyance as his cell phone beeped in his ear, indicating that he had another call waiting. When he checked the caller I.D., it read: incoming call- Maria,

"Nigga, stay in school and leave this street shit to me. Don't ever call me on that bullshit again, aight," he said before disconnecting from his cousin and switching to the other line.

"Yo? Bloody Benny said into the phone once again as his way of greeting. No one replied.

He checked his cell phone to see if the call was still connected. It was.

"Yo?" he repeated himself into the handheld, becoming irritated.

"So. this is what a dead man sounds like," the voice on the other end replied. - Bloody Benny was confused. The caller I.D. had come up as Maria but the person his cell phone had connected him to was clearly not his son's mother,

"Yo, who's this?" Bloody Benny asked harshly,

"Your worst nightmare, you bitch-ass nigga" the voice malevolently shot back.

"Ayo, just outta curiosity;" the mysterious voice continued to say. "How many funerals do you think you're gonna have to attend this week?"

"Oh, I get it," Bloody Benny replied, feigning cheerfulness. "You must have a death wish or something, right? I'ma ask you just one more time nigga; who the fuck is this?"

Bloody Benny could hear the mysterious voice on the other end of the call start to chuckle.

"Nigga, you a bitch... Your baby moms got more heart than you, you fuckin' slob," the voice instigated further.

Bloody Benny was furious now. Who the fuck was this nigga on the phone talking shit to him? And how the fuck did he manage to get a hold of Maria's cell phone? He followed up by asking the next logical question;

"Where's Maria?"

"She's here," the voice answered nonchalantly. "You wanna say hi?" Bloody Benny could hear the phone change hands and then Maria was on the line.

"Benny?" The fear in her voice was as clear as day. "Please help me..."

"What the fuck's going on Maria? Who the fuck's with you?"

"They killed Kato and now they're gonna kill me," she cried into the phone. "Talk to them, please!"

"Who the fuck's Kato?" Bloody Benny yelled, now even more confused. But Maria was gone, and the mysterious voice had returned.

"She's a pretty bitch. That's how you downtown yutes're movin', huh?" the voice remarked mockingly.

In an instant, the situation began to make sense to Bloody Benny. He sneered as he asked the question he already knew the answer to:

"So, it was you at that club with me last night, eh?"

"My cousin got touched in that shit, dawg," the voice said, after a brief pause confirming Bloody Benny's suspicions.

"Oh yeah, well next time we'll try a little harder and make sure you get touched too...Kilo."

Kilo smirked.

"So, you heard about me?"

"Yeah, I heard about you," Bloody Benny responded coolly, thinking back to his conversation with Big Will. "I heard you's a baby; Gerber, Where's Prince at, how's his little brother doing?"

"Yo, suck your mother, bitch," Kilo fired back. "When we find you, just know say that it's me who's gonna clock you!"

Bloody Benny laughed triumphantly. Proud that he had finally struck a nerve with his newfound enemy.

"I'm in these streets all day, nigga. Don't act like you can't find me."

"Nigga I'm in your hood right now; I can't see you...But tell you what, though," Kilo said, mischievously. Bloody Benny could hear a gun being cocked in the background.

"Since you're nowhere to be found, I'm just gonna make your mizzle hold what I got for you and we'll square up when I see you, zeen."

"Yo, if you even dare touch one hair on her-"

BANG!

Bloody Benny could hear the shot resonate through the phone.

"Hello...Hello??" he called out desperately into his handheld, but it was too late. The call had already disconnected.

Bloody Benny pulled over to the shoulder of the freeway and just stared at the screen of his cell phone in shock.

CHAPTER 25

"The Mob is silent..."

After ten excruciatingly long minutes, Zulu had finally finished typing his reasons for beefing Bloody Benny on his big brother's cell phone. Though he was anxious to uncover the truth, Rakim held off on reading what was typed down and instead smiled encouragingly into his kid brother's face.

"Everything's gonna be alright," Rakim assured his younger brother, getting up to leave before a shift change could send in a new nurse with even newer suspicions. He affectionately squeezed Zulu's good shoulder and was genuinely happy to see that his little brother's condition hadn't gone the other way. Rakim knew all too well of the scores of unlucky people who were unable to wake up from gunshot wounds. Not surprisingly, at that very moment, he had plans on adding a few more unlucky souls to that list.

"I'm gonna go deal with this shit, aight; don't watch nuthin'," he continued to say. "Just focus on healin' up and I'll forward back as soon as I can, zeen?"

Eyes shining with admiration, Zulu painfully nodded his head that he understood. Not wanting to waste any more time, Rakim marched out of the Intensive Care Unit with renewed determination. He kept his head low as he strolled past a police officer sweet talking a young nurse by the main set of elevators. Deciding to take the stairs, Rakim kept a downcast gaze in an effort to avoid eye contact. with any old (or potentially new) witnesses.

Just as he was about to hit the exit, a familiar voice unceremoniously called out his government name.

"Ronald!" Jasmine shouted from across the hall.

Rakim froze in disbelief. He turned towards the voice, apprehensively.

"Jasmine?" He asked almost to himself.

What the hell is she doing here? He questioned silently as she sashayed her way towards him. Rakim was quick to notice how all the male eyes in the vicinity were glued to the exotic beauty gliding through the drab hallways of the downtown hospital; including, to Rakim's displeasure, the police officer by the elevators.

"Whatchu doin' here?" Rakim asked casually with a bogus smile, putting up a front for the cop who was now sizing them up. On the surface Rakim was all smiles and manners, but in his eyes the anger and suspicions were on full display. Jasmine walked up and kissed him affectionately on the cheek.

"Just making new friends," she replied innocently, fully aware of the raging emotions burning behind her lover's eyes. "You should come and say hi, the entire family's here."

Rakim, though it was difficult, maintained his phony smile.

This bitch is playing games.

"When did you. get here?" he asked all friendly like. The nosy police officer was still watching.

"Oh, I don't know, an hour ago, maybe," Jasmine replied. "Come and say hi to Alicia, Ronald. She's been waiting, oh so, patiently to see you."

Bingo!

That's what all this was about, Rakim concluded. The bitch is jealous. Jasmine continued to smile sweetly. Rakim smiled back. The cop was still watching.

"So, you met Alicia?' Rakim asked. "When did that happen?"

"Earlier today," Jasmine replied. "She's so beautiful. I've been hanging out with her and her little sister. They're all just so pretty. How come you never mentioned them to me before? Are we keeping secrets from each other now?"

Rakim was barely listening. He was more focused on the cop by the elevators. If the pig decided to card him, a shit load of problems could arise. He stealthily surveyed the cop's next move. If the pig made any headway towards Rakim and Jasmine, Rakim decided that he would just make a break for it down the stairwell. Luckily, the young nurse who the police officer was wooing said something to him recapturing his attention, causing him to instantly forget about Jasmine and Rakim.

Rakim didn't waste any time. He put his arms around Jasmine and ushered her into the stairwell so quickly that not even Jasmine knew what was going on.

Once they were alone, he violently grabbed her by the throat and pinned her against the wall.

"What the fuck're you doin' around here, Jasmine?" he demanded through clenched teeth. He was pissed; beyond pissed. Jasmine was dangerous. She represented a world in which Rakim tried to keep separate from his family. The fact that she was there on a bad-minded-tip caused Rakim to snap.

Jasmine could barely breathe. Prince was gripping her neck so hard that she was sure that if he didn't let up, she would pass out; but she loved it though. She didn't answer Prince because frankly, she was unable to. Instead, she smiled slyly, despite her discomfort, adding to Rakim's anger.

This bitch is losing it, Rakim silently concluded. He released his grip and she fell to the floor. Rakim allowed her to catch her breath. He really hated putting his hands on women, but this bitch was a different breed.

"I'm not playin' with you, Jasmine. Talk," he demanded.

Jasmine got back up slowly and remained silent until she regained her composure. She had never seen Prince lose his temper before.

For years, she had searched in vain for his weak spot, trying to find the Achilles Heel in which to control or destroy him by. First, she had tried with her pussy but that didn't work. Then she had attempted to manipulate him through his friends but in the end, that too had failed. It had never occurred to Jasmine that the only vulnerable area in Prince's life would be his family. He had always kept that part of his life hidden; Out of sight, out of mind. Now that she knew, she planned to exploit it.

"I already told you what it is, Prince," Jasmine said in an icy tone. "You're fuckin' up the money. I'm sorry your bro got touched the other night but the way you and your crew is movin' is fuckin' up the program for everybody. The man dem just got outta the spotlight a day-ago and there you go draggin' us back into the mix of things. The Mob is silent; we're not in it for the notoriety. If you can't run tings properly then I think it's time for someone who can."

"Yeah?" Rakim smirked at her treachery. He had known for years what this power-hungry bitch was about. He was mildly amused to see the snake slither into her true form. "And who can run tings better than me?" he asked, even though he had already caught the play.

Jasmine smiled menacingly.

"Me of course," she said looking him dead in his eyes. "I've been with this shit since day one. I keep it a hundred, 100% of the time. I'm done being the bitch in the background, Prince. It's time for the Queen to take her throne, don't you think?"

Rakim scoffed and shook his head in disgust.

"You're fuckin' delusional," he said. "Do you really think the goons' dem would really take directions from you? I know you think you're smart, baby, but in reality, you're just eye candy for the crew; a trophy to be shown off in the clubs. Don't hurt yourself by overreaching your status. This is a man's game; bitches are too emotional for this shit. Stay in your lane, zeen!"

Jasmine flashed with anger. She reached into her handbag and backed out the .22 before she had even realized what she had done.

Rakim didn't flinch. He had proved his point. He allowed her to squarely aim the pistol at him without even showing the slightest bit of concern. He knew she had it in her to pull the trigger but Rakim didn't care. He wasn't afraid of dying. Long ago, he had suspected that that was one of the reasons why the others in the crew had looked up to him and had allowed him to be their leader after Leeco had been deported. The consensus was that he I was either courageous or just simply crazy. Either way, he was the perfect man for the job.

Jasmines hands trembled as she aimed the .22 caliber at Prince's chest. She knew that she had fucked up by showing him her hand too early. Now she faced a dilemma: If she didn't wet Prince, right there on the spot, she could be damn sure that he'd retaliate.

Prince would either send one of his goons to light her up or he would just end up murdering her himself.

However, if she decided to pull the trigger, the cop, by the elevators would hear the shot ring out and then she would be fucked. Getting locked up for life wasn't a viable option I for Jasmine. There was no such thing as real power in jail.

She lowered the pistol.

Rakim shook his head in disappointment.

"I wanted to give you the benefit of the doubt, Jazz, I really did" he said, pity coloring his tone. "But I knew you was a snake from the jump."

The cool demeanour Jasmine displayed just moments earlier melted away as a single renegade tear escaped from her eye and made its getaway down her cheek. She hated herself for showing this much emotion. She hated herself for looking so weak in front of a boy she had helped cultivate into the game. She looked tip into Rakim's eyes and saw every single man she had ever known who had worn their superiority over her as if simply being male made them dominant, her resolve hardened.

"I'm not playin' the sidelines anymore Prince," Jasmine whispered in an icy tone...

"I want the crown. I'll take it in blood if I have to."

Rakim's eyes narrowed as he sized up his newly uncovered enemy. He held her gaze and nodded his head.

"Come'n get it," he said, making a mental note to body her before the week was over.

Jasmine wiped away the lone tear and placed the .22 back inside her purse.

The lines were drawn in the sand and the masks were off. She knew that the only way she was going to survive a full out war with Prince was to out maneuver him at every turn. She smiled deceptively as her first move formulated in her mind.

"I'll stay here with the family until everything's straightened out, okay?" She said loudly enough so that the cop by the elevators could hear her, swiftly opening the door that led back to the ICU waiting room.

Rakim frowned as he caught the play.

"Bitch, stay away from my brother," he hissed, as he tried to pull her back into the stairwell.

She quickly shifted just out of his reach until she was back in plain view of the police officer who was stilt by the elevators.

"You sure you don't wanna see your brother, Ronald?" she questioned, still speaking loudly for the cop to hear. "I think you should stay with us and calm yourself down. I can tell that you're angry, but revenge is never the solution; just chill out, okay?"

Rakim knew that she was trying to get the cop's attention. He couldn't tell if it was working from where he was standing but for sure he wasn't going to take any chances.

He smiled maliciously at her and nodded his head. Game on.

"Aight, Jasmine," he said finally. "I'll catch you on the rebound."

He turned away and quickly made his way down the flight of stairs. Jasmine and her wicked games could wait Rakim decided.

For now, war was the only thing on his mind.

*****

"Where did you go?" Alicia asked "Jennifer" as she walked back into the waiting room. "Is Prince here yet?"

Jasmine frowned apologetically and shook her head no. "I just got off the phone with him," she lied. "He told me to tell you that he's not coming anymore. Something to do with 'too many cops around the hospital'...I'm sorry."

Jasmine took her seat beside Alicia, as Alicia tried in vain to disguise her disappointment.

"It's alright," Alicia said finally in a bid to downplay her emotions. "It's probably smarter for him to stay off the radar anyhow."

Jasmine nodded out of forged sympathy. "You like him, don't you?"

Despite herself, Alicia began blushing.

She cast a quick glance towards her sister and Kim who were caught up in their own conversation.

"Is it that obvious?" she replied in a hushed tone so that only "Jennifer" could hear.

Jasmine smiled slyly. "Well, its not, not obvious. Your face gets, like, all red every time he's brought up."

"Oh my God, I know!" Alicia groaned, fully embarrassed. "I'm trying not to catch feelings for him, but I can't help it. I can feel myself getting caught up; I don't know what's wrong with me. He's all that I think about now; even when with my boyfriend, well, ex-boyfriend, all that's running through my mind is him."

Jasmine continued to smile and nodded her head as if she understood, even though, deep down behind the deception, all she wanted to do was slap the bitch for being so naïve. This was the reason why so many niggas took advantage of women, she concluded. All these dumb bitches wear their hearts on their sleeves.

Jasmine swallowed her disgust and continued to play the 'you-can-tell-me-anything' role.

"Did you hook up with him yet?" she asked as she leaned in confidentially.

Bashfully, Alicia continued blushing as she nodded her head yes, again casting quick glances at her sister to see if she was listening.

The mere memory of making love to Prince was too much for her to handle. Alicia felt herself becoming aroused as she recalled how his full lips felt on her neck...His hands searching her body. She had never been intimate with another man aside from Jerome before and she seldom entertained the thought. Prince was a game changer. When he came onto her, it wasn't much of a surprise in Alicia's mind that she had caved in a heartbeat. She was tired of the way Jerome had made her feel. She was tired of never being satisfied in bed. She had yearned for that feeling her friends had described; that explosion that came after sex. She had wanted that passion that she had seen so many times in so many movies. In her fantasies, Prince was the man who could deliver that to her. Alicia could envision him bouncing her off the walls, fucking her until she came over and over again. Her sex pulsated and moistened from the-things she could picture him doing to her. Alicia's cheeks grew even redder as she realized that "Jennifer" was still watching.

Jasmine smiled knowingly as if she knew exactly what Alicia had been thinking. She too quickly glanced at Kim and Keisha to keep up the air of confidentiality as she lowered her voice.

"Trust me girl, I get what you're going through. Prince is, like, super fine, I can't lie. If I didn't see him as being more of a brotherly-type I would've, like, probably been one of his ex-lovers or some shit. Mad girls fall for him all the time.

"But I'll tell you one thing; most of them never last. Prince is very...particular. If a girl can't satisfy him, ASAP, then they're cut out of his life, ASAP. He tells me about it, like, all the time. I know what he's looking for in a relationship. If you want him, I can, like, help you."

"You can help me?" Alicia smiled skeptically. "How and why?"

"Well, because you're, like, exactly the type of girl he needs in his life right now," Jasmine replied, running pure game. "You're not from the hood. You're not a ho, from as far as I can tell. You got you're head on your shoulders and I bet you'd, like, treat him right. I wanna see my bro happy; you'd be perfect for him. I'll play the inside man err, woman, and give you all the tips on how to win his heart."

Alicia remained skeptical and it showed in her facial expression. Jasmine determined that she'd have to push harder.

"Look," Jasmine continued to say. "You like him, right?"

Alicia, though still uncertain, nodded shyly.

"Well, okay then. I know he likes you too, so just trust me and I'll, like, do the cupid-thing and sparks will fly. Believe me, I'm a pro at this sort of thing."

Alicia was still unsure. Jasmine sensed this and continued pushing further.

"Okay, do you want him or not?"

"I do want him," Alicia confessed. "But I just don't get why you would want to help me. Like, what's in it for you?"

Jasmine let out a guilty smile.

"Well, to be, like, completely honest, I think you're cool and I wouldn't mind you as a friend...I know it sounds corny or, like, whatever but I don't have too many girlfriends to just, you know, like, kick it with."

Alicia smiled warmly. She felt flattered that someone as pretty as "Jennifer" would want to be her friend. Alicia knew all to well the feeling of loneliness. She had lost most of her friends when she had decided to focus more on her career. Maybe it was time to be more social again, she thought to herself, especially after the events of the previous night. She reached out and hugged "Jennifer".

"If you're looking for a friend, you got one," she said as she embraced her new homie.

Jasmine hugged her back and smiled treacherously over Alicia's shoulder. She was in.

CHAPTER 26

"And what about your friends?..."

Rakim successfully maneuvered out of the hospital without being discovered or apprehended by the police. He maintained a low profile and power walked. away from the building, clutching onto his cell phone as if it were a prize well earned. He was anxious to read what Zulu had typed down but instead, he decided to exercise patience until he was at least a few blocks away. It was better to remain focused in this part of the city. This wasn't his turf. Aside from the pigs, Rakim now had to keep a watchful eye out for bloodthirsty gunmen who Were known to patrol this side of the city. The daylight was fading away and he could feel another potentially violent night creeping into existence.

After reaching a safe distance, Rakim sent a text message to Kilo asking him how far away he was parked. It took less than a minute for Kilo to respond: I'm around. U ready? Where u at?

Rakim instructed his nigga to pick him up at the corner of Bathurst and Queen.

Kilo pulled up a few minutes later. Rakim quickly hopped into the passenger seat. he first thing he had noticed Was Maria's absence.,

"Where's she at?" Rakim questioned both of them in bewilderment.

No one answered.

Both Kilo and Pyro kept silent as Rakim glared at them through the growing darkness.

Drakes newest single bumped on the radio and filled the discomfited silence inside the car's interior as Rakim searched the faces of his brethren's. Finally, he turned and looked eyes with Pyro who was still sitting in the backseat.,

"Where she at?" he asked him again but this time in an icy tone.

Pyro subconsciously glanced at the back of Kilo's head before shaking his own. He reluctantly ignored his homeboy's question and peered outside the window as the downtown city bionics sped by.

Rakim turned and frowned at Kilo who, at the moment was driving intently, refusing to acknowledge his best friend's questioning glare.

Rakim was furious now.

"So wa gwan; the man dem're deaf all of the sudden?" Rakim shouted, drowning out the music. "Where's the bitch?"

After a few moments of uneasy silence, Kilo finally. sighed.

"She's gone, man," he said quietly, averting, his gaze as he continued to focus tensely on the road.

Rakim's eyes narrowed as he processed what Kilo had said.

"What do you mean she's gone?"

"She's gone, man, fuck!" Kilo repeated defensively.

It was now Rakim's turn to remain muted as he mentally digested what he was hearing. For a moment, a part of him desperately wanted to believe that the girl was somewhere alive, perhaps scared shitless, but alive. He could picture the man dem letting her go and her running wildly down the street, tears streaming 'down her pretty face, grateful for another day above ground.

However, the reality of the situation quickly settled in.

Rakim gazed at the side of Kilo's face and studied the man belled known since childhood. Akiel still wore his hat with a tilt. Though his face was a bit chunkier, Rakim could still see the same little menace that he had grown up with.

Through the years, because of their bond, words were seldom needed to express what the other was feeling. It didn't take long for Rakim to fill in the blanks of his homeboy's silence. He knew without being told the apparent truth. The girl was dead. Rakim was a hundred percent certain.

He sat back in the passenger seat of his own car and contemplated the repercussions of Kilo's actions in silence. The brand-new street war that he had found himself in had taken an ugly turn. Women and children were off limits when it came to beef. It was a rule Rakim had adhered to in other conflicts not because he was soft but because he tightly had held onto a sense of Honour.

His temper began to rise as he pictured his friends gunning down a defenseless woman.

He didn't want his name associated with any innocent bodies. He kissed his teeth out of frustration. His niggas should've known better. The tension between Kilo and Rakim was borderline palpable as the 740 BMW made its way back towards the east end.

"Where we going?" Rakim asked Kilo without looking in his direction.

The Drake song ended and after a brief promo for the radio station, an Oliver the Jeweler commercial crackled through the stereo. Kilo drove into the express lane and pressed play on the car's sound system before answering Rakim. Yo Gotti echoed through the whip as the tension between the two continued to rise.

"It's hot downtown, my nigga. We flying back to the ends for the night.

We'll circle back 'round for Benny tomorrow."

Rakim nodded his head derisively.

"So, I guess you callin' all the shots now, huh?"

Kilo ignored Rakim's loaded question and continued to focus intensely on the road. His main goal at this point was to get as far away from the murder scene as possible. He knew that once the police found Maria's lifeless body all hell would break loose.

Rakim took Kilo's continued silence as a diss.

"Yo, you think I'm a waste man, dawg; you don't hear me talkin' to you?"

"I hear you, my nigga," Kilo said, still keeping his eyes on the road. "But you ain't really saying" nothin '."

"Yo, the man dem just need to chill out with all that bickering," Pyro quickly spoke up from the backseat, trying in vain to defuse the escalating quarrel, "Lees just get back to the ends and we'll sort out everything once we're-"

"Nah, fuck that shit!" Rakim cut in. He turned towards Kilo. "So, you wanna hear me say something, dawg, is that it?"

Kilo didn't reply, so Rakim continued, on:

"Aight, so hear what; you move like a fuckin' retard, my yute. From day one you've been all heart and no brains. You look at me like I'm the one who. doesn't know what he's doin' but in reality, it's you who's fuckin' up the most. We playin' chess out here, cuz, not checkers. Can't you see? You're pilin' way too many unnecessary bodies on us, fam.

"You think the bwoy dem're stupid? You think the streets don't talk? We'll, making way too many ripples out here, man; real talk. Real niggas don't mirk unarmed women. That's some goof shit. We gotta."

"Man, fuck you," Kilo interrupted, unable to take anymore verbal abuse.

"You got all the answers, huh? You always think you're the smartest nigga in the room. I do what I got to do because if I don't than no one will. We've both gotten our hands dirty, dawg. The only thing that changed is you getting all soft' n shit.

"Little brother's laid up in the hospital, man, and you wanna let niggas live?" he paused, kissing his teeth and then shaking his head. "Nah man, bodies gotta drop for that shit rude boy. You can move like a bitch on your own time."

Rakim tensed. Yo Gotti continued to verbally spar with the slow methodical beat of his hit song "I Know" as the atmosphere between the two friends dangerously turned violent.

"You callin' me a bitch, man?" Rakim asked way too calmly, setting both of his friends on edge.

Before Kilo could answer, a flash of red and blue lights appeared behind them, followed by the sharp blare of sirens. Automatically the mood shifted

and all three occupants of the BMW were on high alert.
Rakim slid lower into his seat and gaped at the police cruiser through the passenger side mirror as Kilo did the same but through the rear-view.
Rakim swiftly punched in the code for the car's stash box.

"Yo, send the strap!" he instructed Pyro without turning back to look at, him. The red and blue lights continued to bum behind them, evaporating any doubts about whom the cops were targeting.
Pyro discreetly, handed off the .45 as Kilo continued onwards without making any attempt to pull over. The looming police cruiser inched closer with its sirens now on full blast.
Heartbeats were racing as adrenaline soared. Rakim knew that it was in moments like this where one's mettle was really tested. The last time the cops had tried to pull him and his crew over, a high-speed chase had ensued, resulting in a bloody crash that had left one of his friends dead and another locked up for a crazy amount of years. This new situation felt eerily similar to the last. The choice was clear: either they could pull the car over, leaving their fate up to God or they could go all out, throwing caution to the wind. Rakim secured the firearm into the stash box and then fastened his seatbelt. Pyro turned and nervously looked through the car's rear window.

"Yo; I can't go to jail for no murder," he whined from the backseat.
Kilo gritted his teeth as Rakim continued to spy on the cruiser through the passenger side mirror. The sirens seemed to intensify as a decision was silently made. Kilo stepped on the gas pedal and the car accelerated into higher speeds.
The police cruiser pursued.
Kilo recklessly weaved in and out of traffic, causing some of the cars in his way to sway and veer off road. The police cruiser matched Kilo's pace as its sirens continued to wail.

"We gotta get off the highway," Rakim advised, as Kilo continued to navigate through the express lane at a dangerously highspeed.
Silently agreeing, Kilo took the first exit off the express and gunned it down the 401 towards its nearest exit.
The police cruiser kept tow.
Rakim's mind was racing faster than the police chase. He tried to quickly think ahead and map out their next move. Obviously, they couldn't keep this up, he thought to himself.
Back up was probably en route and once there were multiple police cruisers on their tail, the chances of escape would be few, if any. He quickly realized that the safest way out was to abandon his car and flee on foot. Changing his mind, he again stabbed in the code to the stash box and relieved it of its contents.

"Yo, we gotta run. That's the only way we're lose them, man," he warned to of his niggas, as he stuffed his pockets with his emergency money and held onto the handgun.

The unrelenting sirens screamed in the background as Kilo cut through two lanes, causing a minivan to swerve and crash into a neighbouring car and then flew up the exit ramp, running through one stop light after another. He swerved into a residential neighbourhood and dangerously navigated through its streets. Rakim unbuckled his seatbelt and started mentally preparing for what he had planned next.

Kilo swerved into an apartment complex's parking lot and screeched the car to a halt.

Rakim was the first one out but instead of running, he turned towards the police cruiser, .45 in hand, and began firing, giving his boys cover as they jumped out of the BMW.

The police cruiser started to skid and then it lost control, crashing into a nearby parked car as bullets punched holes into its hood and windshield. The officers inside the cruiser ducked for cover as Kilo and Pyro fled in different directions, running as fast as their adrenaline-filled legs could take them.

Rakim continued firing until he emptied his clip, backtracking two steps with every bullet spent. He turned and ran after the last fired round and sprinted towards a pathway that led into another residential area. Government issued Glock 9's began barking behind him and bullets whizzed through the air as the pigs regained their bearings and began firing back.

Rakim ran in zigzags to avoid being shot, making a sharp turn as soon as he exited the pathway.

There were a handful of frightened people on the streets. Most of them ran back into the safety of their homes as Rakim and the sound of sirens mixed with gunfire flew by. A few terrified bystanders cowered behind cars that were parked along the side of the once quiet lane.

Rakim ran past them faster than Usain Bolt. He couldn't tell if the cops were actually on foot chasing him, but he didn't dare look back. Getting caught by the pigs was no longer an option. With the bullet holes that were peppered into their cruiser, Rakim knew that if he was caught, he'd be gunned down on sight. He ran faster, despite the burning sensation in his lungs. Thankfully, the clay had died and nighttime reigned supreme, covering his frenzied getaway in darkness. He hopped a fence and then another, until he was in some stranger's backyard. He paused for a split second and then lunged over another fence.

Suddenly, he was in a soccer field behind a building that appeared to be a school. He crouched low and surveyed the surrounding area as his heart hysterically thumped inside his chest. The police sirens seemed to have multiplied and gave the impression that they were coming from all directions. Rakim frantically tried to catch his breath as he reloaded his handgun, sliding his last remaining clip into place.

Were the cops still chasing him? He couldn't be certain, though he figured at this point an entire division must've been out in full force searching for him and his crew. He looked up and examined the skies for any apparent Signs of a police helicopter. There was none.

Only the glittering moon hung indifferently, suspended in a starless sky.

Relieved, Rakim greedily gulped up the cool evening air as he prepared to continue with his escape. He briskly ran towards the school. The light above the building's side door was smashed in and standing just below it was a pack of young black teens.

Rakim pocketed his firearm into his jacket and ran towards them, He could smell the undeniable scent of marijuana well before he reached the cluster.

"Aiyo, the bwoy dem're chasin' me," he quickly explained. "Lemme moss out with you for a minute and then I'll bounce, zeen?"

The group of teens cautiously eyed Rakim as if he were an alien that had just fallen from the sky. A bottle of Canadian Club sat devilishly on the ground between the young men's feet. The scent of cheap wine whispered the tale of a reckless adolescence as the teenagers began looking at one another in uncertainty. After a few moments of awkward silence, one of the youngsters spoke up: "The cops're, chasin' you," the teen mumbled in a dreamlike state, slurring his words.

It didn't take a rocket scientist to figure out that the kid was high out of his mind. Though he couldn't make it out in the dark, Rakim would've bet a grand that all of their eyes were bloodshot red. He took a deep breath and tried to remain calm.

"Yes," Rakim answered in a measured tone. "The cops are chasing me, and I need to hide out for a minute or two until they pass. I'll give you each a twenty if you agree to let me blend in with you," He spoke slowly to the teens so that they'd understand him through their marijuana-induced fog.

The ringleader looked back at his young friends and then whispered something to the boy standing nearest to him. The ringleader then turned his attention back to Rakim.

"You'll give us twenty bucks each for just letting you par with us?"

Rakim nodded his head.

"How much money do you have on you right now?" the youngster slurred menacingly.

Rakim could hear the hunger in the kid's voice and for the teenager's sake; he silently prayed that the kid wouldn't try anything stupid.

The mounting police sirens continued to fill the air.

Rakim quickly scanned his surroundings and then looked back at the ringleader who now had his hands in his pockets. Rakim pretended not to notice as he casually slid his own into his jacket and palmed the still wane

.45.

"Listen, I don't have time for no bullshit, man," he explained as one of the boys manoeuvred behind him. "Are you gonna help me or not?"

"Yeah, yeah, fo'sho," the young ringleader replied as he backed out a silver 38. Special. "But first we want all your gwop, yo. Empty your pockets."

Rakim sighed and eyed the pistol. The police sirens grew louder as if a cruiser was about to emerge from the corner at any second. The young teen had heart but he lacked experience, Rakim reasoned to himself. The ringleader held the gun at arm's length, just a few inches away from Rakim's chest. If he had known better, he wouldn't have been standing in such close proximity to his intended target.

In a flash Rakim violently lashed out and grabbed the teen's hand, forcing the 38. Special downwards and away from Rakim's body as Rakim simultaneously pulled out his .45 and aimed it at the kid standing behind him. The young ringleader tried in vain to wrestle out of Rakim's iron grip but then Rakim pointed the .45 at the teen's head and the ringleader instantly let go, raising both of his hands into the air. The other young teens followed suit as Rakim trained his firearm at them.

"Right, let's try this again," Rakim said as he' ushered the boy who was standing behind him back amongst his friends.

"I'ma chill here behind you niggas until shit quiets down, zeen. You lil niggas're gonna stand here in front of me and continue to act all normal and shit. The first one of y'all lil niggas to move is the first one to get popped, you understand?"

Rakim quickly fell into position behind the youngsters just as a police cruiser turned the corner and sped up the street in their direction. Rakim pocketed the 38. Special and then cocked his .45 as the cruiser slowed its approach upon seeing the group of loitering teens.

"Aight everybody, just be cool," Rakim whispered, his eyes never leaving the approaching cop car.

For the most part, the teens tried their best to act casual; though with a loaded gun pointed at their backs and a Toronto police cruiser closing in on the front, the notion of acting casual took on an entirely different dimension.

The driver's side window lowered as the police cruiser came to a complete stop just a few yards away from the loitering teens, A flashlight clicked on from inside. The teens were suddenly assaulted by an offensively bright spotlight that moved between the boys as a predator moved between its prey. Rakim ducked lower and arranged himself directly behind one of the teens as the intrusive search light spilled between the gaps of his human shield.

His heart was beating like a jackhammer and his paranoid mind was on overdrive.

Which one of these kids would end up ratting him out, he half-wondered, gripping his handgun tighter as he silently contemplated homicide.

A voice dripping with authority boomed over the ambience of sirens, asking the group of boys what exactly they were up to, huddled in a corner in the dark.

"We just chillin' and waiting for some friends, officer," the ringleader answered, once again acting as the spokesman for the group.

"You boys from around here?" the cop questioned, training his flashlight on the ringleader.

"Yeah, that's my house over there," the ringleader replied, pointing to a house somewhere down the street.

"And what about your friends?" the officer inquired, once again swinging his flashlight from face to face.

The other teens all began speaking at once, all offering a brief description of 'where they lived and how close it was in relation to the school. That didn't seem to appease the investigating police officer.

"Is that marijuana I smell?" the officer remarked after a brief pause.

None of the teens answered right away.

Rakim held his breath and palmed the .45 tighter.

"Okay, nobody moves!" the police officer commanded as lie began to open his car door.

"You fuckin' idiot!" Rakim swore under his breath, rebuking the nosy constable.

He didn't want to kill a cop but at this point his options were limited. If the pig were to spot him, Rakim knew that he'd either be gunned down on sight or sent to prison for life.

None of those options were appealing. This was a do or die situation and Rakim knew what he had to do.

Just as he was about to jump from behind the boys and start spraying, gunshots sounded off somewhere in the distance. The radio inside the police cruiser crackled to life as the dispatcher relayed a police scanner code and location in a hurried tone.

The police cruiser's door slammed shut.

"Go home, nowt" the officer demanded as he pulled away and sped off down the street. Rakim let out a sigh of relief as the cruiser's taillights faded off into the distance.

Rakim peeked up over the shoulders of his human shield. The shots that drew the police cruiser away had sparked up a storm of conflicting emotions from within. On one hand, Rakim was elated and relieved that the shots had shifted the focus off him. Yet on the flipside, the sounds of gunfire meant that one (or both) of his boys was more than likely facing off against the TPS. Rakim silently prayed to Allah for the safety of his friends.

He swallowed his rising panic and ignored the images of his brethren's being shot to death.

"He's gone, man. Can we go now?" one of the teens pleaded without turning around, causing Rakim to refocus.

He emerged from Isis hiding spot and again quickly scanned his surroundings. None of the teens dared to move as they nervously watched the dangerous gunman.

"Aight, you did good," he said as he pocketed his firearm, turning to leave.

"Aiyo," the ringleader timidly spoke up. "Before you go, can- can we get back our strap?"

Rakim scoffed.

"Are you serious?"

The teen kept his head low and avoided eye contact as he pleaded.

"My bad for tryin' to rob you, man. We just- we just tryin' to eat, naw mean?"

Rakim sized up the ringleader and admired his spirit. The kid reminded Rakim of himself when he was that age. He surveyed the other teens as they cowered behind the ringleader.

They posed no threat. Rakim pulled out the .38 Special and emptied the chamber before handing back the pistol.

"Get some new friends," he advised the young wolf as he turned to leave.

"Hey, aiyo!" the ringleader again called out before Rakim could depart.

"What?" Rakim demanded exasperated as he turned back impatiently.

The teen hesitated for a moment but then looked Rakim directly in the eyes:

"Can we- can we still get dem twenties?"

CHAPTER 27

"I want them more than dead..."

Big Will was in a state of shock. He just couldn't believe that any of this was actually real. The downtown nightmare that he thought he had escaped from had somehow followed him home and managed to corrupt the sanctity of his precious abode. The hooligans who had held him captive for hours had, for the most part, taken over his beloved two-bedroom apartment. His sanctuary was lost.
The four trespassers had violated every single room. Big Will's most favourite area, the kitchen, was ransacked and pillaged for its goods. Evidence of the plunder lay scattered across the apartment as if a pack of wild animals had gotten into the pantry and fridge. To make matters worse, the main bedroom was a write off. If Big Will had known in the past that hooking up a PlayStation 4 in his room would've attracted degenerate scum to defile and undermine the very spot where he slept, he probably would've reconsidered.
Big green Glad garbage bags, (his own garbage bags), were filled to the rim with expensive items that the thugs had decided were no longer of any use to the spineless barber. Electronics, shoes, jewelry, even barber tools were thrown into the bags as the intruders helped themselves to whatever they could find.
Big Will was sitting on the floor, not by choice, marveling at the destruction of his home as the goons kept busy entertaining themselves.
At that very moment, he could heat Shells and Mouse inside his bedroom on the verge of arguing as they played his Call of Duty. A series of "hold that pussies" and other offensive names were thrown at each other whenever a video game kill was made.
A third goon was somewhere off in Big Will's kitchen. The sound of sizzling bacon highlighted the mouth-watering aroma that taunted the fat barber's senses, reminding him of his long-forgotten hunger.
Big Will half wondered to himself if the Swiss Chalet delivery boy had understood his urgent but muted cry for help just before he had shut the

door.

Silently, he fantasized that there was a taskforce of police officers downstairs in his lobby, preparing to rescue him (and his apartment) from his horrible nightmare. He pictured the taskforce team, donned in all black bulletproof gear, busting through his front door and shooting each of the intruders dead. He smiled at the image but then quickly straightened Isis expression' as he noticed S.P. grilling him from the side. The psychopath snugly sat on Big Will's favourite couch as if he owned it, petting the barber's pet dog, Tyson. He was watching a pay-per-view porno with the volume on. mute. Big Will promptly averted his gaze and trained his eyes on the titties bouncing up and down on the big screen T.V. The pom actress, a blonde with a pretty face and fake breasts, furiously played with herself and looked into the camera seductively as she rode her male counterpart in the reverse cowgirl position.

Big Will stared at the screen and fixed his eyes onto a dolphin-shaped tattoo just above the starlet's pussy. Through his peripherals, he could still sense S.P.'s homicidal glare.

Out of fear mixed with hunger, his stomach began to chum and nimble. His pet rottweiler growled at the sound: Cautiously, Big Will ventured a look in S.P.'s direction to see if the psycho was still staring at him. He was.

"What' chu lookin' at, fat boy?" S.P. asked menacingly, startling the barber and causing him to quickly return his vision back to the skin flick.

Big Will kept silent. Maybe if I don't answer him, he'll leave me alone, the barber wishfully thought to himself.

"Yo I Yo, fat boy! I'm talkin' to you!"

The fat barber hesitantly tamed his attention back to the light-skinned killer.

"I ju-just wanted to see if Tyson was botherin' you," Big Will stammered. "I heard him growling and-and if you like, I could put him outside on the balcony no problem."

"Did I say he was botherin' me, you fat piece 'a shit!"

S.P. was staring at Big Will as if the barber had been accused of slapping his mother. The hatred and hostility scribbled on the killers face just didn't seem normal, confirming Big Will's suspicions that the downtown hooligan was certifiably insane.

"No, no, you're right," Big Will said, keeping his eyes downcast. "You didn't say that. I'm- I'm sorry, I didn't mean no disrespect."

S.P. continued to stare intimidatingly at the fat barber sitting on the floor. He really wanted to kill him, or at least stab him a few times so that he could watch him bleed.

The overweight barber timidly turned back to the porno. The blonde was now on all fours, her face twisted in either pleasure or pain as her male co-star fucked her from behind. The scene ended with the sweaty male stud climaxing all over the young blonde's tits. The young actress grinned into the camera with a smile as phony as her breasts.

Big Will continued to watch with feigned interest as the next scene started; a busty brunette, who wore too much make-up, twerked and gyrated on screen.

The goon who was in the kitchen, (Big Will privately dubbed him as "The Cook"), walked into the living room with a plate full of bacon ill one hand and a bag full of Wonder bread in the next. Tyson leapt out of S.P.'s lap and began to bark excitedly. The light-skinned killer stood up and shushed the dog. Tyson immediately stopped barking, though his eyes never left the plate of food. "The Cook" and S.P. sat down at Big Will's second-hand dining room table and began to make BLT's without the lettuce or tomatoes.

Tyson longingly followed closely at their heels. Big Will could only follow with his eyes.

The barber's stomach continued to grumble as he watched his two tormenters carelessly take handfuls of his bacon and slap it between two slices of his white bread, devouring the sandwiches without any traces of grace or manners.

This must be a form of torture, Big Will thought to himself. He painfully suffered in silence as the humiliation and hunger drilled holes into his bloated sense of pride and belly. A cell phone began to vibrate and then ring.

S.P. reached into his pocket and pulled out a cheap flip phone.

"Yo?" he said into the mobile with a mouth full of half-chewed bacon.

"Yeah....yeah.... Aight, we'll buzz you in....Done know." S.P. ended the call and then threw the last remaining strips of bacon onto the floor for the dog. Tyson greedily gobbled up the scraps as "The Cook" looked at S.P. questioningly.

"It's Benny," S.P. replied, wiping his greasy hands clean onto Big Will's white tablecloth. "He's here; said he'll be up in a second."

Big Will's stomach dropped at the thought of another downtown gangster in his apartment. This wasn't how things were supposed to unfold. Big Will should've been far removed from this drama. In his mind, he had envisioned Prince and Kilo meeting their ruin on some poorly lit street, far away from his safe and comfortable home, He had planned to remain behind the scenes, the man pulling the strings. Instead, he had somehow become the victim of his own murderous scheme.

Big Will silently cursed his wretched luck He had to somehow escape this self-imposed, recurring nightmare because, as it stood now, his life was expendable. If he was unable to make himself useful in the next few hours, the likelihood of him becoming one of the bodies these killers planned on dropping tonight remained high. His next move, he concluded, was to add some sort of value to his life and fast. Time was running out.

Ominously, the house phone began to ring.

S.P. retrieved the cordless from its base and handed it over to the fat barber.

"Buzz'im up," he commanded with a look that promised swift and immediate violence if the demand wasn't met.

Big Will timidly complied.

S.P. exited the apartment and waited in the hallway for his boss.

"The Cook" threw himself down onto Big Will's couch and began to watch the silent porno playing on Big Will's '52 inch. The busty brunette was on her knees between two men, alternating between sucking one off and stroking. he other.

Big Will shifted his weight on the cold hardwood floor, trying in vain to alleviate his discomfort. He watched Tyson with disdain as the puppy licked at the spot on the floor where the bacon had been dropped.

"Tucking traitor," Big Will spat under his breath. When he had first bought the puppy, he had envisioned a guard dog that would protect him in situations like this.

Instead, all he got was, a useless lap doe. When this was all over, he promised himself that he'd throw the disloyal mutt off his balcony.

The young rottweiler looked up as if he could read his fat master's thoughts and barked once at the overweight barber before scurrying to the front door as it opened.

S.P. crouched down and scooped up the dog as he re-entered the apartment.

Bloody Benny walked in behind him; in his hands, he was carrying two small, red gas canisters. His eyes were ablaze. Bloody Benny's cool and cocky demeanour was now rigid and tense. The fat barber studied the downtown gangster and wondered what had occurred since he had last seen him. Bloody Benny's face was drawn and haggard.

Whatever had gone down had taken it toll on the unstable gangster, Big Will surmised.

Obviously, going to war with the likes of Prince and Kilo was easier said than done.

"Where's Shells and Mouse?" Bloody Benny snapped, his tone causing "The Cook" to straighten up on the couch.

"They in the next room playin' X-Box or some shit," "The Cook" replied, looking at the gas canisters strangely. "What's those for?"

"Well, what the fuck nigga, what're you waitin' for? Go'n get'em!" Bloody Benny shouted, ignoring the question.

"The Cook" jumped up from the couch and hurried into the next room to retrieve his colleagues as Bloody Benny rested the canisters on the dining room table.

Avoiding eye contact, Big Will tried his best to make himself invisible. He could tell that Bloody Benny was in a murderous mood and he didn't want to end up on the wrong side of the downtown gangster's fury.

S.P. reclaimed his seat on the couch with Tyson sitting comfortably on his lap and switched off the porno with the remote control. "The Cook" re-entered the living room, followed by Mouse and Shells.

"Okay," Bloody Benny began. "I want you niggas to listen closely because I don't plan on repeating myself tonight, aight.

"I want these niggas dead. Fuck that, I want them more than dead. I wanna see them suffer. I wanna hear'em scream."

"Why, what happen just now?" Shells asked, sensing something wasn't right.

Bloody Benny took a shallow breath before answering. A single tear slipped from his eye. The room went still.

"Them niggas...them niggas killed Maria," he managed to say before his mouth went completely dry.

The grim news hit the downtown goons like a ton of bricks. Shells and Mouse's mouths dropped open. "The Cook" shook his head in disbelief. S.P. scowled at the revelation, though to Big Will's discomfort, the scowl was solely aimed in his direction.

"When the fuck did that happen?" "The Cook" asked.

"And why? Why would they touch Shorty?" Mouse added. "How did they even get to her in the first place!'

"Who gives a fuck, it's done!" Bloody Benny yelled with raw emotion. "These pussy-ass Scarborough niggas think they can go toe-to-toe with me?' he asked rhetorically. "They think they're grimy? I'm gonna finish'em, ya hear me? I'ma kill every single one of em in their little pussy-ass clique!"

The room remained still. No one dared to speak in the wake of Bloody Benny's murderous rant. From face to face, Bloody Benny glared at each man in the apartment, silently challenging them to oppose his menacing threats.

His eyes rested on Big Will.

"Why's this pussy still alive?" he asked to no one in particular.

At once, S.P. threw Tyson off his lap, jumped up out of his seat and pulled out his gun, aiming it at the petrified barber's head.

"Wait, wait, wait!" Big Will quickly cried out of pure terror. "I can still help you get Prince and Kilo!" -

"We don't need your help," S.P. growled, cocking back the hammer.

"I-I can help you get at Prince's little brother!" Big Will pleaded.

"I'll go to the hospital myself and slap him out for you. Why get your hands dirty when you don't need too?"

"Hold up, hold up," Bloody Benny said, ordering S.P. to stand down. S.P. sucked his teeth and slightly lowered his weapon.

"You'll do what?" Bloody Benny asked with a whisper of a Smile playing on his lips.

"I'll do it. I-I swear I'll do it. Just give me a chance."

"You lying- ass piece of shit," Mouse remarked, "You ain't killin' shit!"

"I'll do it," Big Will repeated, looking directly at Bloody Benny only.

Bloody Benny stared at the fat barber and weighed his proposal over.

"Aight, you got your chance," he answered after moments passed. "S.P.'ll go with you just to make sure everything runs smooth."

Big Will sighed out of relief.

S.P. glared his disapproval.

"I say we just kill the fat goof now. We can handle Zulu later," Shells said, putting to words what S.P. was feeling.

"Did I ask you for your opinion, nigga?" Bloody Benny snapped. He looked at the overweight barber and nodded his head towards the door.

"Go now before I change my mind."

Big Will jumped to his feet quicker than anyone would've expected for someone his size and made his way towards the door. S.P. followed, uttering curses under his breath.

"Aiyo, family!" Bloody Benny called out to the Scotian just before he exited the apartment and while Big Will was outside in the hallway. Either way it goes, make sure you leave that fat pussy-ass nigga with a bullet in his dome, ya hear me?

S.P. smiled and nodded his head before closing the door behind him.

Bloody. Benny turned to the two small red gas canisters on the dining room table.

"Aight," he said to the rest of his goons. "Let's go'n set the Borough on fire."

CHAPTER 28

"Honour thy brother…"

A crowd was quickly forming behind the bright, yellow police tape that had sectioned off the scene of yet another city shooting.
This was the fourth reported gun related incident in the short span of the last twenty-four hours. The sudden spike in gun and gang violence had the city on edge. The media secretly loved it, the cops were put on high alert and the public, according to certain news outlets, was outraged.
Pockets of curious on-lookers clumped together behind the plastic, yellow police tape as they gossiped in hushed tones. Some of them inquired as others speculated, but none knew for certain what had exactly happened in their once quiet neighborhood.
Two stone-faced police officers defended their side of the police barrier as if they anticipated the nosy suburban on-lookers to rush the crime scene at any given moment.
Local city news vans were piling up to the scene as Rakim observed the spectacle from a safe distance. He cautiously stuck to the shadows, hiding in the dark pathway between two houses. From his vantage point, he had a clear view of the scene as the police continued to conduct their investigation. The gossiping crowd slowly parted like the Red Sea as an ambulance drove up to the police tape, waiting to be admitted onto the scene. The fact that an ambulance was slower than a City TV news truck wasn't a surprise to Rakim. He had known scores of men who could've survived but instead died on the spot because the paramedics had failed to rush to their aid in time. He continued to survey the scene. His eyes rested on a police cruiser that seemed to be the focal point of the growing circus. Two men in plain clothes were having a conversation with three uniformed officers, just three steps away from the cruiser. Rakim guessed that the men in plain clothes were detectives by their body language and by the way they dressed. Cheap suits compounded with the air of authority signaled a detective to a gangster as gold chains and bandanas indicated a gangster to a detective. Rakim ignored the bwoy dem and focused his attention on the

police cruiser.

Someone was inside the car.

He squinted to make out who it was. The man in the cruiser's head was down, but Rakim could tell that it was Kilo. He had grown up with the man so he was able to spot his brethren from a mile away.

Rakim sucked his teeth out of disappointment. Unless God intervened, this was probably the last time he would see his nigga on road for a very long time.

A few more curious onlookers continued to filter in behind the yellow police tape. Rakim decided that his presence was an unnecessary risk at this point, as he casually walked away from the scene. He decided to head home in an effort to regroup and take stock of his new situation. Rakim needed an alibi. He hoped that Pyro had escaped too, and that they would be able to link up and plan their next move, but Rakim knew he was thinking optimistically. None the less, he eagerly held onto the little crumbs of hope that ignorance afforded him.

Moving like a U.S. Marine Soldier stranded in the heart of Taliban territory at night, Rakim ducked and dodged the cops until he was safely seated at the back of an East-Bound TTC Red Rocket. It took no less than thirteen stops for Rakim's heart to stop thumping within his chest. It was not until then that he was able to finally compose himself enough to check his phone for any missed calls or text messages. If Pyro had truly gotten away, he'd probably send a message out for a rendezvous, Rakim reasoned. However, aside from a litany of messages from random messages of people asking him if he was going to the "MOB party" in Scarborough that night, there was nothing from his Somalian comrade in his inbox.

"MOB party?" Rakim whispered to himself, thoroughly confused.

"Who the fucks throwing a MOB party?"

He remembered Kilo saying something about it earlier on that day, but he couldn't make sense of it now. There were no special occasions to celebrate. No birthdays or anniversaries. Something was up. At that very moment, by coincidence, one of Rakim's niggas from the M.O.B. rang his line.

"Yo," he answered on the second ring.

"Yo my nigga, wa gwan, where you at? You're fawadin', right?"

JB was a fellow M.O.B. affiliate who hailed from Mornelle court which was located in the North Side of Scarborough. The stalky Lebanese gang member was a self-described pimp that loved to party, so it didn't surprise Rakim to hear the sounds of loud music in the background of the call.

"Fawadin' where?" Rakim asked.

"Caddy's my nigga! You didn't get the invite? Almost the entire crews out here, baby. We just waitin' on you and crazy-ass Kilo. Where you niggas at?"

Rakim was still puzzled so he probed further.

"What's the special occasion?"

"Special occasion? We don't need no special occasion," JB chuckled. "Were on fire right now, my nigga we're the hottest slimes in da city. I guess somebodies just now finally paying homage. And honestly? If you ask me? Its about mother-fuckin' time. These motherfuckas should be organizing parades for us and shit on a weekly basis, Five. Who's more swagged out than us?"

Despite his mood with everything that had just went down, Rakim couldn't help but laugh out loud. JB had always been the comedian of the crew.

"Yeah, yeah I hear you," Rakim smiled into the phone. "Just chill with all that blood talk, Cuz. Keep all that slob-swag in Mornelle, you hear me?"

Rakim could hear JB laugh on the other side of the call.

"Yeah, yeah, whatever. Are you niggas fawadin' or what?" Rakim sighed heavily and then turned serious.

"Yo? Some shit just went down, brother. Keys just got knocked and I'm not too sure if the Warya is doin' any better."

"What? You serious?" JB yelled. "What happened?"

"A whole bunch of fuckery, my nigga, but true say the phone-tings sticky, you know how it go. When we link up, I'll fill you in, in person. You feel me?"

"Yeah, yeah, yeah," JB replied, all business now.

"Who's all there with you?" Rakim inquired as he pulled the yellow string above his head, signaling for the bus to stop.

"Uhmm, right now its just me and Sunny, Gremlin, Rude Bwoy and Cal. Oh-Oh and I think Big-Up just rolled through with a bunch of the older heads too. Why do you need someone to draw for you, my nigga? Ox just called and said he's on his way, I can make him circle back for you, if you want."

"Nah, nah," Rakim answered after a moment's thought. "I'll link up with ya'll niggas in a second. I just need to change clothes and put some shit together...But yo, do me a favor and tell the man dem to be on point tonight. I know I might be buggin', but I feel like something isn't right now, you hear me?"

"Aight, say no more," JB replied over the phone. "Text me when you're close."

Ending the call, Rakim exited off the bus. He searched through the apps on his cellphone and then ordered an Uber to take him the rest of the way home. He wasn't in the mood for partying, but he figured the jam at Caddy's would be his best bet of an alibi if indeed he ever needed one. Feeling exhausted, he walked into a nearby Wendy's and waited for the rideshare.

*****

JB ended the call and regarded Rude Bwoy and Gremlin with a sombre frown.

"What's good bro, you holla at Price and Kilo yet?" Gremlin asked while a thick dark-skinned girl slow whined on his lap, with a glass of hypnotiq in her hand.

"Yo, I think Kilo just got knocked, fam."

"What?"

"Prince just said my man got hemmed up," JB repeated.

Gremlin pushed the dark-skinned girl off him, causing her to spill her drink, while Rude Bwoy searched his face hoping to find another joke in between his words. The thick girl began to berate Gremlin but he simply ignored her, as he stared at JB in disbelief.

"Tell me you're joking right now, man. Don't fuck around with us Jay…"

"Naw man, I'm serious. Real talk. Prince is fawadin' right now, so we'll get the full hunnid in a minute."

The trio stood together in silence as the party around them started to pick up. Girls were slowly starting to trickle in while a classic Sean Paul song swam through the marijuana smoke-filled bar. Each of the three weighed the bad news in their minds, trying to guess what Kilo and Prince had been up to.

"Yo, you think my man got knocked for what happened last night?" Rude Bwoy asked Gremlin referring to the shooting at the club, putting to words what they all suspected.

It was common knowledge that the pigs were in beast-mode after the incident at the docks and all of the media attention it was gaining.

"Fuck if I know," Gremlin answered honestly, hoping that his own minor involvement wasn't enough to have his name smeared up on any arrest warrants.

"So, what should we do?" Rude Bwoy asked, feeling stupid for being at a party while so much bullshit was going on with his crew on the streets. He had known Price and Kilo for years and was itching to bust his gun for his niggas. No one fucked with family.

"Should we just chill out and wait for Prince to get here?" JB decided for the trio.

"When homeboy reaches, we'll know more and we can act accordingly. Until then, lets pour one out for Keys and get turnt in his honour, honour thy brother, right?

"Honour thy brother," The other two repeated in unison, affirming the M.O.B.'s unofficial slogan.

*****

They got to the hospital where Zulu was laid up in, in record time, much to Big Will's dismay.

Why the hell is this happening to me? He whined to himself silently. SP had found a parking space by the church near the hospital. Despite Big Will's protests, SP had insisted in taking the barber's SUV and obstinately refused to let him drive. The journey downtown was bathed in attention-filled silence because neither of the occupants had anything to say to one another. Big Will had spent the ride to the hospital on trying to figure out how he would get himself out of a promise that he had made to a suspected serial-killer.

SP spent his time fanaticizing on how he would kill the fat coward after this was all over.

Exiting the SUV, both men made their way to the hospital with their minds and their adrenaline racing. Big Will felt as if he were on the verge of a panic attack. He couldn't picture himself killing any body. It just wasn't in him. He had only volunteered to kill Zulu, to buy himself some time. He knew that if he didn't add any value to his already expendable life, Bloody Benny would have had him murked in his own apartment. However, his brief respite was drawing to an end with every sullen step the doomed barber took.

He began to inconspicuously search for a way out of his dilemma.

The downtown Toronto landscape was bustling with activity as motorists, cyclists and buses competed for traffic lanes and quicker ETAS.

Big Will contemplated the notion of making a run for it, but quickly nixed the idea as graphic images of his fat-ass being run over by a car crept into his mind. Besides, who was he kidding? There was no way in hell he was going to out-run a downtown gangbanger, who obviously knew this part of the city much better than he did. Likewise, the pedestrians that obliviously shuffled by, offered little hope. No one dared make eye-contact with two black men who clearly looked like they were up to no good. Big Will wanted to scream out to them all: I'm on your side guys! I'm nothing like this homicidal maniac! Please help me! But he knew his plea would fall on deaf ears. The citizens of Canada's largest city would more than likely write the fat man off as another downtown junkie or a poor overweight man suffering from mental illness. Putting it simply, Big Will was fucked. The two-sum cautiously entered the hospital with the worst of intentions.

It was smiles all around for the visitors of Anthony Zulu Anderson in the Intensive Care Unit of St. Michaels hospital. His over-the-top mother and her equally over-bearing friends crowded around him, leaving little-to-no room for anyone else, including his fuming girlfriend Keisha.

Although she was pissed, Keisha couldn't help but feel excited at the sight of her recovering boyfriend. She wasn't going to let these old hags get the better of her and make her wil'out in front of her man. Keisha decided to take Prince's advice and not cause a scene. If she did, she knew Zulu would be vexed with her, so instead, she chilled at the foot of the bed with Kim flanking her rear, trying her best to smile pleasantly and insert herself within Zulu's line of sight. Alicia, however, opted to remain outside in the waiting room with her newfound friend, "Jennifer". She had told Keisha that she wanted to give her and Zulu's mom some privacy. Though, truth be told, she just couldn't handle the drama. There was just way too much underlying negativity between Keisha and Patty. While the Zulu supporters underhandedly bickered for his attention, Alicia and "Jennifer" bonded over shoes, boys and gossip.

Jasmine played the "Jennifer" role to perfection, snaring Alicia slowly into a perfectly crafted pseudo-friendship. Once she was in close, she would strike at Prince through her new naive friend and finally take possession of the M.O.B.

It was a fanatical ambition, but Jasmine was determined to reach her goal and become Queen. She had been sitting with Alicia for almost fifteen minutes, pretending to be caught up in a conversation about shoes or some shit when she noticed Big Will from Cut Creator step off the elevator with another light-skinned man she had never seen before.

Seconds later, Keisha could hear a commotion building up outside in the hallway. But before she could investigate, the same light-skinned stranger that Jasmine had seen busted into the room with a gun in his hand and murder gleaming in his eyes. He pointed the terrifying pistol towards Zulu.

"Yo Zulu Wuddup Blood!"
BAM!!

******

Big Will was fairly certain that this wasn't S.P.'s first rodeo so he was not at all surprised that the light-skinned killer appeared so calm and collect. He, on the other hand, was shitting bricks.

They made their way to the hospital's main desk where the same chubby, redheaded nurse that Rakim had first encountered was still working.

"Go' head and see which room he in," S.P. ordered Big Will, nudging the unwilling barber in the nurse's direction.

Reluctantly, Big Will walked up to the reception desk.

The mean-faced nurse eyed him warily,

"Can I help you?" she questioned him in a not so friendly manner.

"Uhmm," Big Will stammered at this point, it felt as if every eye in the place was on him and knew exactly what he was up to. Fuck it, he decided, as he mustered up every single drop of courage in his being. I'm not playin' the bitch anymore.

"Listen to me," he addressed the nurse in a hushed yet confident tone. "I need you to call the police. Do you see the man right behind me? Well, he has a gun and he's here to murder somebody."

Eyes wide in shock, the redheaded nurse timidly glanced behind the fat black man to behold the killer within their midst.

"I need you to focus!" Big Will whispered sternly, "Call the police now!" With any luck, the fat barber estimated, the cops would get there shortly and finally free him from this awful nightmare. He'd tell them all about Bloody Benny and his murderous intentions. He would explain how the downtown gangsters had forced their way into his apartment and threatened to kill him if he didn't help them in their homicidal scheme.

So, what if that made him a snitch.

He didn't care anymore. He just had to get out of this situation. If anybody had a problem with it, he'd buy a gun, roll up to their baby-mama's crib and just start firing, Fuck it! He didn't give a shit anymore. He was going to re-write the rules and change the game. He was the real shotta...

"Sir?"

He was the real Big Mon...

"Sir?"

Nobody else in their right mind would ever want to fuck with Big Motherfuckin' Will again-

"Sir?" the mean-faced nurse yelled, snapping Big Will back into reality. "I said, can I help you?"

The fat barber shook his head free from the pathetic fantasy and cleared his throat, slightly embarrassed.

"Uhmm, ca-ca-can you tell me which room Anthony An-Anderson's in?"

The redheaded nurse sized up the stuttering obese man contemptuously.

"You'll need to sign in before I can let you up there."

"Sign in?"

"Yes, you will need to sign in, see, the annoyed nurse reiterated. "I'm required to take your name and record your relationship with the patient before I let you up there," she continued to say in a dry monotone. "Is there a problem?"

"No, no. There's no problem," Big Will answered, swallowing the swellings of paranoia. He didn't want to sign his name to any sign-in sheet, but little was the choices he had.

A few moments later, he found himself in the elevator on its way up to the ICU with a psychopathic killer still staring daggers into him.

"I know Benny said he wants you to do this yourself, but I ain't givin' yo fat-ass no gun, no way. We get up there. You point. I shoot. We cut. Aight? Which room he in?"
Stepping off the elevator, Big Will tried not to let the relief show too much as he relayed the room number.
"Will?" he heard somebody call out his name.
He turned and was semi-surprised to find Jasmine from Malvern walking towards him.
Even though he knew her from the hood through mutual friends, he acted as if she were a stranger and tried his best to ignore her. With the shit that was about to go down, he didn't want people to associate his name with Zulu's murder.
S.P. pushed past them and made his way to his intended target, knocking over Jasmine in his wake.
"What the fuck!" Jasmine screeched.
S.P. didn't even look back at her as he barreled down the hallway.
Jasmine was quick to her feet and was in hot pursuit.
"Yo, you fuckin' bitch-ass-nigga, you like knocking women down? You don't have any fuckin' respect?"
Drawn by the ruckus, nurses and patients began to crowd in the hallway.
S.P. didn't give a fuck. So close to his intended target, he experienced tunnel vision right up until he got to the door. If he had been paying attention, he would have noticed that the disturbance in the hallway had attracted within the crowd the same niggas he had gotten into a shoot-out with the night before in the club.

*****

Smurf couldn't believe his eyes. Was that the same nigga from the club last night? It couldn't be...
Smurf had convinced the reluctant Premiere to bring him down to Zulu's room. He had wanted to check up on the little homie and see how the youngin' was holding up.
But this? This was some shit sent from God. Even though it was dark inside the club, Smurf could have picked the light-skinned shooter out of a photo lineup of over a hundred men.
In disbelief, he watched the man that he had exchanged gunfire with, walk right into Zulu's room with what appeared to be revolver in his hand. Everything moved in slow motion from that point for Smurf with all the adrenaline pumping through his veins.
Without a second thought, he reached for Premieres waist and pulled out the gun he knew would be there while simultaneously pushing Premiere out of the way; he took aim and fired just as the light-skinned gunman lifted his own weapon in what appeared to be a clear attempt on Zulu's life.

BAM!

The man went down amidst a contorted symphony of screams from most of the women who witnessed the random act of violence. Smurf, for half of a second, indulged in the early victory, falsely thinking that he had felled the would-be-assassin.

Not so.

The light-skinned shooter, without warning, flipped onto his back and let five fly in Smurf's direction. This time, it was Premiere who pushed Smurf safely out of the way as four slugs whistled over their heads.

One bullet found its mark as it lodged itself into the bouncer's shoulder, causing him to scream out in pain. Premiere fell violently on top of Smurf, pinning the dwarfish gangster underneath his muscular frame.

From the floor, Smurf saw the light-skinned shooter bolt out of Zulu's room and make his way to the stairs, clutching his bleeding neck, firing his pistol back blindly into the hallway. The terrified spectators that had once crowded the hospital's hallway ducked and dived for cover as bullets ricocheted off the walls, ceilings and the generic furniture all around them. In a matter of seconds, the light-skinned shooter had disappeared down the stairwell leaving the aftermath of chaos in his wake. Smurf pushed Premiere off and rushed to Zulu's room. Aside from a collection of old, crying women awkwardly clinging onto Zulu in a vain attempt to shield him from further gunfire, Zulu was unharmed much to Smurf's relief. Two younger black girls cowered in the corner. Smurf assumed that one of them was Zulu's girlfriend.

Jasmine ran up to Smurf s side and surveyed the room while clutching her purse.

"You okay?"

Smurf glanced over at her and nodded his head. He never really liked Jasmine, so he kept the conversation short "Link Prince."

CHAPTER 29

"Light a match and then kill everything you see..."

Bloody Benny was ready for war. He sat very still in the driver seat of his 2013 Range Rover and disparagingly glared at the front entrance to Caddies. Parked in the shadows of the popular Scarborough nightspot, he covertly studied the enemy forces and regarded their ragtag faction with disdain. Fuck the M.O.B., he thought contemptuously.
Fuck Scarborough...fuck the entire east end! If theses pussies really wanted war, then he would deliver it in spades. Bloody Benny vowed to show not only them, but everybody else in the city that he was the true six-god. He would bring hell right to the doorsteps of the men who affronted him. He would make examples out of entire crews. Tonight, was his night to shine and show off his expanding power and wrath. Tonight, was his night for revenge.
Partygoers carelessly filed in and out of the establishment, utterly oblivious of the carnage that lay ahead.
Rolo, the man Big Will had referred to as the "Cook", sat in the passenger seat of the Range Rover and impatiently waited for Bloody Benny's instructions. He desperately wanted to get this shit over with as quickly as possible, especially with the type of firepower they had sitting in the truck. Mouse and Shells were in the back seat holding an AR-15 and a rusty Tech-9, respectively and in addition to himself; there was no telling what the Boss had strapped to his waist. On the floor, the red containers of gasoline that Bloody Benny had introduced into their fold sat menacingly at their feet, with horrible promises of mayhem and destruction.

*****

Inside the ganja smoke-filled nightspot, the party continued to pick up steam.
Big-Up, a long-time affiliate of the M.O.B., generously bought out the bar and offered free drinks to all the associates and members of his crew. Women were rewarded free liquor on the spot not because the embattled

OG was a nice guy, but because Big-Up believed that he'd possibly increase his chances of getting himself laid that night if most of the women were plastered. A lewd twerking contest was in the midst of its second round by the DJ table, much to the delight of the drunken gangsters who gathered around the scantily clad women to watch and take bets. Earlier that night a fight had broken out by the washrooms over a spilt Heineken but was quickly put on ice when security stepped into the fray and flashed their unconventional, matching Berettas.
So far, it was a typical night out in Scarborough.
Standing by the speakers, JB was already way past tipsy as he eagerly eyed the men's washroom. A coked-out snow-bunny was in there giving top to the man dem and JB was next in line.
As if on cue, Gremlin awkwardly stumbled out of the restroom and tried to zip back up his G-Star jeans with his right hand while still holding a half empty bottle of Hennessey in his left. He unevenly staggered towards his colleague.

"You're up, fam," the short gangster said, slurring his words. "You gotta watch out though, man. The bitch is usin' her teeth."
JB chuckled at his nigga's warning as he made his way towards getting his dick wet. Just before he could enter the washroom however, one of the bouncers that he had known from around the way approached him.

"Yo Jay, do you smell that?" the fat bouncer inquired.

"Smell what?"

"It kinda smells like gasoline..."
Slightly annoyed that he was being held up from getting head, JB paused and inhaled sharply. The bouncer was right; there was a faint tang of the petrol odour in the air. It was definitely odd, but it wasn't enough to raise any real concerns in the horny gangster's mind. The only thing JB was interested in was slipping his hood in some drunk girl's mouth before she could reconsider.

"Who cares. It's probably nothing," JB said, shrugging it off. "Do me a favor and go find Rudeboy and tell him I said that he's next."
With that, he headed into the restroom and instantly forgot about the weird gasoline smell as soon as he caught sight of the skinny white girl in the bathroom stall waiting to receive him orally.

*****

"Aight, done," Mouse wheezed out of breath, as he jumped back into the Range Rover. "I splashed it on everything you told me to splash it on. The front... 'round the back... some of dem cars, but yo man, that fuckin' shit stink, I think some of dem bouncers might've even smelled it-"

"Yeah, but did anybody see you? Bloody Benny cut in.

"Nah Boss, we good," the scrawny white boy smiled as he picked back up his automatic weapon.

The downtown gangster nodded his head and continued to scan the front entrance to the club. Most of the patrons were already inside but a few still mingled with the relaxed security guards by the front doors, sharing drinks and cigarettes.

Much to Bloody Benny's surprise, there were no police cruisers in sight and the bouncers seemed to be distracted by all the local pussy surrounding them.

The timing couldn't have been any more perfect.

"Aight, let's go," Bloody Benny said as he gripped his 40 Cal. and exited the Rover.

His men followed suit and hopped out the whip.

At first, no one by the nightspot noticed the four-armed men until Bloody Benny loudly cleared his throat in a dramatic fashion and addressed the sparsely populated crowd.

"Excuse me; ladies and gentlemen...I would like to take this time to introduce myself to some of you who may not know me."

Some of the eyes in the crowd grew wide with shock at the sight of the street sweepers that two of the strangers were carrying.

"These lil niggas," the unhinged gangster said, indicating the men flanking his side and then levelling his gun at the crowd. "These lil niggas call me Boss, but you, you all can call me your worst nightmare!"

CLAP! CLAP! CLAP!

Before anyone could react, Bloody Benny fired three rapid shoots, sending the once oblivious crowd into a frenzied panic.

While his terrified victims scattered, Bloody Benny addressed his men and ordered Mouse and Rolo to head to the rear of the club, while he and Shells covered the front.

"Light a match and then kill everything you see," he commanded through a twisted smile. He let off more shots, instantly killing one of the bouncers and wounding some of the women who were too slow at dodging bullets.

Shells violently discharged his Tech 9 into a Honda Accord that another bouncer had taken cover behind as Bloody Benny fished a dollar store lighter out of his True Religions. He Sparked a flame, which illuminated the murder in his eyes.

"Welcome to hell, pussies!"

*****

The explosion of the gunshots ringing out outside triggered the music inside the club to stop. Some of the women on the dance floor began to scream and panic, but most of the Toronto natives were used to the sounds of urban warfare and took it as their cue to get the fuck out of the way. The once drunken members of the M.O.B. quickly sobered up and took stock of the situation.

Inside the men's restroom, JB roughly snatched his member out of the snow-bunny's mouth and quickly made his way back to the dance floor.

"What the fuck?" he whispered in disbelief.

Was he tripping, or was there really a thick black cloud of smoke sinisterly draping the ceiling? Prince's warnings began to scathingly echo in the back of JB's mind, along with the fat bouncer's questions about the mysterious gasoline smell.

A crush of panic-stricken partygoers rushed the exits. JB pulled out his Baby 9 and headed in the same direction. The harrowing bangs of gunfire continued to beat just outside. From the sound of it, JB estimated that there were at least two automatic weapons causing havoc out there. He quickened his step.

Through the intensifying thick black smoke, JB could just make out the top of Gremlin's head slightly ahead of him. He too was making his way towards the exit but unexplainably stopped just short of the front door. It took a few seconds for JB to process it, but for some arcane reason, the screaming crowd seemed to be running back towards him in the wrong direction. A terrified flood of humanity desperately fought its way back inside the club as JB battled his way up stream. He didn't know what was causing the reversal in the human tide, but it didn't really matter, he continued to press onwards. The more JB advanced, the higher the temperature seemed to rise. Finally, he reached Gremlin's side and was dumbfounded at what he saw. An intensely hot fire raged by the front doors, rendering it nearly impossible for people to exit unharmed. There were several dead bodies scattered around the burning entrance and with the bullets still whizzing in the air, it wasn't difficult to figure out how they got there.

"What the fuck?" JB repeated again, but this time directing his inquires 'at Gremlin.

The Bay Mills gangster didn't reply, but instead pulled out his burner and returned fire.

*****

BAP!...BAP! BAP! BAP!.... BAP! BAP!!

Bloody Benny took cover behind a parked car as the members of the M.O.B. began to shoot back. He laughed to himself manically.

"These pussies think this is a shoot-out," he chuckled to no one in particular, as he reloaded his firearm.

Shells continued to spray the front entrance with semi-automatic rounds, killing scores of innocent bystanders in his assault.

"This is not a fucking shoot-out!" Bloody Benny yelled in a battle cry. "This is a motherfuckin' massacre!"

Despite the bullets flying through the air, the downtown gangster stood back up and obstinately resumed laying his enemies to waste.

*****

Big Up and a few of the other older heads swiftly scrambled to the back doors as soon as the drama began. He figured that if everybody was going out front, then he and his crew would slip out through the back and regroup under less stressful circumstances.

Unfortunately, he figured wrong.

As soon as he and his crew hit the back door and flung it open, bullets began to fly.

Instantly, two of Big Up's colleagues were mowed down by automatic gunfire.

Big Up and the rest of his surviving friends quickly drew their weapons and fired back.

Death and gunplay were nothing new to the Scarborough bandits, but what unfolded next took the seasoned O.G.'s by surprise. Through their pumping adrenaline, the pungent aroma of gasoline fumes didn't register itself in the defending gangsters' minds until the spark of a ricocheted bullet ignited a massive blaze directly in front of them.

"Ah wha di bloodclot!" one of the O.G.s cried out in disbelief as a scorching wave of fire mercilessly engulfed the men closest to the exit.

Big Up watched in horror the flames devouring his comrades through their screams and the smell of their burning flesh. Still, the bullets continued to rain down on them.

One by one the members of the M.O.B. began to fall.

Big Up knew the score. He was a certified veteran in the murder game, so it didn't take him long to realize that, tonight, he was finally playing on the losing team.

He smiled as he took cover by the wall and reloaded his weapon. His fate was sealed but he didn't mind. He was finally about to link back up with his baby brother, so the call of death was a welcomed one.

Relentlessly, the gunfight continued to wage on all around him. They had fought bravely but for the most part, the majority of his niggas were either dead or dying.

Steeling himself against the knowledge of his impending death, Big Up exhaled and jumped into the madness, busting his gun recklessly. Ignoring the pain, he ran full tilt into the fire, squeezing his trigger at his unknown assailants. Immediately, five bullets fatally slammed into him. He gracelessly fell face first to the ground and died on the spot.

*****

The fire raged on. JB, alongside Gremlin, desperately tried.to gain some sort of advantage in their losing gun battle, but the onslaught of their enemy's attack was proving to be too much. Rudeboy, Sunny and a few other younger members of the M.O.B. had frantically joined the fight, however with the thick black smoke obscuring their vision and robbing them of their air supply, the situation appeared bleak.

Bloodcurdling screams permeated the smoky midnight air, punctuated by the crackle of gunfire and the sounds of police sirens in the distance.

Gremlin was the first to go down. A bullet painfully tore through his chest, sending the Bay Mills gangster to the floor. JB ran to his friend's aid but it was too late; there was nothing he could do.

Tears started to well up in JB's eyes, not because of the loss of his homeboy but because the thick black smoke was beginning to take its toll. His body coughed violently, trying to expel the toxic clouds that had invaded his lungs. The heat from the fire and the noxious fumes that it produced made it nearly impossible for him to focus on the shootout. He fell to his knees and gasped for air. He could no longer hear gunshots ringing out outside or the weapons being discharged from, within. The only sounds he could identify were the pathetic squeals of the poor people trapped within the smoldering nightclub.

He tried to look around to see how his surviving friends were holding up but through his burning eyes, he saw nothing but black smoke. JB tried to stand back up, but the fumes were too strong. His body had lost all of its strength and was completely useless without the vital supply of fresh oxygen. He began to slip in and out of consciousness. In resignation, JB slumped to the floor and closed his red, stinging eyes.

The last thought that ran through the gangster's mind was that of the skinny snow-bunny that he had abandoned in the bathroom stall. He silently rebuked himself for not finishing inside her mouth and chuckled sadly for dying an unsatisfied man.

*****

Bloody Benny and his team of ghetto assassins quickly vaulted back into the Range Rover and sped away from the scene, just before the first police cruisers could respond.

The men spent the ride back downtown in silence, each man coming to grips with the atrocities they had just committed. It was only Bloody Benny who wore a twisted smile on his drawn and haggard face. They say revenge is a dish best served cold, but for the unhinged gang leader, retaliation was something better enjoyed in a fiery blaze of glory.

Though he was almost certain that Prince and Kilo were not amongst the people caught up in his flaming, bullet riddled death trap, Bloody Benny still delighted himself in the carnage that he had single-handedly orchestrated. In the city, after tonight, he would become a legend. His name would forever ring out throughout the streets.

If Prince and Kilo were still out there then the war would continue, he reasoned to himself. More bodies would drop. He would ride on the Vern every day until they were dead if he had to. He always finished what he started. His thoughts then turned to Zulu.

Pulling out his cell phone, be dialed S.P.'s number expecting to hear nothing but good news. Instead, disappointingly, the call only delivered the opposite, which left Bloody Benny seething.

"What happened?" Rolo questioned his boss after Bloody Benny disconnected the call, visibly upset.

The downtown gangster didn't respond. His mind was reeling over the new developments. This fuckin' Zulu kid has to die, he determinately thought to himself.

There just wasn't any other option. Prince and Kilo was one thing, but Zulu...That kid had to go. He knew too much, He had seen too much. With only a few words, Bloody Benny feared that Zulu could tear down his entire operation. Therefore, as it was in the beginning, the plan for Bloody Benny remained the same. Zulu had to be muzzled.

No matter what and no matter who had to die, whether it be on his side or theirs, Zulu had to be silenced.

*****

The hospital in which Zulu was saved in and then almost shot was now shrouded in complete chaos. The Toronto Police Services, along with its K9 units, its tactical response teams and an army of overzealous patrolmen descended upon the besieged downtown hospital with a tempered vengeance.

While E.T.F. scoured and cleared each floor, searching for the runaway gunman, St. Michael's was promptly placed under lockdown. Nobody was allowed in and nobody was allowed out. The floor where the shoot-out had occurred served as the epicenter to the mayhem. Over worked detectives who were once tasked with investigating the previous night's events, were called back to the hospital to interrogate a fresh new batch of terrified witnesses.

Alicia, disconcertedly, sat in the middle of it all, wondering to herself how her once quiet life had now turned into a magnet for high profiled shootings. She refused to believe that the affable Prince and his gang of misfits were responsible for it all, but in every case, Alicia grudgingly admitted to herself, they were the only common denominator.

Common sense urged her to cut ties with the charismatic gang banger, but her heart wouldn't allow it. There was something about Prince that she just couldn't get enough of.

Was it the danger or was it the sex? She wasn't sure, but whatever the case, Alicia knew in her heart of hearts that she was, for better or worse, hooked.

She glanced over at Keisha, who was cuddling her best friend Kim, while being interviewed by a police officer and began to feel empathy for her little sister.

At the beginning, Alicia couldn't understand why Keisha was so in love with a man who was so comfortable with living on the outskirts of the law. However, unexpectedly for the older sister, it took only the short span of the last twenty-four hours for her narrow perspective to change.

Thank God for Jennifer, Alicia thought to herself while her new best friend sat next to her, providing her with comfort and support. Alicia, in her ignorance, considered "Jennifer's" presence as a blessing, but "Jennifer's" motives were entirely self-serving.

Blind to the neighboring treachery, Alicia, continued to take in her surroundings.

A forensic team was busy collecting shell casings and dusting for fingerprints by the hallway and stairwell. Extra care was exercised when it came to the blood trail left by the renegade shooter. Samples were meticulously harvested and gathered for evidence.

Bullet holes decorated the walls behind the doctors and nurses who attended to Premiere and the shell-shocked eyewitnesses, which included the inconsolable Patty and her bevy of hysterical friends. Zulu's melodramatic mother played up her audience and secretly loved the attention she was receiving.

The authorities had relocated Zulu to a more secured section of the hospital and placed him under heavy police guard. According to "Jennifer", the police had also detained Prince's friend Smurf and her "fat friend" from Malvern. The cops were questioning them on their involvement in the shooting. Alicia could have sworn she had seen the fat man crying while being detained.

Outside, the growing media circus contended with each other for the coveted viewership of the masses. Each serving out the few precious facts that were in turn fed to them by second-hand witnesses and their cherished police sources.

Alicia looked away from the window and down at her visibly shaking hands. All this madness was beginning to take its toll. She had sent a text to Prince, filling him in on all the craziness going on at the hospital. Through the text messages, Alicia could tell that Prince was upset by the news, which was completely understandable. In the last forty-eight hours someone, for the second time, had tried to kill his younger brother, so it was fair to say that he had probably seen-better days. Alicia wanted to comfort him and help relieve some of his stress. They agreed to meet up with each other at her apartment as soon as she was released from the hospital. Almost over an hour had passed before an overwhelmed police officer made her way over to Alicia and "Jennifer" and informed them that they were cleared to go. Keisha and Kim opted to stay by Zulu's side despite Alicia's protests, but eventually the older sister relented and promised to return to the hospital as soon as Keisha called.

In the parking lot, after ducking and dodging the press, Alicia and "Jennifer" exchanged cell phone numbers and promises of linking up with each other in the future before parting ways.

Alicia jumped into her car and headed home, unaware of the extra set of eyes clocking her from the other side of the parking lot.

CHAPTER 30

"I couldn't believe my eyes"

In the game of chess, anticipating your enemy's next move is a vital component to victory. Those who neglect this often find themselves losing more than they had originally bargained for. In the back seat of a speeding Uber, Rakim silently condemned himself for not thinking three steps ahead and for allowing his enemy to inflict so much damage to his side of the proverbial chessboard. He realized, bitterly, that he had been too caught up on the offensive, neglecting his flanks and exposing his weaknesses.

Now, he was suffering the consequences.

Ox had called him and had breathlessly informed him of the bloodbath that had just taken place at Caddies. At first, Rakim didn't believe what he was hearing, chalking up Iris friend's dramatics for bad humor. But then the news alerts started to chime in on his cell phone, confirming his nigga's grisly tale. According to the CP24 news app, over a hundred people were murdered in what the press was describing as the bloodiest massacre in modem Canadian history. The police had already begun to link the mass murder to the growing gang war that was shredding apart the city.

Ox had explained that if it had not been for an accident on the 401, he probably would have been laid out with the rest of the crew in the now smoldering Scarborough nightclub. Rakim sat dumbfounded by the news while Ox shouted obscenities over the phone, vowing to gun down every single downtown nigga he knew.

"I mean, what're we gonna do, Prince? We can't just let this shit slide...."
Rakim knew his brethren was right but before he could respond, his cell phone began to vibrate in his hand, indicating that he had just received a new text message.

It was, from Alicia, and what she had to say drained whatever color Rakim had left in his already pale face. Through text messages, Alicia recounted the horror that had played out at the downtown hospital. She made every attempt at reassuring him that his little, brother was safe and unharmed but Rakim was still livid.

The war was slipping out of his control and he was losing way too many men. Between Bloody Benny, the loss of Kilo, a growing threat of jasmine's rebellion and the unwanted attention of the bwoy. dem, Rakim was beginning to feet overwhelmed. In a daze, he told Ox that he would link him back and then made new arrangements with Alicia, planning to meet up with her at her apartment.

"Aiyo, change of plans," Rakim called out to the Uber driver in a shaky voice. "I need you to turn around and bring me to Ajax."

"Hold on, hold on. Wait a minute buddy," the driver said, replying rudely. "This is a ride-share, not a taxi service. You prepaid for Scarborough. I'm not going to Durham Region. If you wanna go to Ajax, then I suggest you get yourself another fucking Uber."

In a flash and without thinking, Rakim punched the back of the Uber driver's head, causing the ride-share to swerve out of its lane. The sudden burst of violence caught both men by surprise.

Utterly terrified, the Uber driver began to change his tune. He begged and pleaded for his life, realizing that the man in the backseat was someone that he didn't want to mess with.

Rakim shook his head, instantly regretting his lack of self-control. He reached inside his pockets and pulled out a stack of one hundred-dollar bills, throwing it into the driver's lap.

"Here, take this," he said apologetically. "I'm just havin' a really rough night. I would appreciate it if we could just move past this and forget all the ugliness that just transpired...Do me a favor and take the money and bring me to where I want to go... Or we can, regretfully, continue on the path we're currently on. Ultimately, it's your choice."

The Uber driver, with one hand on the steering wheel, tenderly rubbed the back of his head. He wordlessly counted the hundreds that was thrown onto his lap and decided to take the money.

"Okay buddy," the driver said while making a U-turn. "Just don't hurt me, okay pal."

"Deal," Rakim replied, nodding his head and then refocusing back on his cell phone.

It was 2:15 in a morning that would forever be engraved in the forefront of the afflicted gangster's mind. Rakim sat in silence and reflected on the last forty-eight hours.

He needed to regain control of the situation. He needed to end this war with Bloody Benny before anybody else from his side got hurt. He closed his eyes and meditated.

In order for Rakim to find an ending, he realized that he would first have to understand the beginning. Suddenly remembering his brother, he opened his eyes, scrolled through his cell phone to where Zulu had typed in his story, and began to read...

*****

Yo brother, I know I should have showed you this earlier, but I didn't think shit was so deep...You done know me n Blacks have been doin' our thing on the Sherbourne strip...The herein game had me and homeboy caking. N since Blacks fucks with dam Regent yutes, things, 4 a time were movin' smoothly...Blacks introduced me n Beads 2 some nigga named Bloody Benny n everything wee lit. I mean, I never really liked the Benny yute because he seemed weird n shit, but Blacks fucked with him hard, plus the money was rollin' in so I never complained...

Rakim shook his head at that while the Uber flew steadily down the 401. He had always communicated to Zulu to trust his gut when it came to niggas outside the set. If his wayward brother had actually listened to him, many of his current problems would have been averted. Instead, here they were; Zulu laid up in the hospital with bullet wounds and' Rakim twisting in the wind with most of his crew slaughtered. Shaking his head, he continued to read on...

One night though, Zulu narrated. There was this crony-ass party on Shuter. Bloody Benny n all his goons were there. Mad bitches—Mad weed...Mad liquor...Everyone got wasted, so we Just decided 2 crash there 4 the night. I wake up the next morning n everyone's passed out around me. l tried 2 wake Blacks n dem up so we could dip but niggas were dead 2 the world n shit. I looked around the spot n some of the blood-niggas were there 2, but Bloody Benny was nowhere 2 be found. At first, I thought nothing of it because, like I said, l just wanted 2 get outta there... So, I tell Blacks n Beads that I was going 2 use the john n that they better be reedy 2 bounce as soon as I fawaded back because I wasn't plannin' on stayin' there any longer than I needed 2. I mean, you know how Keisha gets sometimes… So anyways, I make my way 2 the bathroom n bust the door, but you'd never believe what I saw...Yo, Rakim, no word of a lie, l saw Bloody Benny fuckin' the shit outta some dude, right there on the bathroom floor! l couldn't believe my eyes! This nigga was balls deep in a man's ass big bro. Balls deep!

The cell phone almost fell from Rakim's hands, as his eyes grew wide with shock.

"What the fuck!" he whispered to himself loud enough to draw a curious glance from the terrified Uber driver in the rear-view mirror. The artificial glow emanating from Rakim's smartphone highlighted the multitude of questions currently plaguing the gangsters mind. Bloody Benny? A fish? Incredulously, Rakim re-read his brother's narration but it only delivered the same message: Bloody Benny was gay. Rakim shook his head and continued reading...

Before I could close the door, Bloody Benny locked eyes wit me n the look of terror in his eyes was plain 2 see. I never said anything though...I Just shut the door n damn near ran back 2 where the men dem were sleeping. A few minutes later, Bloody Benny n the dude he was bangin', waltz right back into the spot as if nothing ever happened.

Yo, Rakim, after that, the whole time I was there, Bloody Benny was just grillin' me fam... I guess he was tryin' to figure me out or whatever... Honestly, I didn't care. I just wanted 2 get the fuck outta there. A couple days fly by n I still haven't shown the man dem what I saw. I don't know why... Maybe I figured it just wasn't my place 2 blow up homeboy's spot, you know? But then, Blacks started movin' all weird with me n shit. He starts hinting that Bloody Benny thinks there's n rat in the crew n I try 2 ignore the sideway looks he's givin' me. In turn, I try 2 drop hints of my own that maybe Bloody Benny isn't all that he says he Is, but again, I'm not tryin' to expose nigga's sexual preferences. I mean, it wasn't my place 2 say. Anyways, Blacks ends up tellin' me that Bloody Benny has a couple of bricks he tryin' to let go of for cheap, so I tell him 2 set up the deal...We went down there n that's when shit went downhill... I'm sry bro... I know I should've shown u the play from time. Looking back at it now I feel so stupid for letting these niggas run up on me like that... should've been on point...I'm sry. But yo, whatever u plan 2 do next just make sure ur careful wit It. I know ur a savage on dem streets, hit please don't gat twined up 4 me...

Too late little bro, Rakim thought to himself as he sat in silence, quietly fuming over what he just read. All because of one man's secret, a pointless war had been ignited which resulted in unnecessary Violence and a rash of senseless killings. With this new information, he began to think back and everything now became crystal clear, From the first time he had met Bloody Benny, Rakim had always felt that there was something off about the downtown gangster. The incident with Bloody Benny's cell partner in the East Detention Center began to make more sense. Though it wasn't for certain, Rakim was pretty sure that Bloody Benny had fucked his crack head celly and then hid his actions by having the drug addict killed.

Rakim laughed aloud in disbelief.

He understood why Bloody Benny was so hell-bent on guarding his secret the dangerous subculture of Toronto's underworld would never be as accepting as the rest of society. Rakim reflected on these startling new developments as the Uber exited off the highway and onto Westney Road. He finally learned the answers to the questions he had been searching for, but now a completely new chapter had opened up. If Rakim was to survive and ultimately win this war, he knew what he had to do. As much as he hated to admit it, Kilo was right. It was time to refocus. It was time to put in that work. It was time to honour his brother.

EPILOGUE

"Gotta little bit of street in you"

As the ultra-violent night finally drew to a merciful end, in downtown Ajax, Rakim's Uber quietly pulled up to Alicia's apartment building. At this time of the night, unlike its big city counterpart, the streets of Durham region were deserted.

A cool summer breeze blew through the quiet, east-end parking lot as Rakim exited the ride-share.

He ignored the look of relief that was pathetically painted on the Uber driver's face and instead focused on carefully scanning his surroundings. Aside from the rows and rows of unoccupied vehicles, the darkened parking lot appeared vacant. Looking back down at his S10, he texted Alicia's number, informing her that he was downstairs.

As the ride-share pulled away, Rakim stood by the front doors to the building's lobby, oblivious to the fact that somebody was secretly watching him. His phone vibrated in his hands with Alicia's reply. Apparently, her apartment building's buzzer was broken, so she would have to meet him downstairs to let him in.

In an attempt to calm his nerves, Rakim sparked a cigarette and waited patiently in the shadows with his eyes fixed on the horizon and his mind fixed on revenge.

It took Alicia a few minutes to make her way downstairs. Dressed in a modest, white tank top, sky blue Lululemon tights and an old pair of all white, retro Jordan 3s, she opened the lobby's door, but stopped short of inviting Rakim in, once she seen the lit cigarette in his hand.

Knowingly, Rakim smirked. "I guess I can't smoke this upstairs, huh?"

Alicia shook her head and smiled back, apologetically.

"We can chill out here until you're finished, though."

Still smiling and agreeing to the compromise, Rakim nodded his head, He leaned against the building's brick wall and wordlessly invited Alicia to join him. Thirty seconds passed by without either one of them uttering a single word to each other. They basked in the comfortable silence between them and reflected on the chaos that they had both just been through.

A sluggish racoon indifferently sauntered by the couple a few feet away in the parking lot Rakim absentmindedly followed the nocturnal creature's progress with his eyes, as he casually took pulls off his Du'maurier.

"So," Alicia said, finally breaking the silence. "How you holding up?"

Rakim exhaled a cloud of smoke into the early morning air and seriously gave thought to the question before answering.

"I'll be fine," he answered at length with a forced smile. "How're you holdin'?"

Alicia regarded him skeptically and then shook her head.

"Listen Prince, you don't gotta act all tough with me. What you've been through tonight alone is more than enough to make even the strongest of us to go insane. I'm not saying that I expect you to cry on my shoulder or anything, but I do wanna let you know that I'm here for you." She took a hold of his free hand and stared at him until he was forced to meet her eye to eye. "Seriously though," she said, full of compassion. "I'm here."

Rakim moved in front of her with his back facing the street and stared into her hazel brown eyes. This is a bad bitch, he admitted to himself, studying the beautiful woman in front of him as he threw away his spent cigarette. Any man would be lucky to have this girl by his side. He brought her hand to his lips and kissed it softly.

"I hear you baby girl, and you're right. I can't lie, I'm shakin' it right now, but I ain't the only one. You've been through a lot too these past couple of days. To be real with you, I admire your strength. There's not too many women built like you nowadays.

"You're smart... sexy and if I'm not in mistaken, you do gotta little bit of street in you."

Rakim stabbed his finger playfully into her chest to emphasize his point. Alicia couldn't control the smile that tugged at her lips. She continued to stare deep into his brown eyes as he gently leaned into her for a kiss.

She was falling for this man and she couldn't help it.

At that very moment, two things ran through Alicia's mind. The first was the realization that she was in love with the gangster that stood before her. The second was the confusion she felt at the sight of her ex-boyfriend Jerome power walking towards them with a gun in his hand.

"Jerome?" she called out in disbelief. "What are you-"

CLAP!...CLAP!
CLAP!
CLAP!
CLAP!

To be continued...

GLOSSARY

The following are words and/or terms used within the book:
- Aq or Aqi: Brother in Arabic
- Ballin': Rich/ Showing off your wealth
- Batty Bwoy: Homosexual male
- Beast: Police officer
- Big Mon: Big Man/ Boss
- Bing: Jail
- Boogie: Take leave/ Exit
- Boom: A person, generally a male
- Brown Boy: Canadian $100 bill
- Bucket: Provincial jail
- Burner: Gun
- Bwoy Dem: Police officer(s)
- Caking: Getting money
- Catty or Catties: A female
- Century Sam or Centuries: A cigar used for marijuana use
- Crib: House/Home
- Cuz: Short form for cousin/ Crip slang
- D.L. : Down Low
- D.T.F.: Down to fuck
- Daps: Handshake
- Deh pun: Short form for "here on"
- Dime(s): An exceptionally beautiful woman
- Ends: Neighbourhood
- Ganja: Marijuana/Weed
- Gat: Gun
- Girt: Harm
- Giving Top: Performing oral sex
- Goof: Idiot
- Gov'y: Short form for "government"
- Hammer: Handgun
- Heat: Gun
- Hoodrat: Female of ill-repute (usually from a poor section of a city)
- Jam: Party
- Jubies: Females
- Juice: Alcohol

- Lah'd: Lord
- Man dem: Team/Crew etc.
- Milly: Short form for militant
- Mirk: Kill/Murder
- Moss out: Hang out or to conceal
- O.G. Original gangster/ title given to older gangsters
- Older head: Seasoned gang member
- O.T.: Out of Town
- Par: See Moss out
- Passa passa: Gossip
- Piff: Marijuana
- Pig(s): Police officer(s)
- Pitch: Kill/Murder
- Plugged in: Knowledgeable of a situation or engaged
- Pree: Observe/Watch
- Props: Close handed handshake (fist bump)
- Right hand man: Best friend
- Road Dog: Friend outside of prison or jail
- Rock or rocking: Wear or wearing
- Rude Boy or Bwoy: Gangster or thug
- Salaah: Islamic prayer
- Shook: Scared/Frightened
- Shotta: Gangster/Shooter
- Snaking: Betrayal
- Snow-bunny: Caucasian female
- Splurt: Leave/Exit from scene
- Stoley: Stolen Vehicle
- Strap: Gun
- Strapped: Armed with a weapon (usually a handgun)
- Taped up: Armed with a weapon (usually a handgun)
- Touch Road: Released from incarceration
- Wa gwan: Short form for "What's going on"
- Wha'chu: Short form for "what are you"
- Whip: Car/Vehicle
- Ya zee it: Short form for "You see it" or (Do you understand)
- Yaw'd: Jamaica
- Yaw'di: A Jamaican immigrant
- Yute: Short form for youth (usually male)
- Zeen: Okay
- Zuked: Poisoned (usually by taking bad drugs)

ABOUT THE AUTHOR

Warren is a 33-year-old male who grew up in Malvern. Malvern is a neighbourhood located in Scarborough, Ontario. This book was written while Warren was serving a prison sentence for a murder that he was originally acquitted of. After being released and found not guilty, two years later Warren was recharged and sentenced to 25-years. During this time, he used his time behind bars to craft this novel. This was Warren's way of leaving the streets and moving out of the lifestyle and into a more positive lifestyle. After winning his second appeal, Warren was released in 2018 with time served. After his release from prison he began working with multiple organizations offering peer-mentorship to troubled youths. He also has and continues to speak at multiple events about his experience and how to help youths steer clear from the gang-lifestyle and to help them to live a productive future.

Made in United States
Orlando, FL
07 December 2022